THE
RANDOM HOUSE
BOOK OF
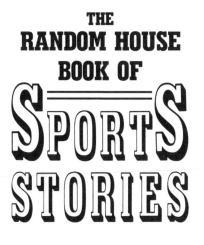

THE
RANDOM HOUSE
BOOK OF
SPORTS
STORIES

Selected by
L. M. SCHULMAN

Illustrated by
THOMAS B. ALLEN

RANDOM HOUSE 🏠 NEW YORK

To Janet, a good sport
—*L. S.*

For the Frank Deford family
—*T. A.*

Library of Congress Cataloging-in-Publication Data:
The Random House book of sports stories / selected by L. M. Schulman ;
illustrated by Thomas B. Allen.   p.   cm.
Summary: Presents a collection of sports stories by such authors
as Ernest Hemingway, Ring Lardner and John Updike.
ISBN 0-394-82874-7 (trade) ISBN 0-394-92874-1 (lib. bdg.)
1. Sports stories. 2. Children's stories, American. [1. Sports—
Fiction. 2. Short stories.] I. Schulman, L. M. II. Allen,
Thomas B. (Thomas Burt), ill. III. Random House (Firm)
IV. Title: Book of sports stories.
PZ5.R194 1990 [Fic]—dc20 89-12834 CIP AC

Manufactured in the United States of America   10 9 8 7 6 5 4 3 2 1

Copyright acknowledgments appear on page 247.

Contents

Foreword

Our world is sports-crazy.

All around the globe people eagerly head for soccer fields, football fields, baseball diamonds, tennis courts, and basketball courts, to play harder than they would ever dream of working. We fill every seat in huge stadiums, screaming louder at the actions of others than we would if our own fates and fortunes were on the line. We spend countless hours indoors, staring at the glare of sports on TV while the sun shines ignored outside. We read newspapers from back to front, skipping the news of the world to get the sport pages first. We pay star athletes more than presidents, worship them like gods and goddesses, and even call them "immortals," as if sports had turned these very human men and women into superhuman beings.

Why?

I strongly suspect that we are so crazy about sports because we are not that crazy about our lives. We find in sports what we do not find in our lives. Rules that are clear and firm, with cheating not only penalized but scorned. A fair chance for every player to show his or her true worth, with skill and strength, courage and determination, properly rewarded. A beginning and an end that frames the action for our eyes and understanding. And above all, a final score.

No wonder that storytellers have found sports a fertile field in which to root their work. For their purpose too is to provide us with what our daily lives do not.

To read a story is to watch a game created by a writer. We begin with its opening words and follow it to its outcome as eagerly as any fan leaning forward at the starter's gun or the cry of "Play ball!" And if the story is good, if the author has the talent and does not cheat, we see life as we long to see it, as clearly as if we sat in a box seat or in front of a giant TV, held spellbound by the action and by our hunger to know the results. Who won? Who lost? How, what, and why?

This book is your ticket to sixteen such games. They are games played in a wide range of styles, from the raw power of Jack London to the screwball humor of James Thurber, from the fierce honesty of Ernest Hemingway to the finely honed insights of John Updike. They are games of youth and games of age, games of love and games of hate, games of discovery and games of disillusion. They are games in which games of every kind play a vital part, but their victories and defeats go far beyond numbers on a scoreboard. And most important, they are games at which you, the reader, cannot remain a spectator. For it is every writer's goal to turn a reader into a member of his or her team. These writers do—in stories that take you out of yourself and into their games to win the prize that both sports and art can grant: the sense of going the limit to live life at its peak.

—L. M. Schulman

viii

THE
RANDOM HOUSE
BOOK OF

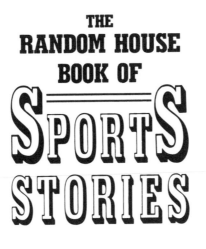

SPORTS
STORIES

James Thurber

YOU COULD LOOK IT UP

Move over, mighty Casey.
A new baseball legend is coming to bat.

It all begun when we dropped down to C'lumbus, Ohio, from Pittsburgh to play a exhibition game on our way out to St. Louis. It was gettin' on into September, and though we'd been leadin' the league by six, seven games most of the season, we was now in first place by a margin you could 'a' got it into the eye of a thimble, bein' only a half a game ahead of St. Louis. Our slump had given the boys the leapin' jumps, and they was like a bunch a old ladies at a lawn fete with a thunderstorm comin' up, runnin' around snarlin' at each other, eatin' bad and sleepin' worse, and battin' for a team average of maybe .186. Half the time nobody'd speak to nobody else, without it was to bawl 'em out.

Squawks Magrew was managin' the boys at the time, and he was darn near crazy. They called him "Squawks" 'cause when things was goin' bad he lost his voice, or perty near lost it, and squealed at you like a little girl you stepped on her doll or somethin'. He yelled at everybody and wouldn't listen to nobody, without maybe it was me. I'd been trainin' the boys for ten year, and he'd take more lip from me than from anybody else. He knowed I was smarter'n him, anyways, like you're goin' to hear.

This was thirty, thirty-one year ago; you could look it up, 'cause it was the same year C'lumbus decided to call itself the Arch City, on account of a lot of iron arches with electric-light bulbs into 'em which stretched acrost High Street. Thomas Albert Edison sent 'em a telegram, and they was speeches and maybe even President Taft opened the celebration by pushin' a button. It was a great week for the Buckeye capital, which was why they got us out there for this exhibition game.

Well, we just lose a double-header to Pittsburgh, 11 to 5 and 7 to 3, so we snarled all the way to C'lumbus, where we put up at the Chittaden Hotel, still snarlin'. Everybody was tetchy, and when Billy Klinger took a sock at Whitey Cott at breakfast, Whitey throwed marmalade all over his face.

"Blind each other, whatta I care?" says Magrew. "You can't see nothin' anyways."

C'lumbus win the exhibition game, 3 to 2, whilst Magrew set in the dugout, mutterin' and cursin' like a fourteen-year-old Scotty. He bad-mouthed everybody on the ball club and he bad-mouthed everybody offa the ball club, includin' the Wright brothers, who, he claimed, had yet to build a airship big enough for any of our boys to hit it with a ball bat.

"I wisht I was dead," he says to me. "I wisht I was in heaven with the angels."

I told him to pull hisself together, 'cause he was drivin' the boys crazy, the way he was goin' on, sulkin' and bad-mouthin' and whinin'. I was older'n he was and smarter'n he was, and he knowed it. I was ten times smarter'n he was about this Pearl du Monville, first time I ever laid eyes on the little guy, which was one of the saddest days of my life.

Now, most people name of Pearl is girls, but this Pearl du Monville was a man, if you could call a fella a man who was only thirty-four, thirty-five inches high. Pearl du Monville was a midget. He was part French and part Hungarian, and maybe even part

Bulgarian or somethin'. I can see him now, a sneer on his little
pushed-in pan, swingin' a bamboo cane and smokin' a big cigar.
He had a gray suit with a big black check into it, and he had a
gray felt hat with one of them rainbow-colored hatbands onto it,
like the young fellas wore in them days. He talked like he was
talkin' into a tin can, but he didn't have no foreign accent. He
might 'a' been fifteen or he might 'a' been a hunderd, you couldn't
tell. Pearl du Monville.

After the game with C'lumbus, Magrew headed straight for
the Chittaden bar—the train for St. Louis wasn't goin' for three,
four hours—and there he set, drinkin' rye and talkin' to this bartender.

"How I pity me, brother," Magrew was tellin' this bartender.
"How I pity me." That was alwuz his favorite tune. So he was
settin' there, tellin' this bartender how heartbreakin' it was to be
manager of a bunch a blindfolded circus clowns, when up pops
this Pearl du Monville outa nowheres.

It give Magrew the leapin' jumps. He thought at first maybe
the D.T.'s had come back on him; he claimed he'd had 'em once,
and little guys had popped up all around him, wearin' red, white
and blue hats.

"Go on, now!" Magrew yells. "Get away from me!"

But the midget clumb up on a chair acrost the table from
Magrew and says, "I seen that game today, Junior, and you ain't
got no ball club. What you got there, Junior," he says, "is a side
show."

"Whatta ya mean, 'Junior'?" says Magrew, touchin' the little
guy to satisfy hisself he was real.

"Don't pay him no attention, mister," says the bartender. "Pearl
calls everybody 'Junior,' 'cause it alwuz turns out he's a year older'n anybody else."

"Yeh?" says Magrew. "How old is he?"

"How old are you, Junior?" says the midget.

"Who, me? I'm fifty-three," says Magrew.

"Well, I'm fifty-four," says the midget.

Magrew grins and asts him what he'll have, and that was the beginnin' of their beautiful friendship, if you don't care what you say.

Pearl du Monville stood up on his chair and waved his cane around and pretended like he was ballyhooin' for a circus. "Right this way, folks!" he yells. "Come on in and see the greatest collection of freaks in the world! See the armless pitchers, see the eyeless batters, see the infielders with five thumbs!" and on and on like that, feedin' Magrew gall and handin' him a laugh at the same time, you might say.

You could hear him and Pearl du Monville hootin' and hollerin' and singin' way up to the fourth floor of the Chittaden, where the boys was packin' up. When it come time to go to the station, you can imagine how disgusted we was when we crowded into the doorway of that bar and seen them two singin' and goin' on.

"Well, well, well," says Magrew, lookin' up and spottin' us. "Look who's here. . . . Clowns, this is Pearl du Monville, a monseer of the old, old school. . . . Don't shake hands with 'em, Pearl, 'cause their fingers is made of chalk and would bust right off in your paws," he says, and he starts guffawin' and Pearl starts titterin' and we stand there givin' 'em the iron eye, it bein' the lowest ebb a ball-club manager'd got hisself down to since the national pastime was started.

Then the midget begun givin' us the ballyhoo. "Come on in!" he says, wavin' his cane. "See the legless base runners, see the outfielders with the butter fingers, see the southpaw with the arm of a little chee-ild!"

Then him and Magrew begun to hoop and holler and nudge each other till you'd of thought this little guy was the funniest guy than even Charlie Chaplin. The fellas filed outa the bar without a word and went on up to the Union Depot, leavin' me to handle Magrew and his new-found crony.

Well, I got 'em outa there finely. I had to take the little guy along, 'cause Magrew had a holt onto him like a vise and I couldn't pry him loose.

"He's comin' along as masket," says Magrew, holdin' the midget in the crouch of his arm like a football. And come along he did, hollerin' and protestin' and beatin' at Magrew with his little fists.

"Cut it out, will ya, Junior?" the little guy kept whinin'. "Come on, leave a man loose, will ya, Junior?"

But Junior kept a holt onto him and begun yellin', "See the guys with the glass arms, see the guys with the cast-iron brains, see the fielders with the feet on their wrists!"

So it goes, right through the whole Union Depot, with people starin' and catcallin', and he don't put the midget down till he gets him through the gates.

"How'm I goin' to go along without no toothbrush?" the midget asts. "What'm I goin' to do without no other suit?" he says.

"Doc here," says Magrew, meanin' me—"doc here will look after you like you was his own son, won't you, doc?"

I give him the iron eye, and he finely got on the train and prob'ly went to sleep with his clothes on.

This left me alone with the midget. "Lookit," I says to him. "Why don't you go on home now? Come mornin', Magrew'll forget all about you. He'll prob'ly think you was somethin' he seen in a nightmare maybe. And he ain't goin' to laugh so easy in the mornin', neither," I says. "So why don't you go on home?"

"Nix," he says to me. "Skiddoo," he says, "twenty-three for you," and he tosses his cane up into the vestibule of the coach and clam'ers on up after it like a cat. So that's the way Pearl du Monville come to go to St. Louis with the ball club.

I seen 'em first at breakfast the next day, settin' opposite each other; the midget playin' Turkey in the Straw on a harmonium and Magrew starin' at his eggs and bacon like they was a uncooked bird with its feathers still on.

"Remember where you found this?" I says, jerkin' my thumb at the midget. "Or maybe you think they come with breakfast on these trains," I says, bein' a good hand at turnin' a sharp remark in them days.

The midget puts down the harmonium and turns on me. "Sneeze," he says; "your brains is dusty." Then he snaps a couple drops of water at me from a tumbler. "Drown," he says, tryin' to make his voice deep.

Now, both them cracks is Civil War cracks, but you'd of thought they was brand new and the funniest than any crack Magrew'd ever heard in his whole life. He started hoopin' and hollerin', and the midget started hoopin' and hollerin', so I walked on away and set down with Bugs Courtney and Hank Metters, payin' no attention to this weak-minded Damon and Phidias acrost the aisle.

Well, sir, the first game with St. Louis was rained out, and there we was facin' a double-header next day. Like maybe I told you, we lose the last three double-headers we play, makin' maybe twenty-five errors in the six games, which is all right for the intimates of a school for the blind, but is disgraceful for the world's champions. It was too wet to go to the zoo, and Magrew wouldn't let us go to the movies, 'cause they flickered so bad in them days. So we just set around, stewin' and frettin'.

One of the newspaper boys come over to take a pitture of Billy Klinger and Whitey Cott shakin' hands—this reporter'd heard about the fight—and whilst they was standin' there, toe to toe, shakin' hands, Billy give a back lunge and a jerk, and throwed Whitey over his shoulder into a corner of the room, like a sack a salt. Whitey come back at him with a chair, and Bethlehem broke loose in that there room. The camera was tromped to pieces like a berry basket. When we finely got 'em pulled apart, I heard a laugh, and there was Magrew and the midget standin' in the doorway and givin' us the iron eye.

"Wrasslers," says Magrew, cold-like, "that's what I got for a ball club, Mr. Du Monville, wrasslers—and not very good wrasslers at that, you ast me."

"A man can't be good at everythin'," says Pearl, "but he oughta be good at somethin'."

This sets Magrew guffawin' again, and away they go, the midget taggin' along by his side like a hound dog and handin' him a fast line of so-called comic cracks.

When we went out to face that battlin' St. Louis club in a double-header the next afternoon, the boys was jumpy as tin toys with keys in their back. We lose the first game, 7 to 2, and are trailin', 4 to 0, when the second game ain't but ten minutes old. Magrew set there like a stone statue, speakin' to nobody. Then, in their half a the fourth, somebody singled to center and knocked in two more runs for St. Louis.

That made Magrew squawk. "I wisht one thing," he says. "I wisht I was manager of a old ladies' sewin' circus 'stead of a ball club."

"You are, Junior, you are," says a familyer and disagreeable voice.

It was that Pearl du Monville again, poppin' up outa no-wheres, swingin' his bamboo cane and smokin' a cigar that's three sizes too big for his face. By this time we'd finely got the other side out, and Hank Metters slithered a bat acrost the ground, and the midget had to jump to keep both his ankles from bein' broke.

I thought Magrew'd bust a blood vessel. "You hurt Pearl and I'll break your neck!" he yelled.

Hank muttered somethin' and went on up to the plate and struck out.

We managed to get a couple runs acrost in our half a the sixth, but they come back with three more in their half a the seventh, and this was too much for Magrew.

"Come on, Pearl," he says. "We're gettin' outa here."

"Where you think you're goin'?" I ast him.

"To the lawyer's again," he says cryptly.

"I didn't know you'd been the lawyer's once, yet," I says.

"Which that goes to show how much you don't know," he says.

With that, they was gone, and I didn't see 'em the rest of the day, nor know what they was up to, which was a God's blessin'. We lose the nightcap, 9 to 3, and that puts us into second place plenty, and as low in our mind as a ball club can get.

The next day was a horrible day, like anybody that lived through it can tell you. Practice was just over and the St. Louis club was takin' the field, when I hears this strange sound from the stands. It sounds like the nervous whickerin' a horse gives when he smells somethin' funny on the wind. It was the fans ketchin' sight of Pearl du Monville, like you have prob'ly guessed. The midget had popped up onto the field all dressed up in a minacher club uniform, sox, cap, little letters sewed onto his chest, and all. He was swingin' a kid's bat and the only thing kept him from lookin' like a real ballplayer seen through the wrong end of a microscope was this cigar he was smokin'.

Bugs Courtney reached over and jerked it outa his mouth and throwed it away. "You're wearin' that suit on the playin' field," he says to him, severe as a judge. "You go insultin' it and I'll take you out to the zoo and feed you to the bears."

Pearl just blowed some smoke at him which he still has in his mouth.

Whilst Whitey was foulin' off four or five prior to strikin' out, I went on over to Magrew. "If I was as comic as you," I says, "I'd laugh myself to death," I says. "Is that any way to treat the uniform, makin' a mockery out of it?"

"It might surprise you to know I ain't makin' no mockery outa the uniform," says Magrew. "Pearl du Monville here has been made a bone-of-fida member of this so-called ball club. I fixed it up with the front office by long-distance phone."

"Yeh?" I says. "I can just hear Mr. Dillworth or Bart Jenkins agreein' to hire a midget for the ball club. I can just hear 'em." Mr. Dillworth was the owner of the club and Bart Jenkins was the secretary, and they never stood for no monkey business. "May I be so bold as to inquire," I says, "just what you told 'em?"

"I told 'em," he says, "I wanted to sign up a guy they ain't no pitcher in the league can strike him out."

"Uh-huh," I says, "and did you tell 'em what size of a man he is?"

"Never mind about that," he says. "I got papers on me, made out legal and proper, constitutin' one Pearl du Monville a bone-of-fida member of this former ball club. Maybe that'll shame them big babies into gettin' in there and swingin', knowin' I can re-place any one of 'em with a midget, if I have a mind to. A St. Louis lawyer I seen twice tells me it's all legal and proper."

"A St. Louis lawyer would," I says, "seein' nothin' could make him happier than havin' you makin' a mockery outa this one-time baseball outfit," I says.

Well, sir, it'll all be there in the papers of thirty, thirty-one year ago, and you could look it up. The game went along without no scorin' for seven innings, and since they ain't nothin' much to watch but guys poppin' up or strikin' out, the fans pay most of their attention to the goin's-on of Pearl du Monville. He's out there in front a the dugout, turnin' handsprings, balancin' his bat on his chin, walkin' a imaginary line, and so on. The fans clapped and laughed at him, and he ate it up.

So it went up to the last a the eighth, nothin' to nothin', not more'n seven, eight hits all told, and no errors on neither side. Our pitcher gets the first two men out easy in the eighth. Then up come a fella name of Porter or Billings, or some such name, and he lammed one up against the tobacco sign for three bases. The next guy up slapped the first ball out into left for a base hit, and in come the fella from third for the only run of the ball game so far. The crowd yelled, the look a death come onto Magrew's face again, and even the midget quit his tomfoolin'. Their next man fouled out back a third, and we come up for our last bats like a bunch a schoolgirls steppin' into a pool of cold water. I was lower in my mind than I'd been since the day in Nineteen-four when Chesbro threw the wild pitch in the ninth inning with a man on third and lost the pennant for the Highlanders. I knowed something just as bad was goin' to happen, which shows I'm a clairvoyun, or was then.

When Gordy Mills hit out to second, I just closed my eyes. I opened 'em up again to see Dutch Muller standin' on second, dustin' off his pants, him havin' got his first hit in maybe twenty times to the plate. Next up was Harry Loesing, battin' for our pitcher, and he got a base on balls, walkin' on a fourth one you could 'a' combed your hair with.

Then up come Whitey Cott, our lead-off man. He crotches down in what was prob'ly the most fearsome stanch in organized ball, but all he can do is pop out to short. That brung up Billy Klinger, with two down and a man on first and second. Billy took a cut at one you could 'a' knocked a plug hat offa this here Carnera with it, but then he gets sense enough to wait 'em out, and finely he walks, too, fillin' the bases.

Yes, sir, there you are; the tyin' run on third and the winnin' run on second, first a the ninth, two men down, and Hank Metters comin' to the bat. Hank was built like a Pope-Hartford and he couldn't run no faster'n President Taft, but he had five home runs to his credit for the season, and that wasn't bad in them days. Hank was still hittin' better'n anybody else on the ball club, and it was mighty heartenin', seein' him stridin' up towards the plate. But he never got there.

"Wait a minute!" yells Magrew, jumpin' to his feet. "I'm sendin' in a pinch hitter!" he yells.

You could 'a' heard a bomb drop. When a ball-club manager says he's sendin' in a pinch hitter for the best batter on the club, you know and I know and everybody knows he's lost his holt.

"They're goin' to be sendin' the funny wagon for you, if you don't watch out," I says, grabbin' a holt of his arm.

But he pulled away and run out towards the plate, yellin', "Du Monville battin' for Metters!"

All the fellas begun squawlin' at once, except Hank, and he just stood there starin' at Magrew like he'd gone crazy and was claimin' to be Ty Cobb's grandma or somethin'. Their pitcher stood out there with his hands on his hips and a disagreeable look on his face, and the plate umpire told Magrew to go on and get a batter up. Magrew told him again Du Monville was battin' for Metters, and the St. Louis manager finely got the idea. It brung him outa his dugout, howlin' and bawlin' like he'd lost a female dog and her seven pups.

Magrew pushed the midget towards the plate and he says to him, he says, "Just stand up there and hold that bat on your shoulder. They ain't a man in the world can throw three strikes in there 'fore he throws four balls!" he says.

"I get it, Junior!" says the midget. "He'll walk me and force in the tyin' run!" And he starts on up to the plate as cocky as if he was Willie Keeler.

I don't need to tell you Bethlehem broke loose on that there ball field. The fans got onto their hind legs, yellin' and whistlin', and everybody on the field begun wavin' their arms and hollerin' and shovin'. The plate umpire stalked over to Magrew like a traffic cop, waggin' his jaw and pointin' his finger, and the St. Louis manager kept yellin' like his house was on fire. When Pearl got up to the plate and stood there, the pitcher slammed his glove down onto the ground and started stompin' on it, and they ain't nobody can blame him. He's just walked two normal-sized human bein's, and now here's a guy up to the plate they ain't more'n twenty inches between his knees and his shoulders.

The plate umpire called in the field umpire, and they talked a while, like a couple doctors seein' the bucolic plague or somethin' for the first time. Then the plate umpire come over to Magrew with his arms folded acrost his chest, and he told him to go on and get a batter up, or he'd forfeit the game to St. Louis. He pulled out his watch, but somebody batted it outa his hand in the scufflin', and I thought there'd be a free-for-all, with everybody yellin' and shovin' except Pearl du Monville, who stood up at the plate with his little bat on his shoulder, not movin' a muscle.

Then Magrew played his ace. I seen him pull some papers outa his pocket and show 'em to the plate umpire. The umpire begun lookin' at 'em like they was bills for somethin' he not only never bought it, he never even heard of it. The other umpire studied 'em like they was a death warren, and all this time the St. Louis manager and the fans and the players is yellin' and hollerin'.

Well, sir, they fought about him bein' a midget, and they fought about him usin' a kid's bat, and they fought about where'd he been all season. They was eight or nine rule books brung out and everybody was thumbin' through 'em, tryin' to find out what it says about midgets, but it don't say nothin' about midgets, 'cause this was somethin' never'd come up in the history of the game before, and nobody'd ever dreamed about it, even when they has nightmares. Maybe you can't send no midgets in to bat nowadays, 'cause the old game's changed a lot, mostly for the worst, but you could then, it turned out.

The plate umpire finely decided the contrack papers was all legal and proper, like Magrew said, so he waved the St. Louis players back to their places and he pointed his finger at their manager and told him to quit hollerin' and get on back in the dugout. The manager says the game is percedin' under protest, and the umpire bawls, "Play ball!" over 'n' above the yellin' and booin', him havin' a voice like a hog-caller.

The St. Louis pitcher picked up his glove and beat at it with his fist six or eight times, and then got set on the mound and studied the situation. The fans realized he was really goin' to pitch to the midget, and they went crazy hoopin' and hollerin' louder'n ever, and throwin' pop bottles and hats and cushions down onto the field. It took five, ten minutes to get the fans quieted down again, whilst our fellas that was on base set down on the bags and waited. And Pearl du Monville kept standin' up there with the bat on his shoulder, like he'd been told to.

So the pitcher starts studyin' the setup again, and you got to admit it was the strangest setup in a ball game since the players cut off their beards and begun wearin' gloves. I wisht I could call the pitcher's name—it wasn't old Barney Pelty nor Big Jack Powell nor Harry Howell. He was a big right-hander, but I can't call his name. You could look it up. Even in a crotchin' position, the ketcher towers over the midget like the Washington Monument.

The plate umpire tries standin' on his tiptoes, then he tries crotchin' down, and he finely gets hisself into a stanch nobody'd even seen on a baseball field before, kinda squattin' down on his hanches.

Well, the pitcher is sore as a old buggy horse in fly time. He slams in the first pitch, hard and wild, and maybe two foot higher'n the midget's head.

"Ball one!" hollers the umpire over 'n' above the racket, 'cause everybody is yellin' worsten ever.

The ketcher goes on out towards the mound and talks to the pitcher and hands him the ball. This time the big right-hander tries a undershoot, and it comes in a little closer, maybe no higher'n a foot, foot and a half above Pearl's head. It would 'a' been a strike with a human bein' in there, but the umpire's got to call it, and he does.

"Ball two!" he bellers.

The ketcher walks on out to the mound again, and the whole infield comes over and gives advice to the pitcher about what they'd do in a case like this, with two balls and no strikes on a batter that oughta be in a bottle of alcohol 'stead of up there at the plate in a big-league game between the teams that is fightin' for first place.

For the third pitch, the pitcher stands there flat-footed and tosses up the ball like he's playin' ketch with a little girl.

Pearl stands there motionless as a hitchin' post, and the ball comes in big and slow and high—high for Pearl, that is, it bein' about on a level with his eyes, or a little higher'n a grown man's knees.

They ain't nothin' else for the umpire to do, so he calls, "Ball three!"

Everybody is onto their feet, hoopin' and hollerin', as the pitcher sets to throw ball four. The St. Louis manager is makin' signs and faces like he was a contorturer, and the infield is givin' the pitcher some more advice about what to do this time. Our boys who was on base stick right onto the bag, runnin' no risk of bein' nipped for the last out.

Well, the pitcher decides to give him a toss again, seein' he come closer with that than with a fast ball. They ain't nobody ever seen a slower ball throwed. It come in big as a balloon and slower'n any ball ever throwed before in the major leagues. It come right in over the plate in front of Pearl's chest, lookin' prob'ly big as a full moon to Pearl. They ain't never been a minute like the minute that followed since the United States was founded by the Pilgrim grandfathers.

Pearl du Monville took a cut at that ball, and he hit it! Magrew give a groan like a poleaxed steer as the ball rolls out in front a the plate into fair territory.

"Fair ball!" yells the umpire, and the midget starts runnin' for first, still carryin' that little bat, and makin' maybe ninety foot an hour. Bethlehem breaks loose on that ball field and in them stands. They ain't never been nothin' like it since creation was begun.

The ball's rollin' slow, on down towards third, goin' maybe eight, ten foot. The infield comes in fast and our boys break from their bases like hares in a brush fire. Everybody is standin' up, yellin' and hollerin', and Magrew is tearin' his hair outa his head, and the midget is scamperin' for first with all the speed of one of them little dash-hounds carryin' a satchel in his mouth.

The ketcher gets to the ball first, but he boots it on out past the pitcher's box, the pitcher fallin' on his face tryin' to stop it, the shortstop sprawlin' after it full length and zaggin' it on over towards the second baseman, whilst Muller is scorin' with the tyin' run and Loesing is roundin' third with the winnin' run. Ty

Cobb could 'a' made a three-bagger outa that bunt, with everybody fallin' over theirself tryin' to pick the ball up. But Pearl is still maybe fifteen, twenty feet from the bag, toddlin' like a baby and yeepin' like a trapped rabbit, when the second baseman finely gets a holt of that ball and slams it over to first. The first baseman ketches it and stomps on the bag, the base umpire waves Pearl out, and there goes your old ball game, the craziest ball game ever played in the history of the organized world.

Their players start runnin' in, and then I see Magrew. He starts after Pearl, runnin' faster'n any man ever run before. Pearl sees him comin' and runs behind the base umpire's legs and gets a holt onto 'em. Magrew comes up, pantin' and roarin', and him and the midget plays ring-around-a-rosy with the umpire, who keeps shovin' at Magrew with one hand and tryin' to slap the midget loose from his legs with the other.

Finely Magrew ketches the midget, who is still yeepin' like a stuck sheep. He gets hold of that little guy by both his ankles and starts whirlin' him round and round his head like Magrew was a hammer thrower and Pearl was the hammer. Nobody can stop him without gettin' their head knocked off, so everybody just stands there and yells. Then Magrew lets the midget fly. He flies on out towards second, high and fast, like a human home run, headed for the soap sign in center field.

Their shortstop tries to get to him, but he can't make it, and I knowed the little fella was goin' to bust to pieces like a dollar watch on a asphalt street when he hit the ground. But it so happens their center fielder is just crossin' second, and he starts runnin' back, tryin' to get under the midget, who had took to spiralin' like a football 'stead of turnin' head over foot, which give him more speed and more distance.

I know you never seen a midget ketched, and you prob'ly never even seen one throwed. To ketch a midget that's been throwed by a heavy-muscled man and is flyin' through the air, you got to run under him and with him and pull your hands and arms back and down when you ketch him, to break the compact of his body, or you'll bust him in two like a matchstick. I seen Bill Lange and Willie Keeler and Tris Speaker make some wonderful ketches in my day, but I never seen nothin' like that center fielder. He goes back and back and still further back and he pulls that midget down outa the air like he was liftin' a sleepin' baby from a cradle. They wasn't a bruise onto him, only his face was the color of cat's meat and he ain't got no air in his chest. In his excitement, the base umpire, who was runnin' back with the center fielder when he ketched Pearl, yells, "Out!" and that give hysteries to the Bethlehem which was ragin' like Niagry on that ball field.

Everybody was hoopin' and hollerin' and yellin' and runnin', with the fans swarmin' onto the field, and the cops tryin' to keep order, and some guys laughin' and some of the women fans cryin', and six or eight of us holdin' onto Magrew to keep him from gettin' at that midget and finishin' him off. Some of the fans pick up the St. Louis pitcher and the center fielder, and starts carryin' 'em around on their shoulders, and they was the craziest goin's-on knowed to the history of organized ball on this side of the 'Lantic Ocean.

I seen Pearl du Monville strugglin' in the arms of a lady fan with a ample bosom, who was laughin' and cryin' at the same time, and him beatin' at her with his little fists and bawlin' and yellin'. He clawed his way loose finely and disappeared in the forest of legs which made that ball field look like it was Coney Island on a hot summer's day.

That was the last I ever seen of Pearl du Monville. I never seen hide nor hair of him from that day to this, and neither did nobody else. He just vanished into the thin of the air, as the fella says. He was ketched for the final out of the ball game and that was the end of him, just like it was the end of the ball game, you might say, and also the end of our losin' streak, like I'm goin' to tell you.

That night we piled onto a train for Chicago, but we wasn't snarlin' and snappin' any more. No, sir, the ice was finely broke and a new spirit come into that ball club. The old zip come back with the disappearance of Pearl du Monville out back a second base. We got to laughin' and talkin' and kiddin' together, and 'fore long Magrew with laughin' with us. He got a human look onto his pan again, and he quit whinin' and complainin' and wishtin' he was in heaven with the angels.

Well, sir, we wiped up that Chicago series, winnin' all four games, and makin' seventeen hits in one of 'em. Funny thing was, St. Louis was so shook up by that last game with us, they never did hit their stride again. Their center fielder took to mis-judgin' everything that come his way, and the rest a the fellas followed suit, the way a club'll do when one guy blows up.

'Fore we left Chicago, I and some of the fellas went out and bought a pair of them little baby shoes, which we had 'em golded over and give 'em to Magrew for a souvenir, and he took it all in good spirit. Whitey Cott and Billy Klinger made up and was fast friends again, and we hit our home lot like a ton of dynamite and they was nothin' could stop us from then on.

I don't recollect things as clear as I did thirty, forty year ago. I can't read no fine print no more, and the only person I got to check with on the golden days of the national pastime, as the fella says, is my friend, old Milt Kline, over in Springfield, and his mind ain't as strong as it once was.

He gets Rube Waddell mixed up with Rube Marquard, for one thing, and anybody does that oughta be put away where he won't bother nobody. So I can't tell you the exact margin we win the pennant by. Maybe it was two and a half games, or maybe it was three and a half. But it'll all be there in the newspapers and rec-ord books of thirty, thirty-one year ago and, like I was sayin', you could look it up.

Toni Cade Bambara

RAYMOND'S RUN

*Flying feet have to take you far when
you're racing against the odds.*

I don't have much work to do around the house like some girls. My mother does that. And I don't have to earn my pocket money by hustling; George runs errands for the big boys and sells Christmas cards. And anything else that's got to get done, my father does. All I have to do in life is mind my brother Raymond, which is enough.

Sometimes I slip and say my little brother Raymond. But as any fool can see he's much bigger and he's older too. But a lot of people call him my little brother cause he needs looking after cause he's not quite right. And a lot of smart mouths got lots to say about that too, especially when George was minding him. But now, if anybody has anything to say to Raymond, anything to say about his big head, they have to come by me. And I don't play the dozens or believe in standing around with somebody in my face doing a lot of talking. I much rather just knock you down and take my chances even if I am a little girl with skinny arms and a squeaky voice, which is how I got the name Squeaky. And if things get too rough, I run. And as anybody can tell you, I'm the fastest thing on two feet.

There is no track meet that I don't win the first-place medal. I used to win the twenty-yard dash when I was a little kid in kindergarten. Nowadays, it's the fifty-yard dash. And tomorrow I'm subject to run the quarter-meter relay all by myself and come in first, second, and third. The big kids call me Mercury cause I'm the swiftest thing in the neighborhood. Everybody knows that—except two people who know better, my father and me. He can beat me to Amsterdam Avenue with me having a two-fire-hydrant head start and him running with his hands in his pockets and whistling. But that's private information. Cause can you imagine some thirty-five-year-old man stuffing himself into PAL shorts to race little kids? So as far as everyone's concerned, I'm the fastest and that goes for Gretchen, too, who has put out the tale that she is going to win the first-place medal this year. Ridiculous. In the second place, she's got short legs. In the third place, she's got freckles. In the first place, no one can beat me and that's all there is to it.

I'm standing on the corner admiring the weather and about to take a stroll down Broadway so I can practice my breathing exercises, and I've got Raymond walking on the inside close to the buildings, cause he's subject to fits of fantasy and starts thinking he's a circus performer and that the curb is a tightrope strung high in the air. And sometimes after a rain he likes to step down off his tightrope right into the gutter and slosh around getting his shoes and cuffs wet. Then I get hit when I get home. Or sometimes if you don't watch him he'll dash across traffic to the island in the middle of Broadway and give the pigeons a fit. Then I have to go behind him apologizing to all the old people sitting around trying to get some sun and getting all upset with the pigeons fluttering around them, scattering their newspapers and upsetting the wax paper lunches in their laps. So I keep Raymond on the inside of me, and he plays like he's driving a stagecoach which is O.K. by me so long as he doesn't run me over or interrupt my breathing exercises, which I have to do on account of I'm serious about my running, and I don't care who knows it.

Now some people like to act like things come easy to them, won't let on that they practice. Not me. I'll high-prance down 34th Street like a rodeo pony to keep my knees strong even if it does get my mother uptight so that she walks ahead like she's not with me, don't know me, is all by herself on a shopping trip, and I am somebody else's crazy child. Now you take Cynthia Procter for instance. She's just the opposite. If there's a test tomorrow, she'll say something like, "Oh, I guess I'll play handball this afternoon and watch television tonight," just to let you know she ain't thinking about the test. Or like last week when she won the spelling bee for the millionth time, "A good thing you got 'receive,' Squeaky, cause I would have got it wrong. I completely forgot about the spelling bee." And she'll clutch the lace on her blouse like it was a narrow escape. Oh, brother. But of course when I pass her house on my early morning trots around the block, she is practicing the scales on the piano over and over and over and over. Then in music class she always lets herself get bumped around so she falls accidently on purpose onto the piano stool and is so surprised to find herself sitting there that she decides just for fun to try out the ole keys. And what do you know—Chopin's waltzes just spring out of her fingertips and she's the most surprised thing in the world. A regular prodigy. I could kill people like that. I stay up all night studying the words for the spelling bee. And you can see me any time of day practicing running. I never walk if I can trot, and shame on Raymond if he can't keep up. But of course he does, cause if he hangs back someone's liable to walk up to him and get smart, or take his allowance from him, or ask him where he got that great big pumpkin head. People are so stupid sometimes.

So I'm strolling down Broadway breathing out and breathing in on counts of seven, which is my lucky number, and here comes Gretchen and her sidekicks: Mary Louise, who used to be a friend of mine when she first moved to Harlem from Baltimore and got beat up by everybody till I took up for her on account of her mother and my mother used to sing in the same choir when they were young girls, but people ain't grateful, so now she hangs out with the new girl Gretchen and talks about me like a dog; and Rosie, who is as fat as I am skinny and has a big mouth where Raymond is concerned and is too stupid to know that there is not a big deal of difference between herself and Raymond and that she can't afford to throw stones. So they are steady coming up Broadway and I see right away that it's going to be one of those Dodge City scenes cause the street ain't that big and they're close to the buildings just as we are. First I think I'll step into the candy store and look over the new comics and let them pass. But that's chicken and I've got a reputation to consider. So then I think I'll just walk straight on through them or even over them if necessary. But as they get to me, they slow down. I'm ready to fight, cause like I said I don't feature a whole lot of chitchat, I much prefer to just knock you down right from the jump and save everybody a lotta precious time.

"You signing up for the May Day races?" smiles Mary Louise, only it's not a smile at all. A dumb question like that doesn't deserve an answer. Besides, there's just me and Gretchen standing there really, so no use wasting my breath talking to shadows.

"I don't think you're going to win this time," says Rosie, trying to signify with her hands on her hips all salty, completely forgetting that I have whupped her behind many times for less salt than that.

"I always win cause I'm the best," I say straight at Gretchen who is, as far as I'm concerned, the only one talking in this ventriloquist-dummy routine. Gretchen smiles, but it's not a smile, and I'm thinking that girls never really smile at each other because they don't know how and don't want to know how and there's probably no one to teach us how, cause grownup girls don't know either. Then they all look at Raymond who has just brought his mule team to a standstill. And they're about to see what trouble they can get into through him.

"What grade you in now, Raymond?"

"You got anything to say to my brother, you say it to me, Mary Louise Williams of Raggedy Town, Baltimore."

"What are you, his mother?" sasses Rosie.

"That's right, Fatso. And the next word out of anybody and I'll be *their* mother too." So they just stand there and Gretchen shifts from one leg to the other and so do they. Then Gretchen puts her hands on her hips and is about to say something with her freckle-face self but doesn't. Then she walks around me looking me up and down but keeps walking up Broadway, and her sidekicks follow her. So me and Raymond smile at each other and he says, "Giddyap" to his team and I continue with my breathing exercises, strolling down Broadway toward the ice man on 145th with not a care in the world cause I am Miss Quicksilver herself.

I take my time getting to the park on May Day because the track meet is the last thing on the program. The biggest thing on the program is the Maypole dancing, which I can do without, thank you, even if my mother thinks it's a shame I don't take part and act like a girl for a change. You'd think my mother'd be grateful not to have to make me a white organdy dress with a big satin sash and buy me new white baby-doll shoes that can't be taken out of the box till the big day. You'd think she'd be glad her daughter ain't out there prancing around a Maypole getting the new clothes all dirty and sweaty and trying to act like a fairy or a flower or whatever you're supposed to be when you should be trying to be yourself, whatever that is, which is, as far as I am concerned, a poor black girl who really can't afford to buy shoes and a new dress you only wear once a lifetime cause it won't fit next year.

I was once a strawberry in a Hansel and Gretel pageant when I was in nursery school and didn't have no better sense than to dance on tiptoe with my arms in a circle over my head doing umbrella steps and being a perfect fool just so my mother and father could come dressed up and clap. You'd think they'd know better than to encourage that kind of nonsense. I am not a strawberry. I do not dance on my toes. I run. That is what I am all about. So I always come late to the May Day program, just in time to get my number pinned on and lay in the grass till they announce the fifty-yard dash.

I put Raymond in the little swings, which is a tight squeeze this year and will be impossible next year. Then I look around for Mr. Pearson, who pins the numbers on. I'm really looking for Gretchen if you want to know the truth, but she's not around. The park is jam-packed. Parents in hats and corsages and breast-pocket handkerchiefs peeking up. Kids in white dresses and light blue suits. The parkies unfolding chairs and chasing the rowdy kids from Lenox as if they had no right to be there. The big guys with their caps on backwards, leaning against the fence swirling the basketballs on the tips of their fingers, waiting for all these crazy people to clear out the park so they can play. Most of the kids in my class are carrying bass drums and glockenspiels and flutes. You'd think they'd put in a few bongos or something for real like that.

Then here comes Mr. Pearson with his clipboard and his cards and pencils and whistles and safety pins and fifty million other things he's always dropping all over the place with his clumsy self. He sticks out in a crowd because he's on stilts. We used to call him Jack and the Beanstalk to get him mad. But I'm the only one that can outrun him and get away, and I'm too grown for that silliness now.

"Well, Squeaky," he says, checking my name off the list and handing me number seven and two pins. And I'm thinking he's got no right to call me Squeaky, if I can't call him Beanstalk.

"Hazel Elizabeth Deborah Parker," I correct him and tell him to write it down on his board.

"Well, Hazel Elizabeth Deborah Parker, going to give some-one else a break this year?" I squint at him real hard to see if he is seriously thinking I should lose the race on purpose just to give someone else a break. "Only six girls running this time," he continues, shaking his head sadly like it's my fault all of New York didn't turn out in sneakers. "That new girl should give you a run for your money." He looks around the park for Gretchen like a periscope in a submarine movie. "Wouldn't it be a nice gesture if you were . . . to ahhh . . ."

I give him such a look he couldn't finish putting that idea into words. Grownups got a lot of nerve sometimes. I pin number seven to myself and stomp away, I'm so burnt. And I go straight for the track and stretch out on the grass while the band winds up with "Oh, the Monkey Wrapped His Tail Around the Flagpole," which my teacher calls by some other name. The man on the loudspeaker is calling everyone over to the track and I'm on my back looking at the sky, trying to pretend I'm in the country, but I can't, because even grass in the city feels hard as sidewalk, and there's just no pretending you are anywhere but in a "concrete jungle" as my grandfather says.

The twenty-yard dash takes all of two minutes cause most of the little kids don't know no better than to run off the track or run the wrong way or run smack into the fence and fall down and cry. One little kid, though, has got the good sense to run straight for the white ribbon up ahead so he wins. Then the second-graders line up for the thirty-yard dash and I don't even bother to turn my head to watch cause Raphael Perez always wins. He wins before he even begins by psyching the runners, telling them they're going to trip on their shoelaces and fall on their faces or lose their shorts or something, which he doesn't really have to do since he is very fast, almost as fast as I am. After that is the forty-yard dash which I used to run when I was in first grade. Raymond is hollering from the swings cause he knows I'm about to do my thing cause the man on the loudspeaker has just announced the fifty-yard dash, although he might just as well be giving a recipe for angel food cake cause you can hardly make out what he's saying for the static. I get up and slip off my sweat pants and then I see Gretchen standing at the starting line, kicking her legs out like a pro. Then as I get into place I see that ole Raymond is on line on the other side of the fence, bending down with his fingers on the ground just like he knew what he was doing. I was going to yell at him but then I didn't. It burns up your energy to holler.

Every time, just before I take off in a race, I always feel like I'm in a dream, the kind of dream you have when you're sick with fever and feel all hot and weightless. I dream I'm flying over a sandy beach in the early morning sun, kissing the leaves of the trees as I fly by. And there's always the smell of apples, just like in the country when I was little and used to think I was a choo-choo train, running through the fields of corn and chugging up the hill to the orchard. And all the time I'm dreaming this, I get lighter and lighter until I'm flying over the beach again, getting blown through the sky like a feather that weighs nothing at all. But once I spread my fingers in the dirt and crouch over the Get on Your Mark, the dream goes and I am solid again and am telling myself, Squeaky you must win, you must win, you are the fastest thing in the world, you can even beat your father up Amsterdam if you really try. And then I feel my weight coming back just behind my knees then down to my feet then into the earth and the pistol shot explodes in my blood and I am off and weightless again, flying past the other runners, my arms pumping up and down and the whole world is quiet except for the crunch as I zoom over the gravel in the track. I glance to my left and there is no one. To the right, a blurred Gretchen, who's got her chin jutting out as if it would win the race all by itself. And on the other side of the fence is Raymond with his arms down to his side and the palms tucked up behind him, running in his very own style, and it's the first time I ever saw that and I almost stop to watch my brother Raymond on his first run. But the white ribbon is bouncing toward me and I tear past it, racing into the distance till my feet with a mind of their own start digging up footfuls of dirt and brake me short. Then all the kids standing on the side pile on me, banging me on the back and slapping my head with their May Day programs, for I have won again and everybody on 151st Street can walk tall for another year.

"In first place . . ." the man on the loudspeaker is clear as a bell now. But then he pauses and the loudspeaker starts to whine. Then static. And I lean down to catch my breath and here comes Gretchen walking back, for she's overshot the finish line too, huffing and puffing with her hands on her hips taking it slow, breathing in steady time like a real pro and I sort of like her a little for the first time. "In first place . . ." and then three or four voices get all mixed up on the loudspeaker and I dig my sneaker into the grass and stare at Gretchen who's staring back, we both wondering just who did win. I can hear old Beanstalk arguing with the man on the loudspeaker and then a few others running their mouths about what the stopwatches say. Then I hear Raymond yanking at the fence to call me and I wave to shush him, but he keeps rattling the fence like a gorilla in a cage like in them gorilla movies, but then like a dancer or something he starts climbing up nice and easy but very fast. And it occurs to me, watching how smoothly he climbs hand over hand and remembering how he looked running with his arms down to his side and with the wind pulling his mouth back and his teeth showing and all, it occurred to me that Raymond would make a very fine runner. Doesn't he always keep up with me on my trots? And he surely knows how to breathe in counts of seven cause he's always doing it at the dinner table, which drives my brother George up the wall. And I'm smiling to beat the band cause if I've lost this race, or if me and Gretchen tied, or even if I've won, I can always retire as a runner and begin a whole new career as a coach with Raymond as my champion. After all, with a little more study I can beat Cynthia and her phony self at the spelling bee. And if I bugged my mother, I could get piano lessons and become a star. And I have a big rep as the baddest thing around. And I've got a roomful of ribbons and medals and awards. But what has Raymond got to call his own?

So I stand there with my new plans, laughing out loud by this time as Raymond jumps down from the fence and runs over with his teeth showing and his arms down to the side, which no one before him has quite mastered as a running style. And by the time he comes over I'm jumping up and down so glad to see him—my brother Raymond, a great runner in the family tradition. But of course everyone thinks I'm jumping up and down because the men on the loudspeaker have finally gotten themselves together and compared notes and are announcing "In first place—Miss Hazel Elizabeth Deborah Parker." (Dig that.) "In second place—Miss Gretchen P. Lewis." And I look at Gretchen wondering what the "P" stands for. And I smile. Cause she's good, no doubt about it. Maybe she'd like to help me coach Raymond; she obviously is serious about running, as any fool can see. And she nods to congratulate me and then she smiles. And I smile. We stand there with this big smile of respect between us. It's about as real a smile as girls can do for each other, considering we don't practice real smiling every day, you know, cause maybe we too busy being flowers or fairies or strawberries instead of something honest and worthy of respect . . . you know . . . like being people.

William T. Tilden II

THE PHANTOM DRIVE

Nobody was better at playing tennis
than "Big Bill" Tilden. Or better at writing about it.

The departed shade of the Old Champion idly strummed with one hand on the golden strings of his celestial harp and arranged the folds of his celestial robes around him with the other.

It was nearly twenty years, as time is reckoned on earth, since he had left that sphere of strife and sorrow to join the heavenly chorus. Throughout all that time something seemed to be still calling from the world below. Heaven was not quite heaven to him. True, he had never succeeded in reasoning out the void in his existence. He only knew that on earth was something which he should never have left behind and which now day by day grew more insistent in his desires.

The harp was mute now as the shade of the Old Champion strove to recall the world and its details, while he sat, his hands folded in his lap. Out in space in the Celestial City or what ever it was, some lively shade newly arrived from earth, hurled a spectre clod of cloud toward him. "Look out," the spirit voice rang out distinctly. The Old Champion ducked and lifted the harp in protection.

"Twang," the cloud impinged against the golden strings. The sound stirred memories in the earthly consciousness of the departed spirit of the Old Champion. Some time, some where on earth he had heard a sound like that and now it soothed the longing in his soul. What had it been and from whence had it come? Strings, but not golden, no, yellowish and inside a piece of wood.

Suddenly the shade of the Old Champion rose hastily from the golden chair, dropping the protesting harp at his feet. He remembered now—what was it called—oh yes, racquet; a tennis racquet, his old dearly loved tennis racquet, why had he not brought it with him twenty years before? Oh yes, he knew, he had given it away, to that delightful American whom he defeated only after the most bitter match of his whole life, given it as a memento of that match, and now his beloved racquet might be lost, gone forever. No, he would find it, he would go seek it.

He started off posthaste for the Heavenly Office only to remember that but a year before he had applied for leave to visit the earth and had been informed that it would be two centuries before his turn would come. No, he could not get permission to go.

He turned the matter over carefully in his mind. Two centuries from now the racquet might be lost or destroyed beyond recall. Only that day the shade of King Tut had informed him that many treasures were lost before his grave had been discovered and that their loss weighed heavily on him. No, it was now or never for the Old Champion. Very well, he would take a chance. He would be A. W. O. L. from Heaven.

A short, stocky and very much fluttered boy of eighteen stood at the referee's desk on the club-house porch at Westside Club, Forest Hills, Long Island. His light brown hair waved in an unruly manner over his clear gray eyes while at the moment, a puzzled frown wrinkled not only his forehead but also the short nose below it. He addressed the impressive-looking gentleman seated at the table on which was spread out the big draw sheet of the tournament.

It was the opening day of the Lawn Tennis Championship of the United States, the presiding gentleman at the table was none other than Mr. Hyrock, former President of the Tennis Association and one of its foremost figures.

"Name?"

"Yes, sir; I'm Bobby Whitlock." The boy finally found his voice.

"Oh, you're Whitlock. Glad you're here. You play Richard Thomas on the Championship Court at three o'clock. You'll find your locker assigned upstairs. Thomas is here. Dress at once, please."

Mr. Hyrock dismissed the boy with a nod and turned back to his table.

Bobby Whitlock climbed the stairs to the locker-room in a daze. He had to play Dick Thomas. This was Bobby's first tournament, while Dick Thomas had been a prominent figure in American tennis for twenty years. Thomas had been very young when he gained fame, a boy wonder when at sixteen he had carried the famous Old Champion, A. W. Smith, to that memorable five-set battle at Wimbledon just before the latter's lamentable death.

Thomas at thirty-six was still one of the greatest players in America, second only to Billy Jolson himself. Bobby could not believe he was really to play Thomas. There must be some mistake. Almost in a dream he located his locker and automatically began to undress. The clean-cut athletic man at the end of his corridor of lockers turned to watch him as the youngster drew out his only racquet from his tennis bag.

"Playing in the tournament?" The man spoke in a friendly quiet voice that stilled Bobby's nerves.

"Yes, at least I'm trying to." The boy's fingers were undoing the clasps on the racquet cover. "I'm not worrying much. I'll get licked first round."

"Oh, you'll do better than that," the man laughed, as he drew on his tennis shirt, his back to the boy. "Who do you play?"

"Nobody—I guess."

The man turned sharply at the note of the suffering boy's voice. The youngster stood staring at the racquet in his hand, three strings across the center dangling hopelessly and helplessly. The boy turned his head. "It's my only one."

"Never mind that racquet. We'll fix you up. Who did you draw?"

"Dick Thomas!"

"That's great. What's your name?"

"Whitlock, Bobby Whitlock."

"All right, Bobby, try one of my racquets, I'm Thomas!"

The boy flushed suddenly and drew back. "Oh, I couldn't, Mr. Thomas."

"Why not? Don't be foolish, try this one and see if it suits."

Thomas tossed over a Wright and Ditson which was the model he had used for years.

"Thank you." Bobby pitched it up and swung it gingerly. It felt a club in his hand, the handle many sizes too big. It seemed to weigh a ton.

Thomas anxiously watched the boy. "Too heavy. Sorry—mine are all alike, I'm afraid."

"That's quite all right, Mr. Thomas, I'll use my own anyway."

"You can't, Bobby, it's impossible. Here, let me feel it."

Bobby tossed the bat to Thomas. Dick looked at it in momentary amusement. How old-fashioned it seemed in these days. It was an old Pim, cherished doubtless by Bobby's father for many years before it descended to Bobby. Where had he seen a racquet like that recently, Dick asked himself. Somewhere. He turned to the bell. The locker boy responded to the summons.

"Tell George the professional to send me my old racquet which he just strung up and has on exhibition in his office."

"Your own Wright and Ditson, Mr. Thomas?"

"No, the old English racquet; George will know."

The boy hurried off and Dick turned to Bobby.

"I have a racquet for you. It was given to me by the famous Old Champion, Smith, after he beat me at Wimbledon in 1903. Queer thing. It was my first big match, just as this is yours, and as it happened it was his last, poor old fellow. He died suddenly the following week. I've treasured the racquet, the frame is still good as new. Last week this club wanted me to allow the racquet to be placed on exhibition during the tournament so I had George string it up. I'm going to let you use it."

"Thanks a lot, Mr. Thomas, but I'd better not. Something might happen to it."

"I'll take a chance. Here it is, try it."

Bobby grasped the bat eagerly. It was almost a duplicate of his own.

"Gee, it's wonderful."

"Anyway it's a Pim, like yours and almost the same balance and weight. Come on, it's time to start," and grabbing his racquet in one hand and Bobby by the other, Dick Thomas hurried for the stairs.

The departed shade of the Old Champion was again on earth. He had slipped through the Golden Gate unobserved while St. Peter was assisting the victims of a volcano eruption in the South Seas. His departure was not only unobserved but actually opportune for his discarded harp found immediate use among the new arrivals.

The Old Champion was not completely happy. He enjoyed his invisibility on earth and made the most of it by indulging a spirit of mischief that had long been part of his nature, but full joy was not his. He could not recall the name of the young American to whom he had entrusted his beloved racquet. His twenty years' sojourn in Heaven, where music was the only language, had seriously interfered with his ability to read or to understand spoken words. Gradually these things came back from the hidden recesses of his memory and he finally succeeded in recalling enough to enjoy the papers over people's shoulders.

It was during a short stop in Boston that he finally recalled his friend's name. He was engrossed in the sporting news of a young lady's paper which was held enticingly in front of her in the lobby of the Copley Plaza while she flirted skillfully around the corner of it with a gentleman, seated near-by, when suddenly a headline caught the Old Champion's attention.

"AMERICAN TENNIS CHAMPIONSHIP STARTS TODAY."

"Richard Thomas accorded honor of opening classic against young Whitlock."

Richard Thomas! That was the name he sought. In his excitement the Old Champion reached out and seized the paper.

The girl screamed and leaped to her feet. The gentleman dashed to her aid.

"What's the matter?"

The girl laughed self-consciously. "Nothing. Nothing at all. Only my paper shook suddenly and I—well, I just screamed. I couldn't help it."

The man smiled reassuringly. "Sit down, here with me. It's all right."

The Old Champion hovered in space over the settee. Where was Thomas playing? Oh, yes, there it was, Forest Hills, Long Island. Silently he floated out into space for New York.

The great stands were well filled for the opening match of the Championship when Dick Thomas and Bobby Whitlock entered the Championship enclosure. The famous veteran was tremendously popular and his marvelous comeback during the present season had aroused popular sentiment to fever heat.

Bobby Whitlock felt somewhat like the sacrificial lamb as he heard the yell of welcome to his famous opponent rise from the multitude in the stands.

Into this colorful scene floated the departed shade of the Old Champion. This earthly existence seemed very real now and he yearned for the touch of the turf under his feet and the sound of the ball on his racquet and the feel of its impact on the strings.

The two players were warming up, rallying in preparation for the match. He hovered over the head of the boy, watching Thomas across the net, as he had done so many years before in his last match on earth.

It was the same graceful, dashing Dick, not much older in appearance. If only he, the Old Champion, were there in Bobby Whitlock's place! Suddenly the racquet in the boy's hand drew his attention. Could it be? Yes, there on the handle was the old scratch from a spike which he himself had made once when he had dropped the racquet and carelessly kicked it. It was his beloved old bat before his eyes. He must feel it once more in his hands. No! It was too late, already the umpire was calling play. Well, he would take one chance.

Invisibly he floated down and melted around the boy's body, his ghostly hand gripping the handle alongside Bobby's. Up flashed the racquet; a lightning service totally unlike anything Bobby had ever hit, sped through Thomas's court—

"15-love."

Bobby himself, to say nothing of Thomas and the expectant gallery, seemed stunned. Something unusual was about to take place.

It certainly did!

The departed shade of the Old Champion was in the mood of a schoolboy playing "hookey," out for a good time. Never in all his years on earth had the Old Champion felt more like playing tennis. Never had he played better. He swept Bobby's willing, tireless young body around the court, making marvelous shots from all directions and places. Furiously Dick Thomas fought to stop the mad, capricious attack. The tremendous booming drive that raked his court held the veteran anchored to the base-line.

The Old Champion had been a confirmed base-line player. His marvelous driving had earned for him the nickname of the "Driving King" and the "Driving Demon." Back into his old style

the departed shade automatically fell, once the racquet was between his fingers.

The gallery sat and marveled. Even the critics could not understand Bobby's game. There was one grizzled pen-wielder who sat spellbound among the press group. "Look," he said over and over again. "Watch! It is the reincarnation of Old Man Smith!"

"Gosh, what a wallop!" announced one youngster audibly to his father, as that tremendous forehand crashed its way past Thomas.

"That's nothing, Son. Wait till you see Ruth smash a baseball. This guy ain't so hot," and father chewed viciously on the end of an unlighted cigar.

Everywhere among the players the question was asked, where had Bobby learned the old style game? How well the youngster played it and how certain his racquet technique! Billy Jolson finally arose from his seat in the committee box just as Bobby scored a sizzling placement to win the second set.

"It is wonderful," he said. "I have only once seen a game like it and that was old J. C. Parke, the Englishman. They say A. W. Smith was even better than Parke from the back court. How'd the kid get that way?"

In the committee box sat three former Davis Cup men, stars of nearly twenty-five years before.

"I tell you that boy's game is a facsimile of old Al Smith's. I played him at Wimbledon back in '98 and if ever I saw a game reproduced it's out before you now."

"Maybe his soul is back in the boy's body," another cut in.

The Davis Cup veteran turned away in disgust. "Laugh all you want, but if I didn't know better I'd say Old Smith was out there today. It's marvelous!"

The match was short and sweet. Bobby Whitlock was announced winner, 6-4, 6-3, 7-5, while the multitude which had assembled to watch his annihilation stayed to cheer the new hero.

Bobby was the sensation of the moment. The press sang his praises long and loud. The departed shade of the Old Champion read all the story over the shoulders of various unsuspecting men in the lobby of the Vanderbilt Hotel and chuckled in silent celestial glee. One story, that of the veteran reporter, a man of thirty years' experience in tennis, amused him particularly.

"Not since the days of the famous English star, A. W. Smith, has such a terrific forehand drive been seen on the courts. The style of young Whitlock is strangely reminiscent of the great Englishman. It almost seemed as if Smith's hand might have been directing the racquet. The believers in reincarnation may well claim Whitlock as proof of the return of Champion Smith.

"A curious angle to the case is the fact that Whitlock claims that his whole game yesterday was different from any he ever played before. His future performances will be closely watched by the Davis Cup Committee, as he seems destined for the heights of tennis fame."

The Old Champion hugged his celestial body in an ecstasy of joy. There was still one man on earth who remembered him at his best and rejoiced to see his game again. He decided to stay on and win for the lad if he could, and he believed it was possible.

The succeeding days certainly seemed to justify his faith. Bobby marched on in state to the semi-finals, where he, or rather the Old Champion, put a decisive and artistic finish to young Richard Vincey with so perfect a display of driving that the press again proclaimed the return of the Driving King.

Meanwhile Bobby, fondly as he clung to the Old Champion's racquet, had his own old one restrung in case of accident.

The day of the finals dawned bright and warm. The strings of cars poured out to Forest Hills early in the day. Long lines of eager fans formed at the gates by ten o'clock. By two o'clock every available inch of room was packed with an eager public, ready for the big tennis battle of all time, for Billy Jolson, the great defending champion from California, was to meet Bobby Whitlock, the Driving Demon, for the American title.

Around the court in the linesmen positions sat no less than

five former American champions, while Eddie Congdon, the doyen of umpires, graced the chair. Mr. Hyrock was net umpire, while even the ball-boys were of the chosen few.

Bobby stepped into the enclosure to be met by a yell of welcome that almost deafened him. Over his head the Old Champion grinned a celestial grin and dropped into position to play.

Billy Jolson, alert, wiry, nervous, eager, strode from the clubhouse and greeted Bobby cordially. The two men faced the battery of photographers, self-conscious and anxious to start.

"What will you have?" Jolson tossed his racquet in the air.

"Rough."

"It's smooth. I'll serve," Jolson cried.

"I'll start here."

The warm-up was short and snappy. Jolson seemed in unusually fine form, but Bobby had his customary speed and swapped drive for drive.

"Linesmen ready! Players ready! Play!" cried Congdon from the chair as Jolson stepped up to the line to serve.

The match was on!

The Old Champion quickly found he was up against a stiffer opponent than any he had ever met when he was playing in the flesh.

Modern tennis was a step beyond anything he had ever known, at least tennis as Billy Jolson played it. In the old days the Old Champion used to stand back and swap shots with his opponent until at last he found an opening through which to punch his terrific drive. In the old days his opponent rarely came in to the net for a kill or forced him seriously.

Jolson defied all the rules the Old Champion knew of how the game should be played. In the first place there was no weakness to Jolson's game and, what was worse, in the second he never left openings for the other to hit through. One could never tell what Jolson would do. The old game of one great shot was done. The defending champion chopped, lobbed, cut and rushed the net in such a bewildering variety of tactics that the Old Champion felt all at sea.

Even his tremendous drive, played with all the power of Bobby's splendid young body, was unable to cope with Jolson's marvelous game. For a while he hung even. The first six games were divided to three all but only by the most tremendous efforts on the part of the celestial guide. Finally Jolson drove furiously to Bobby's forehand and came in. It gave the Old Champion his favorite opening down the sideline for his fast-passing drive.

Smash! Twang! The ball shot by Jolson so fast he hardly saw it. For a moment it shook even his iron nerve. His attack faltered slightly and the Old Champion jumped at his opening so ably that Bobby won the set, 6-4.

Jolson was annoyed. It was so ridiculous for an unheard-of youngster to spring from nowhere and walk away like this with the American Championship. Doggedly, silently, grimly, he set out to wear down the boy he faced.

Every point found Bobby chasing the ball from corner to corner as Jolson relentlessly pushed home his attack. The Old Champion was tired, disgusted and so hot that he began to wonder if he really had not made a mistake and missed the earth in his descent and gone all the way down. He could not find a chance to use his tremendous drive, for Bobby's legs never carried Bobby's body to the place where the Old Champion was anything more than an also-ran. Panting, puffing, protesting physically, Bobby dropped the second set, 6-3, and the third, 6-4.

The ten-minute rest gave him a meager chance to recover his lost breath and the Old Champion a new lease on his grip of the racquet. The final struggle would be bitter.

"One all."

"Two all."

"Three all."

"Four all."

The games mounted with monotonous regularity. Both players held service against the most violent assaults of their opponent. It was a battering, all-powerful, awe-inspiring brand of tennis. The two greatest forehands in the world locked in a death grip, neither yielding an inch.

Jolson was cleverly offering up soft short shots at unexpected moments that disconcerted Bobby and nearly caused the Old Champion to pass away, if he had not already done that some years before. The gallery was tense, strung to the height of nervous excitement. All present realized that if Bobby pulled even by winning the set, his youth and daring might avail against Jolson.

The defending champion realized his position more acutely than anyone else. He knew it was now or never. Throughout the eight games which were divided, Jolson fought a growing weakness, by a dogged determination such as only he possesses.

In the ninth game, Bobby reached 30-40 on Jolson's delivery. Two wonderful drives, and a net by Jolson, had accounted for his points. It was now or never.

Jolson drove down the center line, figuring that an unexpected delivery to strength instead of the expected offering to weakness might catch Bobby napping. What a chance! The Old Champion saw his favorite opening, deep in Jolson's backhand corner, there awaiting his shot. Violently he pulled back Bobby's arm and viciously he smote the ball with that marvelous drive that had written tennis history twenty years before.

Crash! Crack! A splintering of wood and the ball fell short and soft in the net. Bobby stood staring at the broken frame in his hand. Then with a muttered cry he flung it under the umpire's chair and picked up his own old bat.

"Deuce," cried the umpire.

"I'm sorry." Jolson came in to the net. "Want to hit a few with that racquet?"

"No, that's all right. Go on!"

The Old Champion was hovering over his beloved racquet. It

was gone beyond repair. Never again could it respond to his wishes. If only he had never left Heaven for this!

The Old Champion floated back to the boy's side. His ghostly hand fell in position on the boy's racquet. Somehow it felt all wrong. He knew it was almost the same as his old one but it felt absolutely out of tune. Jolson served and he and Bobby swung.

The ball flashed far out over the base-line. The Old Champion almost wept as he flapped in Bobby's wake as the boy hopelessly chased Jolson's pitiless drives. He realized something which up to then he had not known. Material things were useless to him. Sentiment and love, alone carried in the world of which he was now a part. It had been his deep affection for his old racquet which made it possible for him to play so well. That particular bit of gut and wood gone, he was helpless.

The press next day commented on the complete collapse of Whitlock's game after he broke his racquet. The final score of 4-6, 6-3, 6-4, 6-4, hardly told the whole story of the debacle.

Dick Thomas hurried up to Bobby before he left the court, after shaking hands with Jolson.

"Well played, Bobby!"

"Thank you, Mr. Thomas. I'm terribly sorry about the racquet. It was yours I broke."

"That's all right, Bobby, don't worry about it. I'm going to ask you to accept it from me as a souvenir of this tournament."

"Thank you, Mr. Thomas. I never played like this before. I may never again, but somehow I feel as if someone has taught me something I didn't know before. I feel I have learned that big drive so I can always make it. For a while it didn't seem as if it belonged to me, but now it does."

"That's fine, Bobby. Where's the racquet?"

"Under the umpire's chair."

"No it isn't."

"Why it must be. I threw it there!"

Bobby hurried over, pulling on his sweater as he came.

"It isn't though, Bobby."

The racquet had disappeared.

The wearied shade of the Old Champion wandered anxiously along the Golden Gate of Heaven. It was locked. He saw no chance of getting in and he needed rest. Even strumming on a harp would have appealed to him as undue exercise at the moment. Suddenly a hand fell on his shoulder. He turned to find the Guardian of the Gate, keys in hand, beside him.

"Where have you been?" chanted the Guardian.

The Old Champion spoke curtly.

"A. W. O. L."

"Splendid, so have I! What's that in your hand?"

The Old Champion gazed down at the twisted piece of wood and strings he clutched unconsciously in his right hand. Then, with a start, remembrance of his afternoon spent, returned to him. He started back from the Guardian of the Gate.

"A tennis racquet, my old one I used on earth."

"Ah, tennis! Fine! You can teach me to play."

"No," cried the Old Champion fiercely. "No. On earth tennis may be heaven, but if this modern game they call tennis gets into Heaven it may turn it into Hades. Let me in."

Wonderingly the Guardian of the Gate unlocked the golden lock with the golden key and the two shades A. W. O. L. from Heaven entered, one to resume his watch at the Gate, the other to search for the nearest harp.

The racquet lay unheeded by the Gate of Heaven.

Ernest Hemingway

MY OLD MAN

When you bet your heart on a horse race,
odds are you're riding for a fall.

I guess looking at it, now, my old man was cut out for a fat guy, one of those regular little roly fat guys you see around, but he sure never got that way, except a little toward the last, and then it wasn't his fault, he was riding over the jumps only and he could afford to carry plenty of weight then. I remember the way he'd pull on a rubber shirt over a couple of jerseys and a big sweat shirt over that, and get me to run with him in the forenoon in the hot sun. He'd have, maybe, taken a trial trip with one of Razzo's skins early in the morning after just getting in from To-rino at four o'clock in the morning and beating it out to the stables in a cab and then with the dew all over everything and the sun just starting to get going, I'd help him pull off his boots and he'd get into a pair of sneakers and all these sweaters and we'd start out.

"Come on, kid," he'd say, stepping up and down on his toes in front of the jock's dressing room, "let's get moving."

Then we'd start off jogging around the infield once, maybe, with him ahead, running nice, and then turn out the gate and along one of those roads with all the trees along both sides of them that run out from San Siro. I'd go ahead of him when we hit the road and I could run pretty good and I'd look around and he'd be jogging easy just behind me and after a little while I'd look around again and he'd begun to sweat. Sweating heavy and he'd just be dogging it along with his eyes on my back, but when he'd catch me looking at him he'd grin and say, "Sweating plenty?" When my old man grinned, nobody could help but grin too. We'd keep right on running out toward the mountains and then my old man would yell, "Hey Joe!" and I'd look back and he'd be sitting under a tree with a towel he'd had around his waist wrapped around his neck.

I'd come back and sit down beside him and he'd pull a rope out of his pocket and start skipping rope out in the sun with the sweat pouring off his face and him skipping rope out in the white dust with the rope going cloppetty, cloppetty, clop, clop, clop, and the sun hotter, and him working harder up and down a patch of the road. Say, it was a treat to see my old man skip rope, too. He could whirr it fast or lop it slow and fancy. Say, you ought to have seen them look at us sometimes, when they'd come by, going into town walking along with big white steers hauling the cart. They sure looked as though they thought the old man was nuts. He'd start the rope whirring till they'd stop dead still and watch him, then give the steers a cluck and a poke with the goad and get going again.

When I'd sit watching him working out in the hot sun I sure felt fond of him. He sure was fun and he done his work so hard and he'd finish up with a regular whirring that'd drive the sweat out on his face like water and then sling the rope at the tree and come over and sit down with me and lean back against the tree with the towel and a sweater wrapped around his neck.

"Sure is hell keeping it down, Joe," he'd say and lean back and shut his eyes and breathe long and deep, "it ain't like when you're a kid." Then he'd get up and before he started to cool we'd jog along back to the stables. That's the way it was keeping down to weight. He was worried all the time. Most jocks can just about ride off all they want to. A jock loses about a kilo every time he rides, but my old man was sort of dried out and he couldn't keep down his kilos without all that running.

I remember once at San Siro, Regoli, that was riding for Buzoni, came out across the paddock going to the bar for something cool; and flicking his boots with his whip, after he's just weighed in and my old man had just weighed in too, and came out with the saddle under his arm looking red-faced and tired and too big for his silks and he stood there looking at young Regoli standing up to the outdoors bar, cool and kid-looking, and I said, "What's the matter, Dad?" 'cause I thought maybe Regoli had bumped him or something and he just looked at Regoli and said, "Oh, to hell with it," and went on to the dressing room.

Well, it would have been all right, maybe, if we'd stayed in Milan and ridden at Milan and Torino, 'cause if there ever were any easy courses, it's those two. "Pianola, Joe," my old man said when he dismounted in the winning stall after what everyone thought was a hell of a steeplechase. I asked him once. "This course rides itself. It's the pace you're going at, that makes riding the jumps dangerous, Joe. We ain't going any pace here, and they ain't really bad jumps either. But it's the pace always—not the jumps—that makes the trouble."

San Siro was the swellest course I'd ever seen but the old man said it was a dog's life. Going back and forth between Mirafiore and San Siro and riding just about every day in the week with a train ride every other night.

I was nuts about the horses, too. There's something about it, when they come out and go up the track to the post. Sort of dancy and tight looking with the jock keeping a tight hold on them and maybe easing off a little and letting them run a little going up. Then once they were at the barrier it got me worse than anything. Especially at San Siro with that big green infield and the mountains way off and the fat starter with his big whip

and the jocks fiddling them around and then the barrier snapping up and that bell going off and them all getting off in a bunch
and then commencing to string out. You know the way a bunch
of skins gets off. If you're up in the stand with a pair of glasses
all you see is them plunging off and then the bell goes off and it
seems like it rings for a thousand years and then they come
sweeping round the turn. There wasn't ever anything like it for
me.

But my old man said one day, in the dressing room, when
he was getting into his street clothes, "None of these things
are horses, Joe. They'd kill that bunch of skates for their hides
and hoofs up at Paris." That was the day he'd won the Premio
Commercio with Lantorna shooting her out of the field the last
hundred meters like pulling a cork out of a bottle.

It was right after the Premio Commercio that we pulled out
and left Italy. My old man and Holbrook and a fat Italian in a
straw hat that kept wiping his face with a handkerchief were having an argument at a table in the Galleria. They were all talking
French and the two of them was after my old man about something. Finally he didn't say anything any more but just sat there
and looked at Holbrook, and the two of them kept after him, first
one talking and then the other, and the fat Italian always butting
in on Holbrook.

"You go out and buy me a *Sportsman*, will you, Joe?" my old
man said, and handed me a couple of soldi without looking away
from Holbrook.

So I went out of the Galleria and walked over to in front of
the Scala and bought a paper, and came back and stood a little
way away because I didn't want to butt in and my old man was
sitting back in his chair looking down at his coffee and fooling
with a spoon and Holbrook and the big Italian were standing and
the big Italian was wiping his face and shaking his head. And I
came up and my old man acted just as though the two of them
weren't standing there and said, "Want an ice, Joe?" Holbrook

looked down at my old man and said slow and careful, "You son of a bitch," and he and the fat Italian went out through the tables.

My old man sat there and sort of smiled at me, but his face was white and he looked sick as hell and I was scared and felt sick inside because I knew something had happened and I didn't see how anybody could call my old man a son of a bitch, and get away with it. My old man opened up the *Sportsman* and studied the handicaps for a while and then he said, "You got to take a lot of things in this world, Joe." And three days later we left Milan for good on the Turin train for Paris, after an auction sale out in front of Turner's stables of everything we couldn't get into a trunk and a suit case.

We got into Paris early in the morning in a long, dirty station the old man told me was the Gare de Lyon. Paris was an awful big town after Milan. Seems like in Milan everybody is going somewhere and all the trams run somewhere and there ain't any sort of a mix-up, but Paris is all balled up and they never do straighten it out. I got to like it, though, part of it, anyway, and say, it's got the best race courses in the world. Seems as though that were the thing that keeps it all going and about the only thing you can figure on is that every day the buses will be going out to whatever track they're running at, going right out through everything to the track. I never really got to know Paris well, because I just came in about once or twice a week with the old man from Maisons and he always sat at the Café de la Paix on the Opera side with the rest of the gang from Maisons and I guess that's one of the busiest parts of the town. But, say, it is funny that a big town like Paris wouldn't have a Galleria, isn't it?

Well, we went out to live at Maisons-Lafitte, where just about everybody lives except the gang at Chantilly, with a Mrs. Meyers that runs a boarding house. Maisons is about the swellest place to live I've ever seen in all my life. The town ain't so much, but there's a lake and a swell forest that we used to go off bumming in all day, a couple of us kids, and my old man made me a sling shot and we got a lot of things with it but the best one was a magpie. Young Dick Atkinson shot a rabbit with it one day and we put it under a tree and were all sitting around and Dick had some cigarettes and all of a sudden the rabbit jumped up and beat it into the brush and we chased it but we couldn't find it. Gee, we had fun at Maisons. Mrs. Meyers used to give me lunch in the morning and I'd be gone all day. I learned to talk French quick. It's an easy language.

As soon as we got to Maisons, my old man wrote to Milan for his license and he was pretty worried till it came. He used to sit around the Café de Paris in Maisons with the gang, there were lots of guys he'd known when he rode up at Paris, before the war, lived at Maisons, and there's a lot of time to sit around because the work around a racing stable, for the jocks, that is, is all cleaned up by nine o'clock in the morning. They take the first bunch of skins out to gallop them at 5:30 in the morning and they work the second lot at 8 o'clock. That means getting up early all right and going to bed early, too. If a jock's riding for somebody too, he can't go boozing around because the trainer always has an eye on him if he's a kid and if he ain't working he sits around the Café de Paris with the gang and they can all sit around about two or three hours in front of some drink like a vermouth and seltz and they talk and tell stories and shoot pool and it's sort of like a club or the Galleria in Milan. Only it ain't really like the Galleria because there everybody is going by all the time and there's everybody around at the tables.

Well, my old man got his license all right. They sent it through to him without a word and he rode a couple of times. Amiens, up country and that sort of thing, but he didn't seem to get any engagement. Everybody liked him and whenever I'd come into the Café in the forenoon I'd find somebody drinking with him because my old man wasn't tight like most of these jockeys that have got the first dollar they made riding at the World's Fair in

St. Louis in nineteen ought four. That's what my old man would say when he'd kid George Burns. But it seemed like everybody steered clear of giving my old man any mounts.

We went out to wherever they were running every day with the car from Maisons and that was the most fun of all. I was glad when the horses came back from Deauville and the summer. Even though it meant no more bumming in the woods, 'cause then we'd ride to Enghien or Tremblay or St. Cloud and watch them from the trainers' and jockeys' stand. I sure learned about racing from going out with that gang and the fun of it was going every day.

I remember once out at St. Cloud. It was a big two hundred thousand franc race with seven entries and Kzar a big favorite. I went around to the paddock to see the horses with my old man and you never saw such horses. This Kzar is a great big yellow horse that looks like just nothing but run. I never saw such a' horse. He was being led around the paddocks with his head down and when he went by me I felt all hollow inside he was so beautiful. There never was such a wonderful, lean, running built horse. And he went around the paddock putting his feet just so and quiet and careful and moving easy like he knew just what he had to do and not jerking and standing up on his legs and getting wild eyed like you see these selling platers with a shot of dope in them. The crowd was so thick I couldn't see him again except just his legs going by and some yellow and my old man started out through the crowd and I followed him over to the jock's dressing room back in the trees and there was a big crowd around there, too, but the man at the door in a derby nodded to my old man and we got in and everybody was sitting around and getting dressed and pulling shirts over their heads and pulling boots on and it all smelled hot and sweaty and linimenty and outside was the crowd looking in.

The old man went over and sat down beside George Gardner that was getting into his pants and said, "What's the dope,

George?'' just in an ordinary tone of voice 'cause there ain't any use him feeling around because George either can tell him or he can't tell him.

"He won't win," George says very low, leaning over and buttoning the bottoms of his breeches.

"Who will?" my old man says, leaning over close so nobody can hear.

"Kircubbin," George says, "and if he does, save me a couple of tickets."

My old man says something in a regular voice to George and George says, "Don't ever bet on anything I tell you," kidding like, and we beat it out and through all the crowd that was looking in, over to the 100 franc mutuel machine. But I knew something big was up because George is Kzar's jockey. On the way he gets one of the yellow odds-sheets with the starting prices on and Kzar is only paying 5 for 10, Cefisidote is next at 3 to 1 and fifth down the list this Kircubbin at 8 to 1. My old man bets five thousand on Kircubbin to win and puts on a thousand to place and we went around back of the grandstand to go up the stairs and get a place to watch the race.

We were jammed in tight and first a man in a long coat with a gray tall hat and a whip folded up in his hand came out and then one after another the horses, with the jocks up and a stable boy holding the bridle on each side and walking along, followed the old guy. That big yellow horse Kzar came first. He didn't look so big when you first looked at him until you saw the length of his legs and the whole way he's built and the way he moves. Gosh, I never saw such a horse. George Gardner was riding him and they moved along slow, back of the old guy in the gray tall hat that walked along like he was a ring master in a circus. Back of Kzar, moving along smooth and yellow in the sun, was a good looking black with a nice head with Tommy Archibald riding him; and after the black was a string of five more horses all moving along slow in a procession past the grandstand and the pesage. My old man said the black was Kircubbin and I took a good look at him and he was a nice-looking horse, all right, but nothing like Kzar.

Everybody cheered Kzar when he went by and he sure was one swell-looking horse. The procession of them went around on the other side past the pelouse and then back up to the near end of the course and the circus master had the stable boys turn them loose one after another so they could gallop by the stands on their way up to the post and let everybody have a good look at them. They weren't at the post hardly any time at all when the gong started and you could see them way off across the infield all in a bunch starting on the first swing like a lot of little toy horses. I was watching them through the glasses and Kzar was running well back, with one of the bays making the pace. They swept down and around and came pounding past and Kzar was way back when they passed us and this Kircubbin horse in front and going smooth. Gee, it's awful when they go by you and then you have to watch them go farther away and get smaller and smaller and then all bunched up on the turns and then come around towards into the stretch and you feel like swearing and goddamming worse and worse. Finally they made the last turn and came into the straightaway with this Kircubbin horse way out in front. Everybody was looking funny and saying "Kzar" in sort of a sick way and them pounding nearer down the stretch, and then something came out of the pack right into my glasses like a horse-headed yellow streak and everybody began to yell "Kzar" as though they were crazy. Kzar came on faster than I'd ever seen anything in my life and pulled up on Kircubbin that was going fast as any black horse could go with the jock flogging hell out of him with the gad and they were right dead neck and neck for a second but Kzar seemed going about twice as fast with those great jumps and that head out—but it was while they were neck and neck that they passed the winning post and when the numbers went up in the slots the first one was 2 and that meant that Kircubbin had won.

I felt all trembly and funny inside, and then we were all jammed

in with the people going downstairs to stand in front of the board where they'd post what Kircubbin paid. Honest, watching the race I'd forgot how much my old man had bet on Kircubbin. I'd wanted Kzar to win so damned bad. But now it was all over it was swell to know we had the winner.

"Wasn't it a swell race, Dad?" I said to him.

He looked at me sort of funny with his derby on the back of his head. "George Gardner's a swell jockey, all right," he said. "It sure took a great jock to keep that Kzar horse from winning."

Of course I knew it was funny all the time. But my old man saying that right out like that sure took the kick all out of it for me and I didn't get the real kick back again ever, even when they posted the numbers up on the board and the bell rang to pay off and we saw that Kircubbin paid 67.50 for 10. All round people were saying, "Poor Kzar! Poor Kzar!" And I thought, I wish I were a jockey and could have rode him instead of that son of a bitch. And that was funny, thinking of George Gardner as a son of a bitch because I'd always liked him and besides he'd given us the winner, but I guess that's what he is, all right.

My old man had a big lot of money after that race and he took to coming into Paris oftener. If they raced at Tremblay he'd have them drop him in town on their way back to Maisons and he and I'd sit out in front of the Café de la Paix and watch the people go by. It's funny sitting there. There's streams of people going by and all sorts of guys come up and want to sell you things, and I loved to sit there with my old man. That was when we'd have the most fun. Guys would come by selling funny rabbits that jumped if you squeezed a bulb and they'd come up to us and my old man would kid with them. He could talk French just like English and all those kind of guys knew him 'cause you can always tell a jockey—and then we always sat at the same table and they got used to seeing us there. There were guys selling matrimonial papers and girls selling rubber eggs that when you squeezed them a rooster came out of them and one old wormy-looking guy that went by with post-cards of Paris, showing them to everybody, and, of course, nobody ever bought any, and then he would come back and show the under side of the pack and they would all be smutty post-cards and lots of people would dig down and buy them.

Gee, I remember the funny people that used to go by. Girls around supper time looking for somebody to take them out to eat and they'd speak to my old man and he'd make some joke at them in French and they'd pat me on the head and go on. Once there was an American woman sitting with her kid daughter at the next table to us and they were both eating ices and I kept looking at the girl and she was awfully good looking and I smiled at her and she smiled at me but that was all that ever came of it because I looked for her mother and her every day and I made up ways that I was going to speak to her and I wondered if I got to know her if her mother would let me take her out to Auteuil or Tremblay but I never saw either of them again. Anyway, I guess it wouldn't have been any good, anyway, because looking back on it I remember the way I thought out would be best to speak to her was to say, "Pardon me, but perhaps I can give you a winner at Enghien today?" and, after all, maybe she would have thought I was a tout instead of really trying to give her a winner.

We'd sit at the Café de la Paix, my old man and me, and we had a big drag with the waiter because my old man drank whisky and it cost five francs, and that meant a good tip when the sau- cers were counted up. My old man was drinking more than I'd ever seen him, but he wasn't riding at all now and besides he said that whisky kept his weight down. But I noticed he was putting it on, all right, just the same. He'd busted away from his old gang out at Maisons and seemed to like just sitting around on the boulevard with me. But he was dropping money every day at the track. He'd feel sort of doleful after the last race, if he'd lost on the day, until we'd get to our table and he'd have his first whisky and then he'd be fine.

He'd be reading the *Paris-Sport* and he'd look over at me and say, "Where's your girl, Joe?" to kid me on account I had told him about the girl that day at the next table. And I'd get red, but I liked being kidded about her. It gave me a good feeling. "Keep your eye peeled for her, Joe," he'd say, "she'll be back."

He'd ask me questions about things and some of the things I'd say he'd laugh. And then he'd get started talking about things. About riding down in Egypt, or at St. Moritz on the ice before my mother died, and about during the war when they had regular races down in the south of France without any purses, or betting or crowd or anything just to keep the breed up. Regular races with the jocks riding hell out of the horses. Gee, I could listen to my old man talk by the hour, especially when he'd had a couple or so of drinks. He'd tell me about when he was a boy in Kentucky and going coon hunting, and the old days in the States before everything went on the bum there. And he'd say, "Joe, when we've got a decent stake, you're going back there to the States and go to school."

"What've I got to go back there to go to school for when everything's on the bum there?" I'd ask him.

"That's different," he'd say and get the waiter over and pay the pile of saucers and we'd get a taxi to the Gare St. Lazare and get on the train out to Maisons.

One day at Auteuil, after a selling steeplechase, my old man bought in the winner for 30,000 francs. He had to bid a little to get him but the stable let the horse go finally and my old man had his permit and his colors in a week. Gee, I felt proud when my old man was an owner. He fixed it up for stable space with Charles Drake and cut out coming in to Paris, and started his running and sweating out again, and him and I were the whole stable gang. Our horse's name was Gilford, he was Irish bred and a nice, sweet jumper. My old man figured that training him and riding him, himself, he was a good investment. I was proud of everything and I thought Gilford was as good a horse as Kzar. He was a good, solid jumper, a bay, with plenty of speed on the flat, if you asked him for it, and a nice-looking horse, too.

Gee, I was fond of him. The first time he started with my old man up, he finished third in a 2500 meter hurdle race and when my old man got off him, all sweating and happy in the place stall, and went in to weigh, I felt as proud of him as though it was the first race he'd ever placed in. You see, when a guy ain't been riding for a long time, you can't make yourself really believe that he has ever rode. The whole thing was different now, 'cause down in Milan, even big races never seemed to make any difference to my old man, if he won he wasn't ever excited or anything, and now it was so I couldn't hardly sleep the night before a race and I knew my old man was excited, too, even if he didn't show it. Riding for yourself makes an awful difference.

Second time Gilford and my old man started, was a rainy Sunday at Auteuil, in the Prix du Marat, a 4500 meter steeplechase. As soon as he'd gone out I beat it up in the stand with the new glasses my old man had bought for me to watch them. They started way over at the far end of the course and there was some trouble at the barrier. Something with goggle blinders on was making a great fuss and rearing around and busted the barrier once, but I could see my old man in our black jacket, with a white cross and a black cap, sitting up on Gilford, and patting him with his hand. Then they were off in a jump and out of sight behind the trees and the gong going for dear life and the pari-mutuel wickets rattling down. Gosh, I was so excited, I was afraid to look at them, but I fixed the glasses on the place where they would come out back of the trees and then out they came with the old black jacket going third and they all sailing over the jump like birds. Then they went out of sight again and then they came pounding out and down the hill and all going nice and sweet and easy and taking the fence smooth in a bunch, and moving away from us all solid. Looked as though you could walk across on their backs they were all so bunched and going so smooth. Then they bellied over the big double Bullfinch and something came down. I couldn't see who it was, but in a minute the horse was up and galloping free and the field, all bunched still, sweeping around the long left turn into the straightaway. They jumped the stone wall and came jammed down the stretch toward the big water-jump right in front of the stands. I saw them coming and hollered at my old man as he went by, and he was leading by about a length and riding way out, and light as a monkey, and they were racing for the water-jump. They took off over the big hedge of the water-jump in a pack and then there was a crash, and two horses pulled sideways out of it, and kept on going, and three others were piled up. I couldn't see my old man anywhere. One horse kneed himself up and the jock had hold of the bridle and mounted and went slamming on after the place money. The other horse was up and away by himself, jerking his head and galloping with the bridle rein hanging and the jock staggered over to one side of the track against the fence. Then Gilford rolled over to one side off my old man and got up and started to run on three legs with his front off hoof dangling and there was my old man laying there on the grass flat out with his face up and blood all over the side of his head. I ran down the stand and bumped into a jam of people and got to the rail and a cop grabbed me and held me and two big stretcher-bearers were going out after my old man and around on the other side of the course I saw three horses, strung way out, coming out of the trees and taking the jump.

My old man was dead when they brought him in and while a doctor was listening to his heart with a thing plugged in his ears, I heard a shot up the track that meant they'd killed Gilford. I lay down beside my old man, when they carried the stretcher into the hospital room, and hung onto the stretcher and cried and cried, and he looked so white and gone and so awfully dead, and I couldn't help feeling that if my old man was dead maybe they didn't need to have shot Gilford. His hoof might have got well. I don't know. I loved my old man so much.

Then a couple of guys came in and one of them patted me on

the back and then went over and looked at my old man and then pulled a sheet off the cot and spread it over him; and the other was telephoning in French for them to send the ambulance to take him out to Maisons. And I couldn't stop crying, crying and choking, sort of, and George Gardner came in and sat down beside me on the floor and put his arm around me and says, "Come on, Joe, old boy. Get up and we'll go out and wait for the ambulance."

George and I went out to the gate and I was trying to stop bawling and George wiped off my face with his handkerchief and we were standing back a little ways while the crowd was going out of the gate and a couple of guys stopped near us while we were waiting for the crowd to get through the gate and one of them was counting a bunch of mutuel tickets and he said, "Well, Butler got his, all right."

The other guy said, "I don't give a good goddam if he did, the crook. He had it coming to him on the stuff he's pulled."

"I'll say he had," said the other guy, and tore the bunch of tickets in two.

And George Gardner looked at me to see if I'd heard and I had all right and he said, "Don't you listen to what those bums said, Joe. Your old man was one swell guy."

But I don't know. Seems like when they get started they don't leave a guy nothing.

Gerald Kersh

ALI THE TERRIBLE TURK

A champion's skill fades.
But not a champion's pride.

From the gymnasium came the noise of two men shouting to-gether. Kration was roaring with laughter, while Ali grunted with rage. Adam stood between them.

"What's the trouble?" said Fabian.

Ali replied, "There is only two kinds of Cypriot. There is the Cypriot who always giggles, and the Cypriot who never smiles."

"Hoh-hoh-hoh!" laughed Kration.

"The first kind laughs all the time, because he is too stupid to see that he is really something to weep at; the other frowns all the time, because he is too foolish to see how ridiculous he is."

Kration still laughed. Ali went on, at the top of his voice, "They all wave their hair. They have only three trades. There is no Cypriot who is not a barber, a tailor, or a kitchen boy. In the end they all call themselves wrestlers. But damn it, their national sport is dominoes. They bang down the dominoes, and shout—that is the game. They make love to servant girls who take them to the pictures. Then they are national heroes. And they all fight like slaves. *Ptoo*, and *ptoo* on the Cypriot!"

"Big belly!" laughed Kration, showing twenty brilliant teeth.

When Kration laughed he looked like a man who was completely satisfied with himself. The expression of his smiling face said, "If I were not Kration, I would be God Almighty." But as soon as his mouth closed, his face changed. Savagery came into it. He looked strong and ferocious enough to tear himself apart. His hair crouched low on his forehead, trying to obliterate his eyebrows; his eyebrows, colliding over his nose in a spray of black hair, endeavored to smother his eyes; and only the flat, heavy prow of his nose kept his eyes apart—otherwise, they would have snapped at each other. Meanwhile they waited, smoldering; while his upper lip snarled in triumph over the lower, which, from time to time, jumped up and clamped down on it. Turkey, Greece, and Africa waged war in his veins. Even his hair carried on ancient warfare. There was antagonism in his very follicles, and the hair writhed out, enormously thick, twisted, rebellious, kinked, frizzled, and dried up.

He said to Adam, "He too old to hit. I hit him once, he die. One finger enough. Tiss finger: look!" He wagged a forefinger.

"Lay off!" said Fabian.

"He said I was old! He said I was fat."

Fabian grinned. "Old? Fat? Hell, can't we all see you're a two-year-old? Ain't you wasting away to a shadow?"

"You may joke, yes. But let me fight him. I will show him how old I am. . . . *Tfoo,* I say! Didn't your grandmother learn that a Turk was a better man than a Cypriot while your grandfather hid under the bed? Mongrel!"

"You—"

"Hold um!" yelled Fabian, and attached himself, like a mosquito, to Ali's wrist, while Adam threw his arms around Kration and held him. The Cypriot shook himself. Adam's feet left the floor.

"Listen! Listen!" shouted Fabian. "What's the excitement? You two are having a chance to fight it out in the ring. I'm billing you as a surprise item for next show. Why waste your energy down here, mugs? Ali is making a comeback, see? Ali the Terrible Turk, and Kration. See?"

"Good," said Ali.

"No," said Kration, "my friends will laugh at me for fighting an old man."

"Two guineas apiece!" said Fabian.

"No," said Kration.

Ali suggested, "Give him four, my two and his two. I will fight him for nothing."

"Well?" said Fabian.

"Right," said Kration.

Ali sneered. "They can be bought, these champions. *Ptoo!* He would sell his brother and sister for a small cup of coffee. His friends would laugh at him. Hou! They will laugh all the more when I tie him up like a brown-paper parcel."

Kration replied, over his shoulder, "Fat guts, say your prayers."

Adam took Fabian aside, and said, "Seriously, are you going to let those two fight?"

"Why not?"

"It's a crime! Ali's nearly seventy; Kration's not yet thirty. Ali's old, but he won't admit it. And he's sick."

"Boloney! He's a tiger."

"But—"

"What are you worrying about? Afraid he'll drop dead, or something?"

"I'm afraid he'll take a beating, and I don't want to see it."

"Then stay away."

"I'll give you a fiver if you'll call the fight off."

"Are you trying to offer me money to interfere with sport? Besides, there's more than that in it for me."

"Oh, go and drown yourself." Adam went to the dressing room, and found Ali. "Ali, do me a favor. Call this crazy fight off."

"Why?"

"Why? You get nothing for it, and besides, Kration's not a wrestler; he's a roughhouse specialist, a killer."

"Yah? And I am a hangman."

"But, Ali!"

Ali turned with bulging eyes. "Go to the devil! Leave me alone!" he said.

Adam and Nosseross walked through the sharp air of the morning, to the Corner House.

"Oh, my Christ," said Nosseross, "look who's here!"

It was Fabian, somewhat flushed with excitement, drinking coffee at an adjacent table. Even as Nosseross spoke, Fabian cried, "Oh, boy, oh, boy, do my eyes deceive me?" and came to their table. "What, Phil Nosseross, you old crook, you! Listen, Phil, if you want to see a show, come and see the one I'm running. Listen, Phil, you've heard of Ali the Terrible Turk? He's making a comeback. And is that man in form or is he in form? I'll tell you—he's in form. Is this gonna be a needle fight, or is this gonna be a needle fight? Boy, will they tear lumps out of each other!"

Adam said, "I have half a mind to smack you on the nose."

"Go on, then, smack me on the nose!" said Fabian. "Am I supposed to be scared?"

"What is all this, anyway?" asked Nosseross.

"The fight of the century. Ali the Terrible Turk against Kration. Coming?"

"What, old Ali? He must be getting on for seventy. I saw him thirty years ago, and he wasn't anybody's chicken then. But what a fighter!" said Nosseross. "Not much skill, mind you, and no psychology; but what a terror! Heart of a lion, and about as strong as a bear. Is he still alive?"

"You'll see," said Fabian.

"Listen," said Adam, "let me referee that fight."

"I'm refereeing it myself," said Fabian. He grinned at Nosseross: "He's scared in case Ali—"

"It's not that. Poor old Ali's finished, and you know it. He can't win. About the only thing he's got left is his pride. He's only got one eye. The only thing that keeps him going is the fact that he's never been defeated. And now you match him against a man forty years younger. You ought to be ashamed of yourself!"

"Any betting on this fight?" asked Fabian, grinning.

"With you refereeing it?" said Adam. "Thanks."

"Betting?" said Nosseross. "You're crazy. Dog racing is dirty; boxing isn't clean; racing stinks a bit; but wrestling! There hasn't been a straight match in forty years."

Fabian grinned in Adam's face. "I thought you'd be scared to bet on Ali," he said.

"What odds are you laying?"

"Twenties on Kration."

"I'll take you," said Adam. "Give me forty pounds to two."

"You're on."

"Idiot," said Nosseross, when Fabian had gone. "Why d'you let him rib you into giving him two pounds?"

"I'm not so sure. Old Ali'll never lie down while there's breath in him. But I'd give a tenner to have this fight called off," said Adam.

Here, in one of the dressing rooms, Ali was preparing for the fight. Ali was fat, fantastically fat. When he was naked, one could see how malevolently time had dealt with him; blowing him up like a balloon, and dragging him down like a bursting sack. His pectorals hung flabbily, like the breasts of an old woman. His belly sagged!

He brushed his mustache, pinched out a length of Hungarian Pomade, and molded the ends to needle points with a dexterous twirl.

"Kration'll try and grab that," said Adam, "just to give the lads a laugh."

"Let him try!"

"Ali, why not trim it down?"

Ali swore that he would as soon trim down another essentially masculine attribute. He put on a curious belt, nearly a foot wide, made of canvas and rubber. "Pull this tight, please; as tight as you can," he said; and muttered, with an apologetic look, "I do not want the people to be under the impression that I have been getting a leetle bit fat. . . ."

Adam pulled at the straps, and, like toothpaste in a tube, soft fat oozed up above Ali's waistline.

"Ali, is this wise? This belt squeezes your guts together. If Kration hits you, or kicks you there—"

"Let him try." Ali writhed into a set of long black tights, and pulled over them a pair of red silk shorts. "Now, help me with this sash." He held up a long band of frayed red satin, embroidered with Arabic characters. "This was a present from Abdul Hamid. . . ."

"Ali, you're crazy to press your belly in like that!"

"*Ptah!*" Ali drew himself up, and stood with folded arms. "Tell me, do I look good?"

Adam felt the impulse to shed tears. "Fine!"

"One day, I let you sculpture me."

"Thanks, Ali. Listen, Ali; be cautious, for heaven's sake."

"My little friend, you forget that I have won hundreds of fights—that I have never been beaten!"

"I know. But I should hate like hell to see you hurt."

Ali laughed. "Professor Froehner tore one of my ribs right out of the skin, but I beat him; and I fought again next day. In all my life, nobody ever heard me cry out! Nobody ever saw me tap the mat. Leblond had me by the foot in a jujitsu hold. 'Give in, or I break your ankle,' he said. I said, 'Break on, Leblond: Ali never gives in.' And he broke my ankle, and I got up on one foot, and pinned him. I said, 'You cannot hurt Ali. But he whom Ali grips, God forgets!' That is me!"

"Oh, I'm sure you'll win. I've betted on you."

"Good boy! What odds did they lay against me?"

"Very small."

"You're lying. They think I'm an old man. They laugh. Good, let them. And in the end, when they laugh on the other side of the face, I shall laugh, too—I shall laugh right into their eyes and say, 'The old wolf still has teeth.' Do I look good?"

"You look like a champion, Ali, you really do."

Ali laughed, until the fat on his stomach bounced like a cat in a sack. "Ha-ha-ha! I surprised you, eh? . . . They think I'm going to fool about with this Greek, this Cypriot. No. I shall walk in— one, two, three; up with the legs, back with the head—dash him down, pick him up like a child, shake him like a kitten; then over my head, bim-bam, and pin him. Back again—forward with his head, under my arm with it, and *khaaa!* my old stranglehold, un- til his eyes pop out. Then I shall pick him up like a dumbbell, and hold him above my head, and say to the crowd: 'This is the man who thought he could beat Ali the Turk!' Then—"

An open door let in the shouting of a crowd. Legs Mahogany came through, bleeding from the nose, followed by the Black Strangler, who staggered as he walked.

An attendant came in, and said, "Ali!"

Ali put on a dressing gown of quilted red silk, thirty years old, and eroded by moths. "Smart, eh? A woman gave me this in Vienna, in . . . I forget the date. . . ."

Adam whispered: "Give me your glass eye: it's madness to wrestle in one of those things."

"Rubbish! And let him see I have a blind side?"

"Give it to me, I tell you!"

"If you insist, then, take it." Ali slid out his left eye, and gave it to Adam, who put it in his waistcoat pocket. Then he strode, with slow dignity, out to the ringside, while through his head ran the cheerful rhythm of the "March of the Gladiators," the tune to which the old wrestlers at the International Tournaments had strutted in glory round the arenas.

There was a roar of applause. Ali raised his hands to acknowl- edge it, when he saw Kration, already in the ring, bowing and smiling. Ali grasped the ropes and swung himself up. There was a pause. A little trickle of clapping broke out; then laughter, which rose and swelled, pierced by high catcalls and shrill whistles. . . .

"Hoooi! Laurel and 'Ardy!"

"Where d'you get them trousis?"

"Take yer whiskers orf! We can't see yer!"

Somebody began to sing, in a good tenor voice, "It happened on the beach at Belly-Belly!"

Figler's friend, Lew, rose and shouted, in a voice trained in the marketplaces of the earth, "Good old Ali! We remember you!"

Ali tore off his dressing gown and threw it at Adam.

"Go on, laugh!" he cried.

They laughed.

Fabian shrieked into a megaphone, "Ladies and gentlemen! On my right, two hundred and forty pounds of bone, muscle, brain, and nerve, Kration of Cyprus, contender for championship honors! . . . On my left—"

"Father Christmas!" said a voice; and there was another shout of laughter.

"Ali the Terrible Turk, ex-heavyweight champion of the world, now making a sensational comeback—"

"Champion of wot world?" yelled a thin cockney voice.

"Lad-eez and gentlemen! The name of Ali the Terrible Turk was a household word at the beginning of the century—"

"Wot century?"

("That's what you get, if you get old without any money," said Lew to Figler.)

Fabian stepped back. Kration and Ali went to their corners. Kration still smiled. It was best, he decided, to let it seem that this affair was an elaborate joke. Ali was as grim as death.

"Now don't forget—take it easy!" whispered Adam.

Ali replied, "I shall have him pinned within twenty seconds. Count twenty, slowly—"

The gong clanged.

The wrestlers went out into the ring.

Kration advanced with the grace of a dancer. Ali moved slowly, jaws clamped, chin down. They circled about each other, feinting. Then there was a sound like the crack of a whip. Before Ali's fat-clogged, time-laden muscles could coordinate in a counter-attack, Kration had slapped him on the buttocks.

"Get 'im by the 'orns!" somebody shouted.

"Right," said Kration, and grabbed at Ali's mustache. But next moment, a grip like pincers closed on his wrist, a force like an earthquake twirled him around and his hand went back over his head toward his shoulderblades.

Kration broke out into a sweat. It occurred to him that Ali was in savage earnest. He had not sufficient skill to break the hold. Resisting Ali's pressure with all his strength, he butted backward with his head. The hard, round skull, padded with kinky black hair, jolted against Ali's jaw. The Turk snarled and tried to knock Kration's feet from under him; but between himself and his opponent, his vast abdomen stood like a wall. Kration's head jerked back again. In Ali's nose, something like a lever in a pump, and bright red blood began to run onto his mustache.

Kration broke away, whirling around, and in turning, struck Ali on the jaw with his forearm. It seemed to Ali that the Cypriot was swimming in a sea of red water reticulated with a network of dazzling light; and that the voice of this sea was laughter. But even as his brain wavered, his ancient instincts were sending him lumbering after Kration, while his consciousness automatically juggled with the logic of a hundred different forms of attack. . . .

He's too fast: Waste no strength chasing! Get close and crush! His huge right hand hooked Kration's neck. Kration's fingers, forked like a snake's tongue, flickered toward his eyes. Ali ducked. Kration's nails scratched his forehead. Then Ali had his right hand in an irresistible grip. Adam saw his back quiver.

"Flying mare!" screamed a woman's voice.

Ali heaved Kration off his feet by his right arm; stooped to throw him over his shoulder; then stopped. The edge of his belt had cut him short. They stayed, for a moment, in this ignominious posture. Then Kration, wriggling like a python, caught Ali's throat between his biceps and forearm, twisted a leg between Ali's thighs, grunted, tugged; then writhed away as they fell. The Turk's body struck the mat with the dead thud of a falling tree. Something snapped: his belt had burst. Kration uttered a triumphant yell and pulled it away, leaped back and held it over his head.

Laughter roared through the spectators like a wind through the trees. Ali was up, growling. Fabian took the belt from Kration's hands, muttering, as he did so, "Liven it up a bit, can't you, you two? Don't play about like kids in a bloody nursery! Come on, now!"

Kration evaded Ali's slashing right hand, threw himself back against the ropes, and fired himself across the ring like a stone from a catapult. His right shoulder struck Ali in the abdomen. Ali fell backward with a tremendous gasp, but even as he fell, rolled over with a grunt and caught Kration below the ribs in a scissors hold.

Kration felt like a man in a train smash, pinned by a fallen ceiling. He writhed, but Ali held fast. The crowd screamed. Kration breathed in short coughs—*Asssss. . . . Asssss. . . . Assssss.* He tensed all the iron muscles of his stomach. Ali still struggled for breath: every exhalation, blowing through the blood which still ran from his nose, spattered the mat with red drops: *Prup-aghhh . . . prup-aghhh . . .* He realized that he could not hold Kration for more than another ten seconds. Cramp crawled in the muscles of his thighs.

Kration ground the heel of his hand into Ali's mouth, and broke loose; leaped high in the air, and came down backside first. Ali saw him coming, but could not move quickly enough. Kration's two hundred and forty pounds dropped, like a flour sack falling from a loft, onto Ali's chest. Wind rushed out—*Ahffffffff!*—with a fine spray of blood. Darkness descended on the Turk; for

perhaps one second, he became unconscious. His mind floundered up out of a darkness as deep and cold as Siberian midnight. He found himself struggling to his feet.

Adam's voice reached his ears as from an immense distance. "Careful, Ali, careful!" Kration was upon him again, on his blind side, and had caught him in a wrist lock.

Ali's brain flickered and wavered like a candle flame in a draft. There was a countermove; something . . . something . . . he could not remember. He put out all his might, and caught one of the Cypriot's wrists; grunted, "Hup!" like a coal heaver; and used his tremendous weight to spin Kration around and swing him off his feet. As Kration staggered, Ali caught one of his ankles, twirled him around, six inches off the mat, in the manner of an acrobatic dancer, then let go. The Cypriot fell on his face, kicking and heaving like a wounded leopard. "Ahai!" yelled Ali, springing forward as Kration rose to his hands and knees. "Waho!"

"Nice work!" screamed Adam.

Ali had Kration in a headlock. Kration crouched, gathering his strength; then began to strain left and right, in spasmodic jerks. Blood from Ali's nose fell like rain on Kration's back. Both men were red to the waist, slippery with blood. Ali's grip was slipping: Kration was as hard to hold as a flapping sail in a raging wind. . . . Kration's head was free. Ali caught a glimpse of his face, purple, swollen, split by a grin of anger that displayed all his teeth, white as peeled almonds. Then Kration swung his left arm. His hard, flat palm struck Ali in the face: one of his nails scraped the surface of Ali's eye.

A blank, bleak horror came into the heart of the Turk. *My eye! My last eye! If I lose this eye, too!* Then he roared like a maddened lion, buried his fingers in the softer flesh above Kration's hips, lifted him above his head by sheer force, threw him across the ring, and followed him, growling unintelligible insults and spitting blood.

Clang! went the gong.

Ali groped his way back to his corner, and sat limply. Adam

sponged him with cold water, adjusted his sash, and wiped the blood from his face.

"My eye," said Ali, "my eye!"

"It's badly scratched," said Adam.

Ali's eye was closing. The lids, dark and swollen, were creeping together to cover the blood-colored eyeball.

The crowd shouted. One voice screamed, "Carm on, Nelson! Carm on, whiskers!"

Ali sucked up a mouthful of water and, like a spouting whale, sprayed it toward the crowd. "Cowards!" he shouted. "Cowards!"

Figler muttered, "This is disgusting. Let's go."

Lew, shaken by emotion, did not answer, but raised his piercing voice and called to Ali, "Good work, Ali! I've not seen anything better since you beat Red Shreckhorn in Manchester!"

Ali called back, "Thank you for that!"

"Go easy, for God's sake, go easy," said Adam.

The gong sounded. Kration advanced, smiling. To Ali, he looked like a man half-formed out of red dust. He thought: *If I do not get him within five minutes, this eye will close, and then I shall be a man fighting in the dark.* This thought was indescribably terrifying. The curtain of mist was darkening. Now, by straining the muscles of his forehead and cheeks, and holding his mouth wide open, he could barely manage to see.

A voice cried, "Look out Kration! He's going to swallow you!" Another shouted, "Oo-er! Look at 'is whiskers! They're coming unstuck!"

Ali's mustache had, indeed, fallen into a ludicrous Nietzschean droop, matted to a spiky fringe with congealing blood. Kration snarled, leaped in, struck Ali across the neck with a flailing arm, and seized his mustache. He tugged. If the hair had not been slippery with the blood from Ali's nose, Kration might have pulled it out. But it slid through his fingers. Ali, weeping huge tears of pain, grasped blindly, and caught the Cypriot by the biceps of his right arm. The darkness had come. He knew that if he relaxed his grip, he was lost. As Kration jerked back, Ali followed. The Cypriot began to gasp with pain: *Esss-ha; esss-ha. . . .* Everything in Ali's body and soul focused in the five small points of his fingertips. He was blind now, utterly blind, lost in a roaring, spinning ring, dumb with agony, choked with blood, deafened with howls of derision and encouragement which seemed to have no end—and in this world of sickening pain, there was only one real thing, and that was the arm of his enemy, in which he was burying his fingers . . .

They clung together, spinning around and around like two twigs in a whirlpool; the Cypriot groaning now, Ali silent. He felt cold. A ring post ground into his back. He groped with his other hand, and found nothing. The noise of the crowd was becoming fainter; his face seemed to be swelling, while in his breast his heart thundered like horses galloping over a wooden bridge. Something knocked his feet from the mat. He fell, still clutching Kration's arm. The Cypriot said, "For Christ's sake!" Ali replied, "You feel my grip, eh?"

Voices were shouting: "Stop the fight! Stop it!"

Out of his midnight, Ali roared, "Stop nothing! Ali never stops!"

Suddenly he released Kration's biceps, slid his hand down until it reached the wrist, where it shut like a bear trap; swung his other hand to the elbow. The Cypriot's arm broke. Ali heard his scream of pain, but still held on. Kration became limp. Ali held his eye open, with the first and second fingers of his free hand. He could see nothing except an interminable, fiery redness. Somebody tried to prize open his fingers, which still gripped Kration's wrist. Ali struck out blindly. A voice said, "Stop! You've won! It's me, Adam!"

"By God," said Ali, "that Greek went down like bricks."

The crowd was delirious. Fabian said, "You certainly gave those sons-of-bitches their money's worth."

Adam led him back to the dressing room.

Ali found his voice. "Did you see how I beat him? Did you

see how I broke him up? Did you see how I pulled him down? Did you see how his arm went? Did you see my grip? I could have beaten him in the first ten seconds, only I wanted the public to see a *fight*. Did you see my grip? What Ali grips, God forgets!"

"You were great, Ali."

"Now am I fat?"

"No, Ali."

"Now am I old?"

"No, Ali."

"Now have I no teeth?"

"Teeth like a tiger."

"Now can I wrestle?"

"Better than ever, Ali."

"Now am I undefeated?"

"Still undefeated, Ali."

Ali raised his head, brushed back his mustache, twirled it again to fine points, and said, "Nobody on God's earth ever beat me. Nobody ever will. Look at me: If he hadn't scratched my eye, I should be right as rain."

"Have a rest, Ali."

"Close the windows," said Ali, "there's a devil of a cold wind."

The windows were already closed.

Ali muttered, "I wonder if my eye is badly damaged? Get me some boric-acid crystals and a little warm water—" He stopped abruptly and said, "Put your hand on my chest!"

Adam did so. In Ali's chest, he felt something rattling, like a loose plate in a racing engine.

Ali exclaimed, with an astounded expression, "The clock is stopping!"

"Nonsense, Ali! Rest."

Ali struck his vast belly with a colossal fist and murmured, "What a meal for the worms!"

Those were the last words he ever uttered.

That night he died.

Jay McInerney

From RANSOM

*The martial arts—where the real
contest is with yourself.*

From a deep sleep Ransom woke into a sovereign state of anxiety. For a moment he held back on the edge of waking, with the notion of slowing the inevitable. Sunday morning, once the start of the Lord's day.

Ransom slipped on a pair of boxers, washed, shaved and rolled up the bed. He pulled back the doors to the terrace and stepped outside, where two sets of karate gi were hanging from the clothesline. The view from the terrace was the backsides of the houses on the next street, rigged out like galleons with TV antennas and clotheslines. Above the tiled rooftops, the sky was overcast. If it rained, practice would be cancelled.

Beneath the terrace was Kaji's garden, an immaculate plot with stones and dwarf trees that gave the illusion of major landscape. Presiding over the ornamental puddle was a ceramic tanuki, an animal that the Japanese loved inordinately and that seemed to Ransom a bear-raccoon hybrid. The buds of the cherry tree were swollen and showing pink, the tortured yellow branches of the trained pine tipped with a new green. As he looked down, a ferret darted from underneath the house with a piece of paper in its mouth and dashed across the pebbles to the water; it rose on its hind legs to examine the tanuki and test the air. Ransom whistled. The ferret looked up at him, then bolted underneath the fence, leaving the paper behind. Ransom tried to remember if a ferret was a good or bad omen. In Japan, everything was some kind of omen.

The first to arrive, Ransom changed into his gi and began to sweep the parking lot. They only trained inside during rainy season, when there was space reserved for them in the gym. The sensei had no use for padded mats and controlled temperature. Asphalt toughened the soles of the feet and gave you an incentive to stay on them. The winter had been cold and they had often practiced with snow on the ground. The biggest problem in winter was your toes; you couldn't feel them until you jammed one, and then it was like a dentist's drill hitting a nerve. The sensei had a shiatsu method of unjamming toes which involved yanking on them. In November Ransom had broken the middle toe on his left foot. He still taped the toe and favored right kicks. The doctor told him to lay off karate for two months. The sensei told him to tape it and forget about it.

He hoped he would have time to finish sweeping the lot before anyone arrived. He liked having the morning to himself. It would get violent and sweaty soon enough.

Ransom learned how to sweep when he started with the dojo. His first lessons were in bowing and sweeping. Ransom had been desperate to join. The sensei had not been eager to take on a foreign disciple. There were dojos that catered to gaijin but his wasn't one of them. He did not believe gaijin had the stuff. His reluctance convinced Ransom that he had found the right teacher.

Every night for a week Ransom watched them practice. He had not noticed the fighting so much as the grace of movement. The best of the students gave the impression of quadruped balance and intimacy with the ground. They conveyed an extraordinary sense of self-possession. For months Ransom had drifted

across landscapes in a fevered daze, oblivious to almost everything but his own pain and guilt. The dojo with its strange incantations and white uniforms seemed to him a sacramental place, an intersection of body and spirit, where power and danger and will were ritualized in such a way that a man could learn to understand them. Ransom had lost his bearings spiritually, and he wanted to reclaim himself.

Finally Ransom approached the sensei with a speech he had worked up out of the dictionary. It was the only time Ransom would see him entirely at a loss. Later the sensei told Ransom that he would have gotten rid of him if he had known how. The sensei's English and Ransom's Japanese were equally poor; the sensei struggled to explain in Japanese that he was not equipped to handle a foreigner. His was a small dojo. The gaijin-san would feel more at home elsewhere. The sensei repeated this, speaking very slowly, and then retreated into the gym with his clothes under his arm. Ransom was back the next night, and the night after that. The third night, after practice, the sensei gave him a piece of paper with what turned out to be an address, written in both Japanese and painstaking Roman characters. He pointed to his white suit, then to the piece of paper.

Ransom was waiting the next night in his crisp new gi, short in the arms and legs. When the sensei arrived he handed Ransom a broom. Ransom began to sweep the lot. The sensei stepped in several times to correct his technique. Ransom wasn't sure what to make of it. After the seated meditation, the sensei took him off into a corner of the lot. Through Suzuki, a college student who spoke more English than anyone else in the dojo, the sensei explained that bowing was the first skill to be mastered in karate. Suzuki demonstrated the proper bow. It looked simple enough—the all-purpose bob that Ransom had been seeing since he first arrived in the country. The sensei took Ransom over to the post wrapped in hemp. Ransom had seen the others punching it, but the sensei wanted him to practice bowing to it. He spent the next hour doing so, while the others leaped and kicked. The sensei came over several times to watch, shaking his head each time and demonstrating once more. Ransom watched and tried to determine what was different and crucial in the sensei's bow. He wondered if there was an exact angle of inclination, if the thing was codified that far; Ryder told him months later that department stores had machines designed to train their employees to bow correctly. Ransom concentrated on putting as much sincerity and humility into it as he could. After an hour his lower back was aching and his store of sincerity exhausted.

After a closing round of seated meditation, the sensei handed him the broom. Wondering why this was necessary after practice, Ransom swept the lot again from one end to the other.

The next night was the same. While the others followed their secret choreography, Ransom stood in the dunce corner bowing to his post. The sensei came around twice to measure his progress but offered no comment. Ransom's back ached so severely the next day that he could hardly get out of bed. He walked to the public bath hunched over like the old country women he saw sometimes at the bus stops, women who spent their lives bent doubled over in rice fields.

At the end of the third night he was convinced he was being systematically humiliated. The sensei hadn't wanted him in the dojo to begin with. When he came around to watch, Ransom was too stiff to bow fluidly, and the proper mix of humility and sincerity was out of the question.

Practice finished, he was changing into his street clothes when the sensei held out the broom. Ransom continued buttoning his shirt and didn't look up. When he got to the second-to-last button he saw there were three buttonholes left. The sensei saw, too. He held out the broom. Ransom rebuttoned and tucked in his shirt, then took the broom and snapped it in half over his knee. He laid the two halves down at the sensei's feet and was out in the street before he realized he had left his shoes behind.

The shoes were sitting beside the door of the gym when he arrived the next night, under a folded-paperbag tent. Ransom was fifteen minutes early. He had brought a new broom. The sensei arrived as he was beginning to sweep. Ransom continued sweeping. The sensei walked over to the post and began punching. Ransom laid down the broom and approached him. The sensei changed hands and hit the post fifty times before turning to look at Ransom. Ransom drew himself up, clenched his fists at his side and bent deeply from the waist. He kept his head down.

Okay, the sensei said. *Good.*

Roger Angell

TENNIS

Between father and son lies abiding love.
And unending rivalry.

The thing you ought to know about my father is that he plays a lovely game of tennis. Or rather, he used to, up to last year, when all of a sudden he had to give the game up for good. But even last summer, when he was fifty-five years of age, his game was something to see. He wasn't playing any of your middle-aged tennis, even then. None of that cute stuff, with lots of cuts and drop shots and getting everything back, that most older men play when they're beginning to carry a little fat and don't like to run so much. That wasn't for him. He still played all or nothing—the big game with a hard serve and coming right in behind it to the net. Lots of running in that kind of game, but he could still do it. Of course, he'd begun to make more errors in the last few years and that would annoy the hell out of him. But still he wouldn't change—not him. At that, his game was something to see when he was on. Everybody talked about it. There was always quite a little crowd around his court on the weekends, and when he and the other men would come off the court after a set of doubles, the wives would see their husbands all red and puffing. And then they'd look at my old man and see him grinning and not even breathing hard after *he'd* been doing all the running back after the lobs and putting away those overheads, and they'd say to him, "Honestly, Hugh, I just don't see how you do it, not at your age. It's *amazing!* I'm going to take my Steve (or Bill or Tom) off cigarettes and put him on a diet. He's ten years younger and just look at him." Then my old man would light up a cigarette and smile and shake his head and say, "Well, you know how it is. I just play a lot." And then a minute later he'd look around at everybody lying on the lawn there in the sun and pick out me or one of the other younger fellows and say, "Feel like a set of singles?"

If you know north Jersey at all, chances are you know my father. He's Hugh Minot—the Montclair one, not the fellow out in New Brunswick. Just about the biggest realty man in the whole section, I guess. He and my mother have this place in Montclair, thirty-five acres, with a swimming pool and a big vegetable garden and this En-Tout-Cas court. A lovely home. My father got a little name for himself playing football at Rutgers, and that helped him when he went into business, I guess. He never played tennis in college, but after getting out he wanted something to sort of fill in for the football—something he could do well, or do better than the next man. You know how people are. So he took the game up. Of course, I was too little to remember his tennis game when he was still young, but friends of his have told me that it was really hot. He picked the game up like nothing at all, and a couple of pros told him if he'd only started earlier he might have gotten up there in the big time—maybe even with a national ranking, like No. 18 or so. Anyhow, he kept playing and I guess in the last twenty years there hasn't been a season where he missed more than a couple of weekends of tennis in the summertime. A few years back, he even joined one of these fancy clubs in New York with indoor courts, and he'd take a couple of days off from work and go in there just so that he could play in the wintertime. Once, I remember, he played doubles in there with Alice Marble and I think Sidney Wood. He told my mother about that game lots of times, but it didn't mean much to her. She used to play tennis years ago, just for fun, but she wasn't too good and gave it up. Now the garden is the big thing with her, and she hardly ever comes out to their court, even to watch.

I play a game of tennis just like my father's. Oh, not as good. Not nearly as good, because I haven't had the experience. But it's the same game, really. I've had people tell me that when they saw us playing together—that we both made the same shot the same way. Maybe my backhand was a little better (when it was on), and I used to think that my old man didn't get down low enough on a soft return to his forehand. But mostly we played the same game. Which isn't surprising, seeing that he taught me the game. He started way back when I was about nine or ten. He used to spend whole mornings with me, teaching me a single shot. I guess it was good for me and he did teach me a good, all-round game, but even now I can remember that those morning lessons would somehow discourage both of us. I couldn't seem to learn fast enough to suit him, and he'd get upset and shout across at me, "Straight arm! Straight arm!" and then *I'd* get jumpy and do the shot even worse. We'd both be glad when the lesson ended.

I don't mean to say that he was so *much* better than I was. We got so we played pretty close a lot of the time. I can still remember the day I first beat him at singles. It was in June of 1937. I'd been playing quite a lot at school and this was my first weekend home after school ended. We went out in the morning, no one else there, and, as usual, he walked right through me the first set—about 6–1 or so. I played much worse than my regular game then, just like I always did against him for some reason. But the next set I aced him in the second game and that set me up and I went on and took him, 7–5. It was a wonderful set of tennis and I was right on top of the world when it ended. I remember running all the way back to the house to tell Mother about it. The old man came in and sort of smiled at her and said something like "Well, I guess I'm old now, Amy."

But don't get the idea I started beating him then. That was the whole trouble. There I was, fifteen, sixteen years old and getting my size, and I began to think, Well, it's about time you took him. He wasn't a young man any more. But he went right on beating me. Somehow I never played well against him and I knew it, and I'd start pressing and getting sore and of course my game would go blooey.

I remember one weekend when I was in college, a whole bunch of us drove down to Montclair in May for a weekend—my two roommates and three girls we knew. It was going to be a lot of fun. But then we went out for some tennis and of course my father was there. We all played some mixed doubles, just fooling around, and then he asked me if I wanted some singles. In that casual way of his. And of course it was 6–2, 6–3, or some such thing. The second set we were really hitting out against each other and the kids watching got real quiet, just as if it was Forest Hills. And then when we came off, Alice, my date, said something to me. About him, I mean. "I think your father is a remarkable man," she said. "Simply remarkable. Don't you think so?" Maybe she wanted to make me feel better about losing, but it was a dumb question. What could I say except yes?

It was while I was in college that I began to play golf a little. I liked the game and I even bought clubs and took a couple of lessons. I broke ninety one day and wrote home to my father about it. He'd never played golf and he wrote back with some little gag about its being an old man's game. Just kidding, you know, and I guess I should have expected it, but I was embarrassed to talk about golf at home after that. I wasn't really very good at it, anyway.

I played some squash in college, too, and even made the B team, but I didn't try out for the tennis team. That disappointed my father, I think, because I wasn't any good at football, and I think he wanted to see me make some team. So he could come and see me play and tell his friends about it, I guess. Still, we did play squash a few times and I could beat him, though I saw that with time he probably would have caught up with me.

I don't want you to get the idea from this that I didn't have a good time playing tennis with him. I can remember the good days very well—lots of days where we'd played some doubles with friends or even a set of singles where my game was holding up or maybe even where I'd taken one set. Afterward we'd walk back together through the orchard, with my father knocking the green apples off the path with his racket the way he always did and the two of us hot and sweaty while we smoked cigarettes and talked about lots of things. Then we'd sit on the veranda and drink a can of beer before taking a dip in the pool. We'd be very close then, I felt.

And I keep remembering a funny thing that happened years ago—oh, away back when I was thirteen or fourteen. We'd gone away, the three of us, for a month in New Hampshire in the summer. We played a lot of tennis that month and my game was coming along pretty fast, but of course my father would beat me every single time we played. Then he and I both entered the little town championship there the last week in August. Of course, I was put out in the first round (I was only a kid), but my old man went on into the finals. There was quite a big crowd that came to watch that day, and they had a referee and everything. My father was playing a young fellow—about twenty or twenty-one, I guess he was. I remember that I sat by myself, right down beside the court, to watch, and while they were warming up I looked at this man playing my father and whispered to myself, but almost out loud, "Take him! Take him!" I don't know why, but I just wanted him to beat my father in those finals, and it sort of scared me when I found that out. I wanted him to give him a real shellacking. Then they began to play and it was a very close match for a few games. But this young fellow was good, really good. He played a very controlled game, waiting for errors and only hitting out for winners when it was a sure thing. And he went on and won the first set, and in the next my father began to hit into the net and it was pretty plain that it wasn't even

going to be close in the second set. I kept watching and pretty soon I felt very funny sitting there. Then the man won a love game off my father and I began to shake. I jumped up and ran all the way up the road to our cabin and into my room and lay down on my bed and cried hard. I kept thinking how I'd wanted to have the man win, and I knew it was about the first time I'd ever seen my father lose a love game. I never felt so ashamed. Of course, that was years and years ago.

I don't think any of this would have bothered me except for one thing—I've always *liked* my father. Except for this game, we've always gotten along fine. He's never wanted a junior-partner son, either in his office or at home. No Judge Hardy stuff or "Let me light your cigar, sir." And no backslapping, either. There have been times where I didn't see much of him for a year or so, but when we got together (at a ball game, say, or during a long trip in a car), we've always found we could talk and argue and have a lot of laughs, too. When I came back on my last furlough before I went overseas during the war, I found that he'd chartered a sloop. The two of us went off for a week's cruise along the Maine coast, and it was swell. Early-morning swims and trying to cook over charcoal and the wonderful quiet that comes over those little coves after you've anchored for the night and the wind has dropped and perhaps you're getting ready to shake up some cocktails. One night there, when we were sitting on deck and smoking cigarettes in the dark, he told me something that he never even told my mother—that he'd tried to get into the Army and had been turned down. He just said it and we let it drop, but I've always been glad he told me. Somehow it made me feel better about going overseas.

Naturally, during the war I didn't play any tennis at all. And when I came back I got married and all, and I was older, so of course the game didn't mean as much to me. But still, the first weekend we played at my father's—the very first time I'd played him in four years—it was the same as ever. And I'd have sworn I had outgrown the damn thing. But Janet, my wife, had never seen me play the old man before and *she* spotted something. She came up to our room when I was changing afterward. "What's the matter with you?" she asked me. "Why does it mean so much to you? It's just a game, isn't it? I can see that it's a big thing for your father. That's why he plays so much and that's why he's so good at it. But why you?" She was half kidding, but I could see that it upset her. "This isn't a contest," she said. "We're not voting for Best Athlete in the County, are we?" I took her up on that and tried to explain the thing a little, but she wouldn't try to understand. "I just don't like a sorehead," she told me as she went out of the room.

I guess that brings me down to last summer and what happened. It was late in September, one of those wonderful weekends where it begins to get a little cool and the air is so bright. Father had played maybe six or seven sets of doubles Saturday, and then Sunday I came out with Janet, and he had his regular tennis gang there—Eddie Earnshaw and Mark O'Connor and that Mr. Lacy. I guess we men had played three sets of doubles, changing around, and we were sitting there catching our breath. I was waiting for Father to ask me for our singles. But he'd told me earlier that he hadn't been able to get much sleep the night before, so I'd decided that he was too tired for singles. Of course, I didn't even mention that out loud in front of the others—it would have embarrassed him. Then I looked around and noticed that my father was sitting in one of those canvas chairs instead of standing up, the way he usually did between sets. He looked awfully pale, even under his tan, and while I was looking at him he suddenly leaned over and grabbed his stomach and was sick on the grass. We all knew it was pretty bad, and we laid him down and put his cap over his eyes, and I ran back to the house to tell Mother and phone up the doctor. Father didn't say a word when we carried him into the house in the chair, and then Dr. Stockton came and said it was a heart attack and that Father had played his last game of tennis.

You would have thought after that and after all those months in bed that my father would just give up his tennis court—have it plowed over or let it go to grass. But Janet and I went out there for the weekend just last month and I was surprised to find that the court was in good shape, and Father said that he had asked the gang to come over, just so I could have some good men's doubles. He'd even had a chair set up in the orchard, halfway out to the court, so he could walk out there by himself. He walked out slow, the way he has to, and then sat down in the chair and rested for a couple of minutes, and then made it the rest of the way.

I haven't been playing much tennis this year, but I was really on my game there that day at my father's. I don't think I've ever played better on that court. I hardly made an error and I was relaxed and I felt good about my game. The others even spoke about how well I played.

But somehow it wasn't much fun. It just didn't seem like a real contest to me, and I didn't really care that I was holding my serve right along and winning my sets no matter who my partner was. Maybe for the first time in my life, I guess, I found out that it was only a game we were playing—only that and no more. And I began to realize what my old man and I had done to that game. All that time, all those years, I had only been trying to grow up and he had been trying to keep young, and we'd both done it on the tennis court. And now our struggle was over. I found that out that day, and when I did I suddenly wanted to tell my father about it. But then I looked over at him, sitting in a chair with a straw hat on his head, and I decided not to. I noticed that he didn't seem to be watching us at all. I had the feeling, instead, that he was *listening* to us play tennis and perhaps imagining a game to himself or remembering how he would play the point—the big, high-bouncing serve and the rush to the net for the volley, and then going back for the lob and looking up at it and the wonderful feeling as you uncoil on the smash and put the ball away.

Pedro Juan Soto

THE CHAMP

When the rule book is torn up,
only the law of the jungle remains.

The cue made a last swing over the green felt, hit the cue ball and cracked it against the fifteen ball. The stubby, yellowish hands remained motionless until the ball went "clop" into the pocket and then raised the cue until it was diagonally in front of the acned, fatuous countenance: the tight little vaselined curl fell tidily over the forehead, the ear clipped a cigarette, the glance was oblique and mocking, and the mustache's scarce fuzz had been accentuated with pencil.

"Wha' happen, man?" said the sharp voice. "That was a champ shot, hey?"

Then he started to laugh. His squat, greasy body became a cheerfully quaking blob inside the tight jeans and the sweaty T-shirt.

He contemplated Gavilán—the eyes, too wise, didn't look so wise now; the three-day beard tried to camouflage the face's ill temper, but didn't make it; the long-ashed cigarette kept the lips shut tight, obscene words wading in back of them—and enjoyed the feat he had perpetrated. He had beaten him in two straight games. Gavilán had been six months in jail, sure, but that didn't matter now. What mattered was that he had lost two games with him, whom these victories placed in a privileged position. They placed him above the others, over the best players in the neighborhood and over the ones who belittled him for being nothing but a sixteen-year-old, nothing but a "baby." Now nobody could cut him out of his spot in Harlem. He was the *new one*, the successor to Gavilán and other individuals worthy of respect. He was the same as . . . no. He was better, on account of his youth: he had more time and opportunities to surpass all their feats.

He felt like running out into the street and shouting, "I won two straight games from Gavilán! Speak out now! C'mon, say something now!" He didn't do it. He only chalked his cue and told himself it wasn't worth the trouble. It was sunny out, but it was Saturday and the neighbors would be at the market place at this hour of the morning. He would have no more audience than snot-nosed kids and disinterested grannies. Anyway, a little humility suited champs well.

He picked up the quarter Gavilán threw on the felt and exchanged a conceited smile with the scorekeeper and the three spectators.

"Collect yours," he told the scorekeeper, hoping that some spectator would move to the other pool tables to spread the news, to comment how he—Puruco, the too-fat kid with the pimply face and the comic voice—had made a fool of the great Gavilán. It seemed, however, that they were waiting for another show.

He put away his fifteen cents and said to Gavilán, who was wiping his sweaty face, "Play another?"

"Let's," Gavilán said, taking from the rack another cue that he would chalk meticulously.

The scorer took down the triangular rack and shaped up the balls for the next round.

Puruco broke, and immediately began to whistle and pace around the table with a springy walk, almost on the tips of his sneakers.

Gavilán came up to the cue ball with his characteristic heaviness, and centered it, but didn't hit it yet. He simply raised his very shaggy head, his body still bent over the cue and the felt, and said, "Hey, quit the whistle."

"Okay, man," Puruco said, and twirled his cue until he heard Gavilán's shot and the balls went running around and clashed again. None of them went home.

"Ay, bendito," Puruco laughed. "Got this man like dead."

He hit number one, which went in and left number two lined up for the left pocket. Number two also dropped in. He could not stop smiling toward the corners of the parlor. He seemed to invite the spiders, the flies, and the numbers bookies dispersed among the bystanders at the other pool tables, to take a look at this.

He carefully studied the position of each ball. He wanted to win this other set, too, to take advantage of his recent reading of Willie Hoppe's book, and all that month-after-month practicing, when he had been the butt of his opponents. Last year he was just a little pisspot; now the real life was beginning for him, the life of a champ. Once he beat Gavilán, he would lick Mamerto and Bimbo . . .

"Make way for Puruco!" the cool men would say. And he would make it with the owners of the pool parlors, gather good connections. He'd be bodyguard to some, and buddy-buddy to others. Cigarettes and beer for free, he would have. And women, not the scared, stupid chicks who went no further than some squeezing at the movies. From there, right into fame: big man in the neighborhood, the one and only guy for any job—the numbers, the narco racket, the broad from Riverside Drive slumming in the neighborhood, this gang's rumble with that one to settle "manly things."

With a grunt, he missed the three ball and cursed. Gavilán was right behind him when he returned.

"Watch out puttin' foofoo on me!" he said, ruffling up.

And Gavilán:

"Ah, stop that."

"No. Don't give me that, man, just 'cause yuh losin'?"

Gavilán did not answer. He centered the cue ball through the smoke which wrinkled his features, and pocketed two balls in opposite sides.

"See?" Puruco said, and he crossed his fingers to protect himself.

"Shaddup yuh mouth!"

Gavilán tried to ricochet the five in, but failed. Puruco studied the position of his ball and settled for the farthest but surest pocket. While aiming, he realized that he would have to uncross his fingers. He looked at Gavilán suspiciously and crossed his legs to shoot. He missed.

When he looked up, Gavilán was smiling and sucking his upper gums to spit his pyorrhea. Now he had no doubt that he was the victim of a spell.

"No foolin', man. Play it clean." Gavilán gazed at him with surprise, stepping on the cigarette distractedly.

"What's the matter?"

"No," Puruco said. "Don't you go on with that *bilongo!*"

"Hey!" Gavilán laughed. "This one t'inks a lot about witches."

He put the cue behind his back, feinted once, and pocketed the ball easily. He pocketed again in the next shot, and in the next. Puruco began to get nervous. Either Gavilán was recovering his ability, or else that voodoo spell was pushing his cue. If he didn't get to raise his score, Gavilán would win this set.

Chalking his cue, he touched wood three times and awaited his turn. Gavilán missed his fifth shot. Then Puruco eyed the distance. He hit, putting in the eight. He pulled a combination shot to pocket the eleven with the nine. The nine went home later. He caromed the twelve in, and then missed the ten. Gavilán also missed it. Finally Puruco managed to send it in, but for ball thirteen he almost ripped the felt. He added the score in his head. About eight more to call it quits—he could relax a little.

The cigarette went from behind his ear to his lips. When he lit it, turning his back to the table so that the fan would not blow out the match, he saw the sly smile of the scorekeeper. He turned around rapidly and caught Gavilán right in the act: feet lifted off the floor, body leaning against the table rim to make an easy shot. Before he could speak, Gavilán had pocketed the ball.

"Hey, man!"

"Wha' happen?" Gavilán said calmly, eyeing the next shot.

"Don't you pull that on me, boy! You can't beat me that way."

Gavilán raised an eyebrow at him, and bit the inside of his mouth while making a snout.

"Wha's hurtin' you?" he said.

"No, like that no!" Puruco jerked his arms open and almost hit the scorekeeper with his cue. He threw the cigarette down violently and said to the onlookers, "You seen it, right?"

"See wha'?" said Gavilán, unmoved.

"Nothin', that dirty play," squealed Puruco. "T'ink I'm stupid?"

"Aw, man," Gavilán laughed. "Don't you go askin' me, maybe I tell you."

Puruco struck the table rim with the cue.

"With me you gotta play fair. You ain't satisfied with puttin' a spell on me first, but after you put me on with cheatin'."

"Who cheatin'?" Gavilán said. He left the cue on the table and, smiling, moved closer to Puruco. "You say I'm cheatin'?"

"No," Puruco said, changing his tone, babying his voice, wavering on his feet. "But that's no way to play, man. They seen you."

Gavilán turned to the others.

"I been cheatin'?"

Only the scorekeeper shook his head. The others said nothing and looked away.

"But like he's lyin' on the table, man," Puruco said.

Gavilán clutched the T-shirt as if by chance, baring the pudgy back as he pulled him over.

"Me, nobody call me a cheatin' man."

The playing had stopped at all the other pool tables. The rest of the people watched from a distance. Nothing was heard but the buzz of the fan and the flies, and the screaming of children in the street.

"You t'ink a pile of crap like you gonna call me a cheater?" Gavilán said, forcing his fist against Puruco's chest, ripping the shirt. "I let you win two tables so you have somethin' to put on, and now you t'ink you king. Get outta here, jerk," he said between his teeth. "When you grow up we'll see ya."

The push threw Puruco against the plaster wall, where his back smashed flat. The crash filled the silence with holes. Somebody laughed, tittering. Somebody said: "He a bragger."

"An' get outta here before I kick you for good," Gavilán said.

" 'Kay man," Puruco stammered, dropping the cue.

Out he went without daring to raise his eyes, hearing cues clicking again on the tables, and some giggles. On the street, he felt like crying, but held it in. That was for sissies. The blow didn't hurt; that other thing—"When you grow up we'll see ya"—hurt more. He was a full-grown man. If they beat him, if they killed him, let them do it paying no mind at all to his being a sixteen-year-old. He was a man already. He could do a lot of damage, plenty of damage, and he could also survive it.

He crossed over to the other sidewalk, furiously kicked a beer can, his hands, from inside the pockets, pinching his body nailed to the cross of adolescence.

Two sets he had let him win, Gavilán said. Dirty lie. He knew he would lose every one of them to him, from now on, to the new champ. He had pulled the voodoo stuff on account of that, on account of that the cheating, the blow on account of that. Oh, but those three other men would spread the news of Gavilán's fall. After that, Mamerto and Bimbo. Nobody could stop him now. The neighborhood, the whole world, would be his.

When the barrel hoop got trapped between his legs, he kicked it aside. He gave a slap to the kid who came to pick it up.

"Careful, man, or I knock yuh eye out," he growled.

And he went on walking, unconcerned with the mother who cursed him and ran toward the tearful kid. Lips held tight, he inhaled deeply. At his passing, he could see confetti falling and cheers pouring from the closed and deserted windows.

He was a champ. He was on the lookout only for harm.

Ring Lardner

====================

HURRY KANE

Much in baseball has changed. But there have always been fastballs and oddballs.

====================

It says here: "Another great race may be expected in the American League, for Philadelphia and New York have evidently added enough strength to give them a fighting chance with the White Sox and Yankees. But if the fans are looking for as 'nervous' a finish as last year's, with a climax such as the Chicago and New York clubs staged on the memorable first day of October, they are doubtless in for a disappointment. That was a regular Webster 'thrill that comes once in a lifetime,' and no oftener."

"Thrill" is right, but they don't know the half of it. Nobody knows the whole of it only myself, not even the fella that told me. I mean the big sap, Kane, who you might call him, I suppose, the hero of the story, but he's too dumb to have realized all that went on, and besides, I got some of the angles from other sources and seen a few things with my own eyes.

If you wasn't the closest-mouthed bird I ever run acrost, I wouldn't spill this to you. But I know it won't go no further and I think it may give you a kick.

Well, the year before last, it didn't take no witch to figure out what was going to happen to our club if Dave couldn't land a pitcher or two to help out Carney and Olds. Jake Lewis hurt his arm and was never no good after that and the rest of the staff belonged in the Soldiers' Home. Their aim was perfect, but they were always shooting at the pressbox or somebody's bat. On hot days I often felt like leaving my mask and protector in the clubhouse; what those fellas were throwing up there was either eighty feet over my head or else the outfielders had to chase it. I could have caught naked except on the days when Olds and Carney worked.

In the fall—that's a year and a half ago—Dave pulled the trade with Boston and St. Louis that brought us Frank Miller and Lefty Glaze in exchange for Robinson, Bullard and Roy Smith. The three he gave away weren't worth a dime to us or to the clubs that got them, and that made it just an even thing, as Miller showed up in the spring with a waistline that was eight laps to the mile and kept getting bigger and bigger till it took half the Atlantic cable to hold up his baseball pants, while Glaze wanted more money than Landis and didn't report till the middle of June, and then tried to condition himself on wood alcohol. When the deal was made, it looked like Dave had all the best of it, but as it turned out, him and the other two clubs might as well have exchanged photographs of their kids in Girl Scout uniforms.

But Dave never lost no sleep over Glaze or Miller. We hadn't been in Florida three days before him and everybody on the ball club was absolutely nuts about big Kane. Here was a twenty-year-old boy that had only pitched half a season in Waco and we had put in a draft for him on the recommendation of an old friend of Dave's, Billy Moore. Billy was just a fan and didn't know much baseball, but he had made some money for Dave in Texas oil leases and Dave took this tip on Kane more because he didn't want to hurt Billy's feelings than out of respect for his judgment. So when the big sapper showed up at Fort Gregg, he didn't get much of a welcome. What he did get was a laugh. You couldn't look at him and not laugh; anyway, not till you got kind of used to him.

You've probably seen lots of pictures of him in a uniform, but they can't give you no idear of the sight he was the first day he blew in the hotel, after that clean, restful little train ride all the way from Yuma. Standing six foot three in what was left of his stockings, he was wearing a suit of Arizona store clothes that would have been a fair fit for Singer's youngest Midget and looked like he had pressed it with a tractor that had been parked on a river bottom.

He had used up both the collars that he figured would see him through his first year in the big league. This left you a clear view of his Adam's apple, which would make half a dozen pies. You'd have thought from his shoes that he had just managed to grab hold of the rail on the back platform of his train and been dragged from Yuma to Jacksonville. But when you seen his shirt, you wondered if he hadn't rode in the cab and loaned it to the fireman for a wash-cloth. He had a brown paper suitcase held together by bandages. Some of them had slipped and the raw wounds was exposed. But if the whole thing had fell to pieces, he could have packed the contents in two of his vest pockets without bulging them much.

One of the funniest things about him was his walk and I'll never forget the first time we seen him go out to take his turn pitching to the batters. He acted like he was barefooted and afraid of stepping on burrs. He'd lift one dog and hold it in the air a minute till he could locate a safe place to put it down. Then he'd do the same thing with the other, and it would seem about a half-hour from the time he left the bench till he got to his position. Of course Dave soon had him pretty well cured of that, or that is, Dave didn't, but Kid Farrell did. For a whole week, the Kid followed him every step he took and if he wasn't going fast enough, he either got spiked in the heel or kicked in the calf of his hind leg. People think he walks slow yet, but he's a shooting star now compared with when he broke in.

Well, everybody was in hysterics watching him make that first trip and he looked so silly that we didn't expect him to be any

good to us except as a kind of a show. But we were in for a big surprise.

Before he threw a ball, Dave said to him: "Now, go easy. Don't cut loose and take a chance till you're in shape."

"All right," says Kane.

And all of a sudden, without no warning, he whammed a fast ball acrost that old plate that blew Tierney's cap off and pretty near knocked me down. Tierney hollered murder and ran for the bench. All of us were pop-eyed and it was quite a while before Dave could speak. Then he said:

"Boy, your fast one *is* a fast one! But I just got through telling you not to cut loose. The other fellas ain't ready for it and neither are you. I don't want nobody killed this time of year."

So Kane said: "I didn't cut loose. I can send them through there twice as fast as that. I'm scared to yet, because I ain't sure of my control. I'll show you something in a couple more days."

Well, when he said "twice as fast," he was making it a little strong. But his real fast one was faster than that first one he threw, and before the week was over we looked at speed that made it seem like Johnson had never pitched nothing but toy balloons. What had us all puzzled was why none of the other clubs had tried to grab him. I found out by asking him one night at supper. I asked him if he'd been just as good the year before as he was now.

"I had the same stuff," he said, "but I never showed it, except once."

I asked him why he hadn't showed it. He said:

"Because I was always scared they would be a big league scout in the stand and I didn't want to go 'up.' "

Then I said why not, and he told me he was stuck on a gal in Waco and wanted to be near her.

"Yes," I said, "but your home town, Yuma, is a long ways from Waco and you couldn't see much of her winters even if you stayed in the Texas League."

"I got a gal in Yuma for winters," he says. "This other gal is just for during the season."

"How about that one time you showed your stuff?" I asked him. "How did you happen to do it?"

"Well," he said, "the Dallas club was playing a series in Waco and I went to a picture show and seen the gal with Fred Kruger. He's Dallas's manager. So the next day I made a monkey out of his ball club. I struck out fifteen of them and give them one hit—a fly ball that Smitty could have caught in a hollow tooth if he hadn't drunk his lunch."

Of course that was the game Dave's friend seen him pitch and we were lucky he happened to be in Waco just then. And it was Kane's last game in that league. Him and his "during the season" gal had a brawl and he played sick and got himself sent home.

Well, everybody knows now what a whale of a pitcher he turned out to be. He had a good, fast-breaking curve and Carney learned him how to throw a slow ball. Old Kid Farrell worked like a horse with him and got him so he could move around and field his position. At first he seemed to think he was moored out there. And another cute habit that had to be cured was his full wind-up with men on bases. The Kid starved him out of this.

Maybe I didn't tell you what an eater he was. Before Dave caught on to it, he was ordering one breakfast in his room and having another downstairs, and besides pretty near choking himself to death at lunch and supper, he'd sneak out to some lunchroom before bedtime, put away a Hamburger steak and eggs and bring back three or four sandwiches to snap at during the night.

He was rooming at the start with Joe Bonham and Joe finally told on him, thinking it was funny. But it wasn't funny to Dave and he named the Kid and Johnny Abbott a committee of two to see that Kane didn't explode. The Kid watched over him at table and Johnny succeeded Bonham as his roommate. And the way the Kid got him to cut out his wind-up was by telling him, "Now if you forget yourself and use it with a man on, your supper's going to be two olives and a finger-bowl, but if you hold up those runners, you can eat the chef.''

As I say, the whole world knows what he is now. But they don't know how hard we worked with him, they don't know how close we came to losing him altogether, and they don't know the real story of that final game last year, which I'll tell you in a little while.

First, about pretty near losing him: As soon as Dave seen his possibilities and his value to us, he warned the boys not to ride him or play too many jokes on him because he was simple enough to take everything in dead earnest, and if he ever found out we were laughing at him, he might either lay down and quit trying or blow us entirely. Dave's dope was good, but you can't no more prevent a bunch of ball players from kidding a goofer like Kane than you can stop the Century at Herkimer by hollering ''Whoa!'' He was always saying things and doing things that left him wide open and the gang took full advantage, especially Bull Wade.

I remember one night everybody was sitting on the porch and Bull was on the railing, right in front of Kane's chair.

''What's your first name, Steve?'' Bull asked him.

''Well,'' says Kane, ''it ain't Steve at all. It's Elmer.''

''It would be!'' says Bull. ''It fits you like your suit. And that reminds me, I was going to inquire where you got that suit.''

''In Yuma,'' said Kane. ''In a store.''

''A store!'' says Bull.

''A clothing store,'' says Kane. ''They sell all kinds of clothes.''

''I see they do,'' said Bull.

''If you want a suit like it, I'll write and find out if they've got another one,'' says Kane.

''They couldn't be two of them,'' says Bull, ''and if they was, I'll bet Ed Wynn's bought the other. But anyway, I've already got a suit, and what I wanted to ask you was what the boys out West call you. I mean, what's your nickname?''

'' 'Hurry,' '' says the sap. '' 'Hurry' Kane. Lefty Condon named me that.''

"He seen you on your way to the dining-room," said Bull.

Kane didn't get it.

"No," he said. "It ain't nothing to do with a dining-room. A hurricane is a kind of a storm. My last name is Kane, so Lefty called me 'Hurry' Kane. It's a kind of a storm."

"A brainstorm," says Bull.

"No," said Kane. "A hurricane is a big wind-storm."

"Does it blow up all of a sudden?" asked Bull.

"Yeah, that's it," says Kane.

"We had three or four of them on this club last year," said Bull. "All pitchers, too. Dave got rid of them and he must be figuring on you to take their place."

"Do you mean you had four pitchers named Kane?" says the big busher.

"No," said Bull. "I mean we had four pitchers that could blow up all of a sudden. It was their hobby. Dave used to work them in turn, the same afternoon; on days when Olds and Carney needed a rest. Each one of the four would pitch an innings and a half."

Kane thought quite a while and then said: "But if they was four of them, and they pitched an innings and a half apiece, that's only six innings. Who pitched the other three?"

"Nobody," says Bull. "It was always too dark. By the way, what innings is your favorite? I mean, to blow in?"

"I don't blow," says the sap.

"Then," said Bull, "why was it that fella called you 'Hurry' Kane?"

"It was Lefty Condon called me 'Hurry,' " says the sap. "My last name is Kane, and a hurricane is a big wind."

"Don't a wind blow?" says Bull.

And so on. I swear they kept it up for two hours, Kane trying to explain his nickname and Bull leading him on, and Joe Bonham said that Kane asked him up in the room who that was he had been talking to, and when Joe told him it was Wade, one of the smartest ball players in the league, Hurry said: "Well, then, he must be either stewed or else this is a damn sight dumber league than the one I came from."

Bull and some of the rest of the boys pulled all the old gags on him that's been in baseball since the days when you couldn't get on a club unless you had a walrus mustache. And Kane never disappointed them.

They made him go to the club-house after the key to the batter's box; they wrote him mash notes with fake names signed to them and had him spending half his evenings on some corner, waiting to meet gals that never lived; when he held Florida University to two hits in five innings, they sent him telegrams of congratulation from Coolidge and Al Smith, and he showed the telegrams to everybody in the hotel; they had him report at the ball park at six-thirty one morning for a secret "pitchers' conference"; they told him the Ritz was where all the unmarried ball players on the club lived while we were home, and they got him to write and ask for a parlor, bedroom and bath for the whole season. They was nothing he wouldn't fall for till Dave finally tipped him off that he was being kidded, and even then he didn't half believe it.

Now I never could figure how a man can fool themselves about their own looks, but this bird was certain that he and Tommy Meighan were practically twins. Of course the boys soon found this out and strung him along. They advised him to quit baseball and go into pictures. They sat around his room and had him strike different poses and fix his hair different ways to see how he could show off his beauty to the best advantage. Johnny Abbott told me, after he began rooming with him, that for an hour before he went to bed and when he got up, Kane would stand in front of the mirror staring at himself and practicing smiles and scowls and all kinds of silly faces, while Johnny pretended he was asleep.

Well, it wasn't hard to kid a fella like that into believing the dames were mad about him and when Bull Wade said that Evelyn Corey had asked who he was, his chest broke right through his shirt.

I know more about Evelyn now, but I didn't know nothing then except that she was a beautiful gal who had been in Broadway shows a couple of seasons and didn't have to be in them no more. Her room was two doors down the hall from Johnny's and Kane's. She was in Florida all alone, probably because her man friend, whoever he was at that time, had had to go abroad or somewheres with the family. All the ball players were willing to meet her, but she wasn't thrilled over the idear of getting acquainted with a bunch of guys who hadn't had a pay day in four or five months. Bull got Kane to write her a note; then Bull stole the note and wrote an answer, asking him to call. Hurry went and knocked at her door. She opened it and slammed it in his face.

"It was kind of dark," he said to Johnny, "and I guess she failed to recognize me." But he didn't have the nerve to call again.

He showed Johnny a picture of his gal in Yuma, a gal named Minnie Olson, who looked like she patronized the same store where Kane had bought his suit. He said she was wild about him and would marry him the minute he said the word and probably she was crying her eyes out right now, wishing he was home. He asked if Johnny had a gal and Johnny loosened up and showed him the picture of the gal he was engaged to. (Johnny married her last November.) She's a peach, but all Kane would say was, "Kind of skinny, ain't she?" Johnny laughed and said most gals liked to be that way.

"Not if they want me," says Kane.

"Well," said Johnny, "I don't think this one does. But how about your friend, that Miss Corey? You certainly can't call her plump, yet you're anxious to meet her."

"She's got class!" said Kane.

Johnny laughed that off, too. This gal of his, that he's married to now, she's so far ahead of Corey as far as class is concerned—well, they ain't no comparison. Johnny, you know, went to Cornell a couple of years and his wife is a college gal he met at a big house-party. If you put her and Evelyn beside each other you wouldn't have no trouble telling which of them belonged on Park Avenue and which Broadway.

Kane kept on moaning more and more about his gal out West and acting glummer and glummer. Johnny did his best to cheer him up, as he seen what was liable to happen. But they wasn't no use. The big rube "lost" his fast ball and told Dave he had strained his arm and probably wouldn't be no good all season. Dave bawled him out and accused him of stalling. Kane stalled just the same. Then Dave soft-soaped him, told him how he'd burn up the league and how we were all depending on him to put us in the race and keep us there. But he might as well have been talking to a mounted policeman.

Finally, one day during the last week at Fort Gregg, Johnny Abbott got homesick himself and put in a long-distance call for his gal in New York. It was a rainy day and him and Kane had been just laying around the room. Before the call went through Johnny hinted that he would like to be alone while he talked. Kane paid no attention and began undressing to take a nap. So Johnny had to speak before an audience and not only that, but as soon as Kane heard him say "Darling" or "Sweetheart," or whatever he called her, he moved right over close to the phone where he wouldn't miss nothing. Johnny was kind of embarrassed and hung up before he was ready to; then he gave Kane a dirty look and went to the window and stared out at the rain, dreaming about the gal he'd just talked with.

Kane laid down on his bed, but he didn't go to sleep. In four or five minutes he was at the phone asking the operator to get Minnie Olson in Yuma. Then he laid down again and tossed a while, and then he sat up on the edge of the bed.

"Johnny," he says, "how far is it from here to New York?"

"About a thousand miles," said Johnny.

"And how far to Yuma?" said Kane.

"Oh," says Johnny, "that must be three thousand miles at least."

"How much did that New York call cost you?" asked Kane.

"I don't know yet," said Johnny. "I suppose it was around seven bucks."

Kane went to the writing table and done a little arithmetic. From there he went back to the phone.

"Listen, girlie," he said to the operator, "you can cancel that Yuma call. I just happened to remember that the party I wanted won't be home. She's taking her mandolin lesson, way the other side of town."

Johnny told me afterwards that he didn't know whether to laugh or cry. Before he had a chance to do either, Kane says to him:

"This is my last day on this ball club."

"What do you mean?" said Johnny.

"I mean I'm through; I'm going home," says Kane.

"Don't be a fool!" says Johnny. "Don't throw away the chance of a lifetime just because you're a little lonesome. If you stay in this league and pitch like you can pitch, you'll be getting the big money next year and you can marry that gal and bring her East with you. You may not have to wait till next year. You may pitch us into the world's series and grab a chunk of dough this fall."

"We won't be in no world's series," says Kane.

"What makes you think so?" said Johnny.

"I can't work every day," says Kane.

"You'll have help," says Johnny. "With you and Carney and Olds taking turns, we can be right up in that old fight. Without you, we can't even finish in the league. If you won't do it for yourself or for Dave, do it for me, your roomy. You just seen me spend seven or eight bucks on a phone call, but that's no sign I'm reeking with jack. I spent that money because I'd have died if I hadn't. I've got none to throw away and if we don't win the pennant, I can't marry this year and maybe not next year or the year after."

"I've got to look out for myself," says Kane. "I tell you I'm through and that's all there is to it. I'm going home where my gal is, where they ain't no smart Alecks kidding me all the while, and where I can eat without no assistant manager holding me down to a sprig of parsley, and a thimbleful of soup. For your sake, Johnny," he says, "I'd like to see this club finish on top, but I can't stick it out and I'm afraid your only hope is for the other seven clubs to all be riding on the same train and hit an open bridge."

Well, of course Johnny didn't lose no time getting to Dave with the bad news, and Dave and Kid Farrell rushed to the sapper's room. They threatened him and they coaxed him. They promised him he could eat all he wanted. They swore that anybody who tried to play jokes on him would either be fined or fired off the club. They reminded him that it cost a lot of money to go from Florida to Yuma, and he would have to pay his own way. They offered him a new contract with a five-hundred-dollar raise if he would stay. They argued and pleaded with him from four in the afternoon till midnight. When they finally quit, they were just where they'd been when they started. He was through.

"All right!" Dave hollered. "Be through and go to hell! If you ain't out of here by tomorrow noon, I'll have you chased out! And don't forget that you'll never pitch in organized baseball again!"

"That suits me," says Kane, and went to bed.

When Johnny Abbott woke up about seven the next morning, Hurry was putting his extra collar and comb in the leaky suitcase. He said:

"I'm going to grab the eleven-something train for Jacksonville. I got money enough to take me from here to New Orleans and I know a fella there that will see me the rest of the way—if I can find him and he ain't broke."

Well, Johnny couldn't stand for that and he got up and dressed and was starting out to borrow two hundred dollars from me to lend to Kane, when the phone rang loud and long. Kane took off the receiver, listened a second, and then said "Uh-huh" and hung up.

"Who was it?" asked Johnny.

"Nobody," says Kane. "Just one of Bull Wade's gags."

"What did he say?" Johnny asked him.

"It was a gal, probably the telephone operator," said Kane. "She said the hotel was on fire and not to get excited, but that we better move out."

"You fool!" yelled Johnny and run to the phone.

They was no gag about it. The hotel had really caught fire in the basement and everybody was being warned to take the air. Johnny tossed some of his stuff in a bag and started out, telling Kane to follow him quick. Hurry got out in the hall and then remembered that he had left his gal's picture on the dresser and went back after it. Just as he turned towards the door again, in dashed a dame with a kimono throwed over her nightgown. It was Evelyn Corey herself, almost in the flesh.

"Oh, please!" she said, or screamed. "Come and help me carry my things!"

Well, here was once that the name "Hurry" was on the square. He dropped his own suitcase and was in her room in nothing and no-fifths. He grabbed her four pieces of hand baggage and was staggering to the hall with them when a bellhop bounced in and told them the danger was over, the fire was out.

This seemed to be more of a disappointment than Evelyn could stand. Anyway, she fainted—onto a couch—and for a few minutes she was too unconscious to do anything but ask Kane to pour her a drink. He also poured himself one and settled down in the easy chair like he was there for the day. But by now she had come to and got a good look at him.

"I thank you very much," she said, "and I'm so exhausted with all this excitement that I think I'll go back to bed."

Kane took his hint and got up.

"But ain't I going to see you again?" he asked her.

"I'm afraid not," says Evelyn. "I'm leaving here this evening and I'll be getting ready from now till then."

"Where are you headed for?" Kane asked her.

"For home, New York," she said.

"Can't I have your address?" said Kane.

"Why, yes," said Evelyn without batting an eye. "I live at the Ritz."

"The Ritz!" says Kane. "That's where I'm going to live, if they ain't filled up."

"How wonderful!" said Evelyn. "Then we'll probably see each other every day."

Kane beat it down to the dining-room and straight to Dave's table.

"Boss," he said, "I've changed my mind."

"Your what!" says Dave.

"My mind," says Kane. "I've decided to stick."

It was all Dave could do not to kiss him. But he thought it was best to act calm.

"That's fine, Hurry!" he said. "And I'll see that you get that extra five hundred bucks."

"What five hundred bucks?" says Kane.

"The five hundred I promised you if you'd stay," says Dave.

"I hadn't heard about it," said Kane. "But as long as I ain't going home, I'm in no rush for money. Though I'm liable to need it," he says, "as soon as we hit New York."

And he smiled the silliest smile you ever seen.

I don't have to tell you that he didn't live at the Ritz. Or that Evelyn Corey didn't live there neither. He found out she hadn't never lived there, but he figured she'd intended to and had to give it up because they didn't have a suite good enough for her.

I got him a room in my boarding-house in the Bronx and for the first few days he spent all his spare time looking through city directories and different telephone directories and bothering the life out of Information, trying to locate his lost lady. It was when he had practically give up hope that he told me his secret and asked for help.

"She's all I came here for," he said, "and if I can't find her, I ain't going to stay."

Well, of course if you went at it the right way, you wouldn't have much trouble tracing her. Pretty near anybody in the theatrical business, or the people that run the big night clubs, or the head waiters at the hotels and restaurants—they could have put you on the right track. The thing was that it would be worse to get a hold of her than not to, because she'd have give him the air so strong that he would have caught his death of cold.

So I just said that they was no question but what she had gone away somewheres, maybe to Europe, and he would hear from her as soon as she got back. I had to repeat this over and over and make it strong or he'd have left us flatter than his own feet before he pitched two games. As it was, we held him till the end of May without being obliged to try any tricks, but you could see he was getting more impatient and restless all the while and the situation got desperate just as we were starting on our first trip West. He asked me when would we hit St. Louis and I told him the date and said:

"What do you want to know for?"

"Because," he says, "I'm going home from there."

I repeated this sweet news to Dave and Kid Farrell. We finally called in Bull Wade and it was him that saved the day. You remember Bull had faked up a note from Evelyn to Kane down at Fort Gregg; now he suggested that he write some more notes, say one every two or three weeks, sign her name to them, send them to Bull's brother in Montreal and have the brother mail them from there. It was a kind of a dirty, mean thing to do, but it worked. The notes all read about the same—

"Dear Mr. Kane:—I am keeping track of your wonderful pitching and looking forward to seeing you when I return to New

York, which will be early in the fall. I hope you haven't forgotten me."

And so on, signed "Your friend and admirer, Evelyn Corey."

Hurry didn't answer only about half of them as it was a real chore for him to write. He addressed his answers in care of Mr. Harry Wade, such and such a street number, Montreal, and when Bull's brother got them, he forwarded them to Bull, so he'd know if they was anything special he ought to reply to.

The boys took turns entertaining Kane evenings, playing cards with him and staking him to picture shows. Johnny Abbott done more than his share. You see, the pennant meant more to Johnny than to anybody else; it meant the world's series money and a fall wedding, instead of a couple of years' wait. And Johnny's gal, Helen Kerslake, worked, too. She had him to her house to supper—when her folks were out—and made him feel like he was even handsomer and more important than he thought. She went so far as to try and get some of her gal friends to play with him, but he always wanted to pet and that was a little too much.

Well, if Kane hadn't stuck with us and turned out to be the marvel he is, the White Sox would have been so far ahead by the Fourth of July that they could have sat in the stand the rest of the season and let the Bloomer Girls play in their place. But Hurry had their number from the first time he faced them till the finish. Out of eleven games he worked against them all last year, he won ten and the other was a nothing to nothing tie. And look at the rest of his record! As I recall it, he took part in fifty-eight games. He pitched forty-three full games, winning thirty-six, losing five and tying two. And God knows how many games he saved! He had that free, easy side-arm motion that didn't take much out of him and he could pitch every third day and be at his best.

But don't let me forget to credit myself with an assist. Late in August, Kane told me he couldn't stand it no longer to just get short notes from the Corey gal and never see her, and when we started on our September trip West, he was going to steal a week off and run up to Montreal; he would join us later, but he must see Evelyn. Well, for once in my life I had an idear hit me right between the eyes.

The Yuma gal, Minnie Olson, had been writing to him once a week and though he hardly ever wrote to her and seemed to only be thinking of Corey, still I noticed that he could hardly help from crying when Minnie's letters came. So I suggested to Dave that he telegraph Minnie to come East and visit with all her expenses paid, wire her money for her transportation, tell her it would be doing Kane a big favor as well as the rest of us, and ask her to send Kane a telegram, saying when she would reach New York, but to be sure and never mention that she wasn't doing it on her own hook.

Two days after Dave's message was sent, Kane got a wire from El Paso. She was on her way and would he meet her at the Pennsylvania Station on such and such a date. I never seen a man as happy as Hurry was when he read that telegram.

"I knew she was stuck on me," he said, "but I didn't know it was that strong. She must have worked in a store or something since spring to save up money for this trip."

You would have thought he'd never heard of or seen a gal by the name of Evelyn Corey.

Minnie arrived and was just what we expected: a plain, honest, good-hearted, small-town gal, dressed for a masquerade. We had supper with her and Kane her first night in town—I and Johnny and Helen. She was trembling like a leaf, partly from excitement over being in New York and amongst strangers, but mostly on account of seeing the big sap again. He wasn't no sap to her and I wished they was some dame would look at me the way she kept looking at Hurry.

The next morning Helen took her on a shopping tour and got her fixed up so cute that you couldn't hardly recognize her. In the afternoon she went to the ball game and seen Kane shut the Detroit club out with two hits.

When Hurry got a glimpse of her in her Fifth Avenue clothes, he was as proud as if he had bought them himself and it didn't seem to occur to him that they must have cost more than she could have paid.

Well, with Kane happy and no danger of him walking out on us, all we had to worry about was that the White Sox still led us by three games, with less than twenty left to play. And the schedule was different than usual—we had to wind up with a Western trip and play our last thirteen games on the road. I and Johnny and Dave was talking it over one day and the three of us agreed that we would be suckers not to insist on Miss Olson going along. But Dave wondered if she wouldn't feel funny, being the only girl.

"I'll make my gal go, too," said Johnny.

And that's the way it was fixed.

We opened in St. Louis and beat them two out of three. Olds was trimmed, but Carney and Kane both won. We didn't gain no ground, because the White Sox grabbed two out of three from Washington. We made a sweep of our four games in Detroit, while the Sox was winning three from Philadelphia. That moved us up to two and a half games from first place. We beat Cleveland three straight, Kane licking them 6 to 1 and holding Carney's one run lead through the eighth and ninth innings of another game. At the same time, Chicago took three from Boston.

So we finally struck old Chi, where the fans was already counting the pennant won, two and a half games behind and three to go—meaning we had to win all three or be sunk.

I told you how Kane had the Chicago club's number. But I didn't tell you how Eddie Brainard had been making a monkey of us. He had only worked against us six times and had beat us five. His other game was the nothing to nothing tie with Hurry. Eddie is one sweet pitcher and if he had been the horse for work that Kane was, that last series wouldn't have got us nowheres. But Eddie needs his full rest and it was a cinch he wouldn't be in there for more than one game and maybe part of another.

In Brainard's six games against us, he had give us a total of four runs, shutting us out three times and trimming us 3 to 2, 4 to 1 and 2 to 1. As the White Sox only needed one game, it was a cinch that they wouldn't start Eddie against Kane, who was so tough for them, but would save him for Carney or Olds, whichever one worked first. Carney hadn't been able to finish a game with Chicago and Olds' record wasn't much better.

Well, we was having breakfast in our hotel the morning we got in from Cleveland, and Kane sent for Dave to come to the table where him and Johnny Abbott and the two gals was eating.

"Boss," he says, "I'm thinking of getting married and so is Johnny here, but they ain't neither of us can do it, not now anyway, unless we grab some of that world's series jack. And we can't get into the series without we win these three games. So if I was managing this ball club, I'd figure on that and know just how to work my pitchers."

"Maybe I've thought about it a little myself," says Dave. "But I'd like to listen to your idears."

"All right," says Kane. "I'd start Kane today, and I'd start Kane tomorrow, and I'd start Kane the day after that."

"My plan is a little different," said Dave. "Of course you start today, and if you win, why, I want to play a joke on them tomorrow. I intend to start Olds so they'll start Brainard. And if the game is anywheres near close at the end of the third or fourth innings, you're going in. It will be too late for them to take Brainard out and expect him to be as good the third day. And if we win that second game, why, you won't have to beg me to pitch the last one."

You'll think I'm getting long-winded, but they ain't much more to tell. You probably heard the details of those first two games even if you was on the Other Side. Hurry beat them the first one, 7 to 1, and their one run was my fault. Claymore was on second base with two men out in the sixth innings. King hit a foul ball right straight up and I dropped it. And then he pulled a base-hit inside of Bull, and Claymore scored. Olds and Brainard started the second game and at the end of our half of the fourth innings, the score was one and one. Hurry had been warming up easy right along, but it certainly was a big surprise to the Chicago club and pretty near everybody else when Dave motioned him in to relieve Olds. The White Sox never came close to another run and we got to Brainard for one in the eighth, just enough to beat him.

Eddie had pitched his head off and it was a tough one for him to lose. But the best part of it was, he was through and out of the way.

Well, Johnny and Kane had their usual date with the two gals for supper. Johnny was in his bathroom, washing up, when the phone rang. Kane answered it, but he talked kind of low and Johnny didn't hear what he was saying. But when Hurry had hung up, he acted kind of nervous and Johnny asked him what was the matter.

"It's hard luck," said Kane. "They's a friend of mine from Yuma here, and he's in trouble and I've got to go over on the North Side and see him. Will you take both the gals to supper yourself? Because I may not be back till late. And don't tell Min who I'm going to see."

"How could I tell her when you ain't told me?" said Johnny.

"Well," said Kane, "just tell her I'm wore out from working so hard two days in a row and I went right to bed so I'd be all right for tomorrow."

Johnny was kind of worried and tried to coax him not to go. But Kane ducked out and didn't come in till midnight. Johnny tried to find out where he'd been and what had happened, but he said he was too sleepy to talk. Just the same, Johnny says, he tossed around and moaned all night like he was having a nightmare, and he usually slept like a corpse.

Kane got up early and went down to breakfast before Johnny was dressed. But Johnny was still worried, and hustled up and caught him before he was out of the dining-room. He was hoping Hurry would explain his getting in late and not sleeping. Kane wouldn't talk, though, and still acted nervous. So Johnny finally said:

"Hurry, you know what this game today means to me and you ought to know what it means to you. If we get trimmed, a lot of people besides ourselves will be disappointed, but they won't nobody be as disappointed as me. I wished you'd have had a good sleep last night and if you'll take my advice, you'll go up in the room and rest till it's time to go to the ball yard. If you're anywheres near yourself, this Chicago club is licked. And for heaven's sakes, be yourself, or your roomy is liable to walk out into Lake Michigan tonight so far that I can't get back!"

"I'm myself," says Kane and got up and left the table, but not quick enough so that Johnny didn't see tears in his eyes.

That afternoon's crowd beat all records and I was tickled to death to see it, because Hurry had always done his best work in front of crowds that was pulling against him. He warmed up fine and they wasn't nobody on our club, nobody but Kane himself and two others, who didn't feel perfectly confident that we were "in."

The White Sox were starting Sam Bonner and while he had beat us three or four times, we'd always got runs off him, and they'd always been lucky to score at all against Kane.

Bonner went through the first innings without no trouble. And then we got the shock of our lives. The first ball Hurry pitched was high and outside and it felt funny when I caught it. I was used to that old "zip" and I could have caught this one in my bare hand. Claymore took a cut at the next one and hit it a mile to left center for three bases. King hit for two bases, Welsh was safe when Digman threw a ground ball into the seats, and Kramer slapped one out of the park for a homer. Four runs. The crowd was wild and we were wilder.

You ought to have heard us on that bench. "Yellow so-and-so" was the mildest name Hurry got called. Dave couldn't do nothing but just mumble and shake his fists at Kane. We was all raving and asking each other what in hell was going on. Hurry stood in front facing us, but he was looking up in the stand and he acted like he didn't hear one word of the sweet remarks meant for his ears.

Johnny Abbott pulled me aside.

"Listen," he says. "This kid ain't yellow and he ain't wore out. They's something wrong here."

By this time Dave had found his voice and he yelled at Kane: "You so-and-so so-and-so! You're going to stay right in there and pitch till this game is over! And if you don't pitch like you can pitch, I'll shoot you dead tonight just as sure as you're a yellow, quitting—!"

We'd forgot it was our turn to bat and Hildebrand was threatening to forfeit the game before he could get Bull Wade to go up there. Kane still stood in front of us, staring. But pretty soon Dave told young Topping to run out to the bull pen and warn Carney and Olds to both be ready. I seen Topping stop a minute alongside of Kane and look up in the stand where Kane was looking. I seen Topping say something to Kane and I heard Kane call him a liar. Then Topping said something more and Hurry turned white as a sheet and pretty near fell into the dugout. I noticed his hand shake as he took a drink of water. And then he went over to Dave and I heard him say:

"I'm sorry, Boss. I had a bad inning. But I'll be all right from now on."

"You'd better!" says Dave.

"Get me some runs is all I ask," says Kane.

And the words wasn't no sooner out of his mouth when Bull smacked one a mile over Claymore's head and came into the plate standing up. They was another tune on the bench now. We were yelling for blood, and we got it. Before they relieved Bonner, we'd got to him for three singles and a double—mine, if you must know—and the score was tied.

Say, if you think you ever seen pitching, you ought to have

watched Kane cut them through there the rest of that day. Fourteen strike-outs in the last eight innings! And the only man to reach first base was Kramer, when Stout dropped an easy fly ball in the fifth.

Well, to shorten it up, Bull and Johnny Abbott and myself had some luck against Pierce in the seventh innings. Bull and Johnny scored and we licked them, 6 to 4.

In the club-house, Dave went to Hurry and said:

"Have you got anything to tell me, any explanation of the way you looked at the start of that game?"

"Boss," said Kane, "I didn't sleep good last night. Johnny will be a witness to that. I felt terrible in that first innings. I seemed to have lost my 'fast.' In the second innings it came back and I was all right."

And that's all he would say.

You know how we went ahead and took the big series, four games out of five, and how Hurry gave them one run in the three games he pitched. And now you're going to know what I promised to tell you when we first sat down, and I hope I ain't keeping you from a date with that gal from St. Joe.

The world's series ended in St. Louis and naturally I didn't come back East when it was over. Neither did Kane, because he was going home to Yuma, along with his Minnie. Well, they were leaving the next night, though most of the other boys had ducked out right after the final game. Hurry called me up at my house three or four hours before his train was due to leave and asked me would I come and see him and give him some advice. So I went to the hotel and he got me in his room and locked the door.

Here is what he had to say:

On the night before that last game in Chi, a gal called him up and it was nobody but our old friend Evelyn Corey. She asked him to come out to a certain hotel on the North Side and have supper with her. He went because he felt kind of sorry for her. But when he seen her, he lost his head and was just as nuts about her as he'd been at Fort Gregg. She encouraged him and strung him along till he forgot all about poor Minnie. Evelyn told him she knew he could have his pick of a hundred gals and she was broken-hearted because they was no chance for her. He asked her what made her think that, and she put her handkerchief to her eyes and pretended she was crying and that drove him wild and he said he wouldn't marry nobody but her.

Then she told him they had better forget it, that she was broke now, but had been used to luxury, and he promised he would work hard and save up till he had three or four thousand dollars and that would be enough for a start.

"Four thousand dollars!" she says. "Why, that wouldn't buy the runs in my stockings! I wouldn't think of marrying a man who had less than twenty thousand. I would want a honeymoon in Europe and we'd buy a car over there and tour the whole continent, and then come home and settle down in some nice suburb of New York. And so," she says, "I am going to get up and leave you right now because I see that my dream won't never come true."

She left him sitting in the restaurant and he was the only person there outside of the waiters. But after he'd sat a little while—he was waiting till the first shock of his disappointment had wore off—a black-haired bird with a waxed mustache came up to him and asked if he wasn't Hurry Kane, the great pitcher. Then he said: "I suppose you'll pitch again tomorrow," and Kane said yes.

"I haven't nothing against you," says the stranger, "but I hope you lose. It will cost me a lot of money if you win."

"How much?" said Kane.

"So much," says the stranger, "that I will give you twenty thousand dollars if you get beat."

"I can't throw my pals," said Kane.

"Well," said the stranger, "two of your pals has already agreed to throw you."

Kane asked him who he referred to, but he wouldn't tell. Kane don't know yet, but I do. It was Digman and Stout, our shortstopper and first baseman, and you'll notice they ain't with our club no more.

Hurry held out as long as he could, but the thought of Evelyn and that honeymoon in Europe broke him down. He took five thousand dollars' advance and was to come to the same place and get the balance right after the game.

He said that after Johnny Abbott had give him that talk at the breakfast table, he went out and rode around in a taxi so he could cry without being seen.

Well, I've told you about that terrible first innings. And I've told you about young Topping talking to him before he went down to the bull pen to deliver Dave's message to Carney and Olds. Topping asked him what he was staring at and Hurry pointed Evelyn out to him and said she was his gal.

"Your gal's grandmother!" said Topping. "That's Evelyn Corey and she belongs to Sam Morris, the bookie. If I was you, I'd lay off. You needn't tell Dave, but I was in Ike Bloom's at one o'clock this morning, and Sam and she were there, too. And one of the waiters told me that Sam had bet twenty thousand dollars on the White Sox way last spring and had got six to one for his money."

Hurry quit talking and I started to bawl him out. But I couldn't stay mad at him, especially when I realized that they was a fifty-three-hundred-dollar check in my pocket which I'd never have had only for him. Besides, they ain't nothing crooked about him. He's just a bone-headed sap.

"I won't tell Dave on you," I said, and I got up to go.

"Wait a minute," says Kane. "I confessed so I could ask you a question. I've still got that five thousand which Morris paid me in advance. With that dough and the fifty-three hundred from the series, I and Min could buy ourself a nice little home in Yuma. But do you think I should ought to give it back to that crook?"

"No," said I. "What you ought to do is split it with young Topping. He was your good luck!"

I run acrost Topping right here in town not long ago. And the first thing he said was, "What do you think of that goofey Kane? I had a letter from him and a check. He said the check was what he owed me."

"Twenty-five hundred dollars?" I says.

"Two hundred," said Topping, "and if I ever lent him two hundred or two cents, I'll roll a hoop from here to Yuma."

Bruce Brooks

From THE MOVES MAKE THE MAN

In a game you can't win,
what you can't lose is heart.

You probably wonder why the first thing I did wasn't check out the basketball tryouts. Well, I knew that at Parker hoops tryouts did not start until football season was over, which is to say about late November. But then one day after school, when I had stayed after with Madame Dupont in French to get my reflexive verb action down just right, I was walking to my locker and I felt it in the soles of my feet: bammata bammata bammata. Somewhere down that hallway, someone was dribbling basketballs.

Naturally I wanted to go check it out. It is in your body when you love ball. Your hands start to curve and spread, your wrists feel like oiled metal, your feet want to kick up off the ground and you just know you are light and trim and can get up in that sky and stay there. Man, I love it and I was very excited all of a sudden that day.

Lucky, I had worn my high blacks to school instead of my loafers, which I usually do until it's too cold out for canvas which lets the wind whistle through. I had on a pretty old pair of corduroys, getting a little snug, but floppy down at the feet which was bad, and a sweater with a T-shirt underneath. Usually I hate T-shirts and do not wear them under shirts, but with sweaters you got to have something to keep the wool off your skin. Very quickly I thought out what I could do to get in playing shape with my clothes, and then I went quietly down to the place where the dribbling came from and saw, sure enough, that it was the gym. There were two double doors. There was something else too:

Thumbtacked up on the left-hand door was a manila folder opened up and written in crayon BOY'S BASKETBALL TRYOUTS WEDNESDAY THURSDAY. This was Wednesday. I was right on time, baby.

Very fast now, because I heard somebody blow a whistle inside, I ran back to my locker, shucked off my sweater, tightened my laces, and ran into the first classroom I could find.

Sitting behind the desk was old Egglestobbs.

He looked up at me, and smiled one of those smiles that people give you when they think they know just exactly what kind of foolishness you are up to, and you don't know it is foolish yet, being dumber than they.

Scissors, I said. He pretended not to hear me, and leaned back and put his fingertips together under his chin and pooched out his lips, which I guess was his way of studying someone, but to me looked like a pretty weird bunch of body signals.

High excitement, he said, as if he were talking to some great scientist standing beside him. Haste. A great hastiness—notice the angle of the torso.

Notice the fact that I ran in here panting, I said. Any scissors in that desk, Mr. E.?

The spread of the feet is revealing too, he said, nodding slowly and dropping his eyebrows. They enclose an acute, rather than an obtuse, fan of degrees. This of course denotes physical anxiety and not a little emotional disconfidence. He raised his brows and put on this fakey smile which I knew meant he was going to include me in the conversation now. Feeling a little inadequate, are we? Though probably, he said back to his ghost scientist, primarily in a physical sense.

Feeling very late for basketball tryouts, I said, trying not to get sassy, completely in a physical sense. Also feeling the need for a pair of big fat school scissors which I bet you got in that desk drawer if you would just let me check.

I went over and pulled open the drawer, bopping his tummy just a tiny bit, which he probably took as a symbol of my need to disbowel him like the Zulus do in movies, there being all that African stuff in my blood. Especially when I said Hah! and yanked out the big scissors with the red handles and held them up to show him. His eyes got a little wide. But I was already sitting on the floor going to work on my pants.

What are you doing? he said.

Cutting off my trousers.

The abuse of clothing is, of course, symbolic of the will to abuse the corporeal self.

The abuse of these pants legs is so they don't flop on my feet when I go flying past those boys' face in there on my way to a double spin reverse finger roll.

He made a yucky face. Deceit! he said. Bald deceit.

I was through with one leg and started on the other. I heard a whistle again down the hall, and the balls all stopped bouncing. Man, I had to get there!

Basketball, of all games, is the one most dedicated to physical lying, he said.

I never knew anybody who could play while lying, I said, finishing off the leg and pulling the raggedy end pieces off over my sneaks. Most people play it on their physical feet.

He said nothing. I chunked the ends in the trash can, handed him the scissors, which he winced and took with a frown, looking at them like they were a Zulu spear covered in water buffalo blood.

Thanks, Mr. E. Check you later. Keep a cool torso.

What a weary web we weave when we practice to deceive, he said, as I ran out to the hall to get in some deceive-practice. You'll see, boy—the body will be avenged for its servitude to untruth! He might have said more but I didn't hear it, for I had made it to the gym and busted in through those double doors.

I had not been thinking too much about manners and entering nicely, being half worried about what Momma would say when I came home with ruined britches and the other half worried about getting into the gym before the coach made teams up for practice games or whatever he was doing while the balls were quiet. So I just crashed in through the doors, thinking only too late that this was maybe a little reckless. And it was, too.

For there, standing at attention in a row facing me, were a dozen white boys in red and white uniforms and there, turned around to see who was busting down his doors, was this fat white man with a butch haircut wearing white shorts and a red nylon jacket with the collar turned up and a whistle in his mouth. I stopped dead. Everybody was staring hard at me. There was no sound except the doors behind me bonging as they flapped back and forth, slower and slower, until they stopped.

At first the boys' expressions had been all fearful, like the coach had been yelling at them, but they soon got relieved and then very fast got all smug and entertained. In fact a couple of them actually smiled, big private grins, like Here comes a good time.

The coach never smiled. From the start he looked peeved. He looked peeved that someone interrupted him, peeved that it was not Red Auerbach come to observe his coaching method, peeved that instead it was a black kid in ravelly corduroys and a white T-shirt. I began to think he would stare me into the floor unless I said something.

This basketball tryouts? I said. One of the boys let fall the basketball he was holding and grinned. The ball bounced itself down slowly and rolled over towards me.

No, the coach said. This is a meeting of . . . of . . . He was trying to think of something sarcastic. One of the boys helped him out.

Of the Ku Klux Klan, the boy said.

Of the Future Nurses of America, said the coach, ignoring the kid. What does it look like to you? He talked without taking the whistle out of his teeth.

Looks like I'm a little bit late to get a uniform, I said. Sorry, Coach. I was staying after with my French teacher.

Parlez-vous français? said one of the boys and for some reason all of them thought this was marvelous funny and cracked it up. His accent was awful.

You don't walk in here and just GET a uniform, said the coach. He jerked his head towards the kids with the red and white satin on. You earn the right to let your skin touch one of these.

Practice only been going for five minutes, I said. They must earn pretty fast.

He smiled. We scout the P.E. classes and know ahead of time where our talents lie. As a matter of fact, these are not what you would call open tryouts—the most promising prospects are specially invited to participate.

My P.E. class has been playing dodge ball for the two weeks since school started, I said. How is anybody supposed to see what I can do with a basketball?

He shrugged and smiled. One of the kids said, Maybe you'll be invited when the dodge ball team holds tryouts, and they all laughed.

So are you saying I can't try out for the team? I said. I bent down and picked up the ball at my feet, very casual.

I'm afraid it looks that way, the coach said, still talking around his whistle, which tooted a little with the ks at the end of looks.

Well how does this look? I said, twirling the ball in my hands and going straight up, straight as high and trim as could be, waiting until I got to the top to check out the hoop which must have been twenty-five feet away, then cradling the ball and at the last minute pulling my left hand away like Oscar Robertson and snapping that lubricated right wrist and knowing, feeling it right straight through from the tips of the fingers that had let fly the ball and touched it all the way to the last, straight down the front edge of my body to my toes just before they hit the ground again, that the shot was true, feeling the swish and tickle of the net cords rushing quick down my nerves, and landing square and jaunty in time to watch, along with everybody else, as the ball popped through the net without a single bit of deceit, so clean it kicked the bottom of the cords back up and looped them over the rim, which is called a bottoms up and means you shot it perfect and some people even count them three points in street games.

I glanced back at the coach, to find I had been wrong. Not everybody had looked at the ball. For some reason he had kept staring right at me. His expression had not changed. This flustered me a little. Man, I had just hit a shot turned those white boys to jelly inside, you could see it the way they all kind of slunk at the spine when they looked back, but this burrhead fatso had not even bothered to check out my act.

Nice shot, mumbled one of the white kids, but the coach tooted on his whistle and cut him off.

I don't think it was a nice shot, the coach said. Not a nice shot at all.

But jeez, said another kid, Coach, cripes it must be twenty feet. . . .

Typical jig trick shot, said the coach, smiling a very tiny smile behind his whistle. Fancy, one-handed, big jump. Harlem Globetrotter stuff. You like the Globetrotters, boy?

I like basketball, I said.

Trick stuff. Bet you can dribble behind your back, too. Pass between your legs, jigaboo around in the air and shoot with your flat little nose. I bet you play a lot by yourself. He jerked his chin at me. What about it, Meadowlark? You play a lot by yourself?

I play, I said, in a class by myself.

Nobody said anything. The coach chuckled softly. The boys had kind of been with me until I said that, but now I could see them straighten up again. I realized I was being a cocky nigger, true to form as Poke Peters seemed to me.

By yourself, the coach finally said, chuckling and shaking his head. Well I reckon you better get on back to your special class, then, boy, and wait until we refine our crude old five-man sport down to where we have just one-man teams. Then he turned away, picking up a ball nearby and bouncing it once, getting ready to address his troops again.

I'll play any two of you one on two, I said. If I win I get a uniform and a tryout, if I lose I go make the Harlem Globetrotters.

The coach paused, but did not turn around. He started to ignore me and go on with his lecture but about four of the white boys said Hey Coach, let me Coach, I'll take him that is me and Tom will take him Coach, and so on. They were brave as could be at the chance of a little two on one.

The coach thought for a minute. Then he turned back around and looked at me.

Pete and Vic, he said, still looking at me. Two of the boys looked startled. They had not been the volunteers. Probably too good to worry about having to impress the coach.

Yeah Coach? they said.

Pete, you take him man to man, Vic, you zone him under.

But Coach, said one of them, tall and with pimples but he had the look in his eye of a shooter, you can tell them right away.

Come on, Ace, said the other, who was Vic, and him I liked right away because he was a ballhawk like me and wanted to play just to be playing. His eyes were big and smart and he was stocky and moved like a little lion. Stop stalling and let's play him, he said, smacking Pete on the fanny. I'll even take him man to man.

Coach snapped a bounce pass at me but made it bounce right at my feet which hits you in the shins and makes you look foolish if you don't step aside, which I did and gathered it in backhand.

Game to five buckets, he said.

Nigger ball? said Vic, by which he meant make-it-take-it. Then he looked at me, blushing. Sorry, he said, I mean . . .

Nigger ball, said the coach. Win by two.

I whipped a two-handed pass at Pete the tall one and hit him in the chest and he caught it in a hug. Shoot for outs, I said. He dribbled once and sort of looked puzzled, then shrugged and dribbled a couple more times and I saw his mind come right into focus very quick then, and he flowed a couple of steps which technically you are not supposed to when someone gives you a shot for outs but what the heck. He looked at the hoop and I knew I was right about him being the shooter for I saw the look in his eye and sure enough he pumped one up and it banked through.

Yeah, he said, smiling, let's go.

Vic took the ball out behind the line and gave me a check while the other guys sat down on the sideline. I checked it back to Vic and he started to dash off to the right. I flicked the ball with my left hand and pulled back to let him pass right by where it hung in the air, his hand still making the dribble motion, then I snatched it, threw him a head as he turned, went by him the opposite way from his motion and pulled up in Pete's face while he was still trying to figure out how you played a one-man zone. I slanted it off the glass and it zipped through. I came down and slipped around him and caught the ball as it came through the cords and was about to say One–zip when I heard the big whistle.

I looked around. The coach smiled at me. Then very slowly he raised his right hand and placed it behind his neck.

Charge, he said. We'll go the other way.

You're crazy, I said. I didn't touch him. He never even knew I was in the area. I pointed at Pete, who still looked a little puzzled.

Offense initiated contact, he said. White ball.

Asshole, I muttered, which I never curse but was mad.

That's a T, he said, tooting the whistle. Two shots. Pete?

Pete finally woke up, knowing he was to shoot. He hit both free throws.

One bucket to nothing, said the coach. White ball.

This time Vic tried to go right but I blocked him off, forcing him to use his left which most kids cannot yet do, spending most of their time only shooting. Sure enough he sort of stumbled and

made a clumsy crossover and I grabbed the ball again. I was inside him so I just spun right up and popped a twelve-footer, but the whistle was blowing already as I was in the air.

That's a reach, said the coach.

Aw, come on, no it wasn't, said Vic. It was clean, Coach. Vic was actually excited by the steal. He was a lover of the game for sure. Nice grab, he said.

Thanks, I said. But the coach had got the ball and bounced it back at Vic.

A reach, he said. Second personal. White ball.

Well, this time Vic finally got the idea he did not have to drive by me but just get the ball over to Pete for an open shot, and he did and Pete hit it from right underneath and I was down two. He did the same next time, faking the pass first and drawing me off, a nice move, then lofting it over me for a lay-up for the shooter. Three–zip. He tried the same thing next time but this time I pretended to go for the fake and backpedaled and picked Pete up before he could shoot. He went straight up without a fake and I jumped a half second later so I would be at peak just after he let it go and I was and slapped the ball away.

The whistle blew.

Hack, said the coach, shoot two.

Some of the guys on the sideline had clapped when I smacked the shot away, and now they made some Aw, come on! noises. They were okay, I suppose. Too bad they would have to play all year under the burrhead.

Pete hit both of his shots of course. Guys like him turn into beautiful robots when you give them the chance to shoot. I wonder what they do with the rest of their life. They sure don't play defense.

The coach got the ball as it dropped through from the last shot and bounced it back to Vic at the top of the key.

Coach . . . said Vic.

Play it, said the coach.

Vic looked at me and winked. Then he pretended to dribble

but bounced it right into my hands. I turned and drove left behind Pete's back, he was just waiting for his next shot anyway, and flipped it in off the boards with my left hand.

The whistle blew. Pushing off, said the coach, pushing off Pete's back, we'll take it the other way.

I won't take it no way, said Vic disgusted, kicking the ball away when the coach threw it to him. The only thing he pushed off was the floor.

Get back out there, Victor, said the coach, as Vic walked away to the sideline. You want to start this year?

Here's a kid could win us the city, said Vic, and nobody but you cares he's a nigger. Sorry, he said, waving at me.

Sit down, Victor, said the coach, and you won't be standing up in uniform for some time.

Maybe win us the states, he said, to the boys on the ground. They were all staring at the floor. The states, guys! The state championship! Pushing off, my ass, he said, and walked out of the gym.

We will continue as a one on one, said the coach. White ball after the foul. Shoot it, Pete, said the coach, shoving the ball at Pete over by the foul line.

Those were the magic words. I was eight feet away and didn't even try to stop it, but of course it went down anyway. That kid could shoot, I'll hand it to him. I took the ball as it came through the net, snapped a bounce pass at the coach's feet, and turned to go.

Five–nothing, white takes it, he said, as the ball banged off his shins. Take a hike, boy.

Good luck with the Globetrotters, one kid hollered as I pushed on the double doors. Nobody laughed though.

He'll probably make them, said another.

I hope so, said one more.

By then I was through, back in the hall, and the doors were bonging away. The last sound I heard from that gym was the big old scream of the whistle.

Jack London

THE MEXICAN

*Money. Glory. What else
is there to fight for?*

I

Nobody knew his history—they of the Junta least of all. He was their "little mystery," their "big patriot," and in his way he worked as hard for the coming Mexican Revolution as did they. They were tardy in recognizing this, for not one of the Junta liked him. The day he first drifted into their crowded, busy rooms they all suspected him of being a spy—one of the bought tools of the Diaz secret service. Too many of the comrades were in civil and military prisons scattered over the United States, and others of them, in irons, were even then being taken across the border to be lined up against adobe walls and shot.

At the first sight the boy did not impress them favorably. Boy he was, not more than eighteen and not overlarge for his years. He announced that he was Felipe Rivera, and that it was his wish to work for the revolution. That was all—not a wasted word, no further explanation. He stood waiting. There was no smile on his lips, no geniality in his eyes. Big, dashing Paulino Vera felt an inward shudder. Here was something forbidding, terrible, inscrutable. There was something venomous and snakelike in the boy's black eyes. They burned like cold fire, as with a vast, con-

centrated bitterness. He flashed them from the faces of the con-
spirators to the typewriter which little Mrs. Sethby was indus-
triously operating. His eyes rested on hers but an instant—she
had chanced to look up—and she, too, sensed the nameless
something that made her pause. She was compelled to read back
in order to regain the swing of the letter she was writing.

Paulino Vera looked questioningly at Arrellano and Ramos,
and questioningly they looked back and to each other. The indecision of doubt brooded in their eyes. This slender boy was the
Unknown, vested with all the menace of the Unknown. He was
unrecognizable, something quite beyond the ken of honest, ordinary revolutionists whose fiercest hatred for Diaz and his tyr-
anny after all was only that of honest and ordinary patriots. Here
was something else, they knew not what. But Vera, always the
most impulsive, the quickest to act, stepped into the breach.

"Very well," he said coldly. "You say you want to work for
the revolution. Take off your coat. Hang it over there. I will show
you—come—where are the buckets and cloths. The floor is dirty.
You will begin by scrubbing it, and by scrubbing the floors of the
other rooms. The spittoons need to be cleaned. Then there are
the windows."

"Is it for the revolution?" the boy asked.

"It is for the revolution," Vera answered.

Rivera looked cold suspicion at all of them, then proceeded to
take off his coat.

"It is well," he said.

And nothing more. Day after day he came to his work—
sweeping, scrubbing, cleaning. He emptied the ashes from the
stoves, brought up the coal and kindling, and lighted the fires
before the most energetic one of them was at his desk.

"Can I sleep here?" he asked once.

Aha! So that was it—the hand of Diaz showing through! To
sleep in the rooms of the Junta meant access to their secrets, to
the lists of names, to the addresses of comrades down on Mexican soil. The request was denied, and Rivera never spoke of it

again. He slept they knew not where, and ate they knew not where or how. Once Arrellano offered him a couple of dollars. Rivera declined the money with a shake of the head. When Vera joined in and tried to press it upon him, he said:

"I am working for the revolution."

It takes money to raise a modern revolution, and always the Junta was pressed. The members starved and toiled, and the longest day was none too long, and yet there were times when it appeared as if the revolution stood or fell on no more than the matter of a few dollars. Once, the first time, when the rent of the house was two months behind and the landlord was threatening dispossession, it was Felipe Rivera, the scrub boy in the poor, cheap clothes, worn and threadbare, who laid sixty dollars in gold on May Sethby's desk. There were other times. Three hundred letters, clicked out on the busy typewriters (appeals for assistance, for sanctions from the organized labor groups, requests for square news deals to the editors of newspapers, protests against the high-handed treatment of revolutionists by the United States courts), lay unmailed, awaiting postage. Vera's watch had disappeared—the old-fashioned gold repeater that had been his father's. Likewise had gone the plain gold band from May Sethby's third finger. Things were desperate. Ramos and Arrellano pulled their long mustaches in despair. The letters must go off, and the post office allowed no credit to purchasers of stamps. Then it was that Rivera put on his hat and went out. When he came back he laid a thousand two-cent stamps on May Sethby's desk.

"I wonder if it is the cursed gold of Diaz?" said Vera to the comrades.

They elevated their brows and could not decide. And Felipe Rivera, the scrubber for the revolution, continued, as occasion arose, to lay down gold and silver for the Junta's use.

And still they could not bring themselves to like him. They did not know him. His ways were not theirs. He gave no confidences. He repelled all probing. Youth that he was, they could never nerve themselves to dare to question him.

"A great and lonely spirit, perhaps. I do not know, I do not know," Arrellano said helplessly.

"He is not human," said Ramos.

"His soul has been seared," said May Sethby. "Light and laughter have been burned out of him. He is like one dead, and yet he is fearfully alive."

"He has been through hell," said Vera. "No man could look like that who has not been through hell—and he is only a boy."

Yet they could not like him. He never talked, never inquired, never suggested. He would stand listening, expressionless, a thing dead, save for his eyes, coldly burning, while their talk of the revolution ran high and warm. From face to face and speaker to speaker his eyes would turn, boring like gimlets of incandescent ice, disconcerting and perturbing.

"He is no spy," Vera confided to May Sethby. "He is a patriot—mark me, the greatest patriot of us all. I know it, I feel it, here in my heart and head I feel it. But him I know not at all."

"He has a bad temper," said May Sethby.

"I know," said Vera with a shudder. "He has looked at me with those eyes of his. They do not love; they threaten; they are savage as a wild tiger's. I know, if I should prove unfaithful to the cause, that he would kill me. He has no heart. He is pitiless as steel, keen and cold as frost. He is like moonshine in a winter night when a man freezes to death on some lonely mountain top. I am not afraid of Diaz and all his killers; but this boy, of him am I afraid. I tell you true. I am afraid. He is the breath of death."

Yet Vera it was who persuaded the others to give the first trust to Rivera. The line of communication between Los Angeles and Lower California had broken down. Three of the comrades had dug their own graves and been shot into them. Two more were United States prisoners in Los Angeles. Juan Alvarado, the federal commander, was a monster. All their plans did he checkmate. They could no longer gain access to the active revolutionists, and the incipient ones, in Lower California.

Young Rivera was given his instructions and dispatched south.

When he returned, the line of communication was re-established, and Juan Alvarado was dead. He had been found in bed, a knife hilt-deep in his breast. This had exceeded Rivera's instructions, but they of the Junta knew the times of his movements. They did not ask him. He said nothing. But they looked at one another and conjectured.

"I have told you," said Vera. "Diaz has more to fear from this youth than from any man. He is implacable. He is the hand of God."

The bad temper, mentioned by May Sethby, and sensed by them all, was evidenced by physical proofs. Now he appeared with a cut lip, a blackened cheek, or a swollen ear. It was patent that he brawled, somewhere in that outside world where he ate and slept, gained money, and moved in ways unknown to them. As the time passed he had come to set type for the little revolutionary sheet they published weekly. There were occasions when he was unable to set type, when his knuckles were bruised and battered, when his thumbs were injured and helpless, when one arm or the other hung wearily at his side while his face was drawn with unspoken pain.

"A wastrel," said Arrellano.

"A frequenter of low places," said Ramos.

"But where does he get the money?" Vera demanded. "Only today, just now, have I learned that he paid the bill for white paper—one hundred and forty dollars."

"There are his absences," said May Sethby. "He never explains them."

"We should set a spy upon him," Ramos propounded.

"I should not care to be that spy," said Vera. "I fear you would never see me again, save to bury me. He has a terrible passion. Not even God would he permit to stand between him and the way of his passion."

"I feel like a child before him," Ramos confessed.

"To me he is power—he is the primitive, the wild wolf, the

striking rattlesnake, the stinging centipede," said Arrellano.

"He is the revolution incarnate," said Vera. "He is the flame and the spirit of it, the insatiable cry for vengeance that makes no cry but that slays noiselessly. He is a destroying angel moving through the still watches of the night."

"I could weep over him," said May Sethby. "He knows nobody. He hates all people. Us he tolerates, for we are the way of his desire. He is alone . . . lonely." Her voice broke in a half sob and there was a dimness in her eyes.

Rivera's ways and times were truly mysterious. There were periods when they did not see him for a week at a time. Once he was away a month. These occasions were always capped by his return, when, without advertisement or speech, he laid gold coins on May Sethby's desk. Again, for days and weeks, he spent all his time with the Junta. And yet again, for irregular periods, he would disappear through the heart of each day, from early morning until late afternoon. At such times he came early and remained late. Arrellano had found him at midnight, setting type with fresh-swollen knuckles, or mayhap it was his lip, new split, that still bled.

II

The time of the crisis approached. Whether or not the revolution would be depended upon the Junta, and the Junta was hard-pressed. The need for money was greater than ever before, while money was harder to get. Patriots had given their last cent and now could give no more. Section-gang laborers—fugitive peons from Mexico—were contributing half their scanty wages. But more than that was needed. The heartbreaking, conspiring, undermining toil of years approached fruition. The time was ripe. The revolution hung on the balance. One shove more, one last heroic effort, and it would tremble across the scales to victory. They knew their Mexico. Once started, the revolution would take care of itself. The whole Diaz machine would go down like a house of cards. The border was ready to rise. One Yankee, with a hundred I.W.W. men, waited the word to cross over the border and begin conquest of Lower California. But he needed guns. And clear across to the Atlantic, the Junta in touch with them all and all of them needing guns, mere adventurers, soldiers of fortune, bandits, disgruntled American union men, socialists, anarchists, roughnecks, Mexican exiles, peons escaped from bondage, whipped miners from the bullpens of Coeur d'Alene and Colorado who desired only the more vindictively to fight—all the flotsam and jetsam of wild spirits from the madly complicated modern world. And it was guns and ammunition, ammunition and guns—the unceasing and eternal cry.

Fling this heterogeneous, bankrupt, vindictive mass across the border, and the revolution was on. The customhouse, the northern ports of entry, would be captured. Diaz could not resist. He dared not throw the weight of his armies against them, for he must hold the south. And through the south the flame would spread despite. The people would rise. The defenses of city after city would crumple up. State after state would totter down. And at last, from every side, the victorious armies of the revolution would close in on the city of Mexico itself, Diaz's last stronghold.

But the money. They had the men, impatient and urgent, who would use the guns. They knew the traders who would sell and deliver the guns. But to culture the revolution thus far had exhausted the Junta. The last dollar had been spent, the last resource and the last starving patriot milked dry, and the great adventure still trembled on the scales. Guns and ammunition! The ragged battalions must be armed. But how? Ramos lamented his confiscated estates. Arrellano wailed the spendthriftness of his youth. May Sethby wondered if it would have been different had they of the Junta been more economical in the past.

"To think that the freedom of Mexico should stand or fall on a few paltry thousands of dollars," said Paulino Vera.

Despair was in all their faces. José Amarillo, their last hope, a recent convert who had promised money, had been apprehended at his hacienda in Chihuahua and shot against his own stable wall. The news had just come through.

Rivera, on his knees, scrubbing, looked up, with suspended brush, his bare arms flecked with soapy, dirty water.

"Will five thousand do it?" he asked.

They looked their amazement. Vera nodded and swallowed. He could not speak, but he was on the instant invested with a vast faith.

"Order the guns," Rivera said, and thereupon was guilty of the longest flow of words they had ever heard him utter. "The time is short. In three weeks I shall bring you the five thousand. It is well. The weather will be warmer for those who fight. Also, it is the best I can do."

Vera fought his faith. It was incredible. Too many fond hopes had been shattered since he had begun to play the revolution game. He believed this threadbare scrubber of the revolution, and yet he dared not believe.

"You are crazy," he said.

"In three weeks," said Rivera. "Order the guns."

He got up, rolled down his sleeves, and put on his coat.

"Order the guns," he said. "I am going now."

III

After hurrying and scurrying, much telephoning and bad language, a night session was held in Kelly's office. Kelly was rushed with business; also, he was unlucky. He had brought Danny Ward out from New York, arranged the fight for him with Billy Carthey, the date was three weeks away, and for two days now, carefully concealed from the sporting writers, Carthey had been lying up, badly injured. There was no one to take his place. Kelly had been burning the wires east to every eligible lightweight, but they were tied up with dates and contracts. And now hope had revived, though faintly.

"You've got a hell of a nerve," Kelly addressed Rivera, after one look, as soon as they got together.

Hate that was malignant was in Rivera's eyes, but his face remained impassive.

"I can lick Ward," was all he said.

"How do you know? Ever see him fight?"

Rivera shook his head.

"He can beat you up with one hand and both eyes closed."

Rivera shrugged his shoulders.

"Haven't you got anything to say?" the fight promoter snarled.

"I can lick him."

"Who'd you ever fight, anyway?" Michael Kelly demanded. Michael was the promoter's brother, and ran the Yellowstone Poolrooms, where he made goodly sums on the fight game.

Rivera favored him with a bitter, unanswering stare.

The promoter's secretary, a distinctively sporty young man, sneered audibly.

"Well, you know Roberts," Kelly broke the hostile silence. "He ought to be here. I've sent for him. Sit down and wait, though from the looks of you, you haven't got a chance. I can't throw the public down with a bum fight. Ringside seats are selling at fifteen dollars, you know that."

When Roberts arrived it was patent that he was mildly drunk. He was a tall, lean, slack-jointed individual, and his walk, like his talk, was a smooth and languid drawl.

Kelly went straight to the point.

"Look here, Roberts, you've been braggin' you discovered this little Mexican. You know Carthey's broken his arm. Well, this little yellow streak has the gall to blow in today and say he'll take Carthey's place. What about it?"

"It's all right, Kelly," came the slow response. "He can put up a fight."

"I suppose you'll be sayin' next that he can lick Ward," Kelly snapped.

Roberts considered judicially.

"No, I won't say that. Ward's a topnotcher and a ring general. But he can't hash-house Rivera in short order. I know Rivera. Nobody can get his goat. He ain't got a goat that I could ever discover. And he's a two-handed fighter. He can throw in the sleep-makers from any position."

"Never mind that. What kind of a show can he put up? You've been conditioning and training fighters all your life. I take off my hat to your judgment. Can he give the public a run for its money?"

"He sure can, and he'll worry Ward a mighty heap on top of it. You don't know that boy. I do. I discovered him. He ain't got a goat. He's a devil. He's a wizzy-wooz if anybody should ask you. He'll make Ward sit up with a show of local talent that'll make the rest of you sit up. I won't say he'll lick Ward, but he'll put up such a show that you'll all know he's a comer."

"All right." Kelly turned to his secretary. "Ring up Ward. I warned him to show up if I thought it worth while. He's right across at the Yellowstone, throwin' chests and doing the popular." Kelly turned back to the conditioner. "Have a drink?"

Roberts sipped his highball and unburdened himself.

"Never told you how I discovered the little cuss. It was a couple of years ago he showed up out at the quarters. I was getting Prayne ready for his fight with Delaney. Prayne's wicked. He ain't got a tickle of mercy in his make-up. He'd chopped up his pardners something cruel, and I couldn't find a willing boy that'd work with him. I'd noticed this little starved Mexican kid hanging around, and I was desperate. So I grabbed him, slammed on the gloves, and put him in. He was tougher'n rawhide, but weak. And he didn't know the first letter in the alphabet of boxing. Prayne chopped him to ribbons. But he hung on for two sickening rounds, when he fainted. Starvation, that was all. Battered? You couldn't have recognized him. I gave him half a dollar and a square meal. You oughta seen him wolf it down. He hadn't had a bite for a couple of days. That's the end of him, thinks I. But next day he showed up, stiff an' sore, ready for another half and a square meal. And he done better as time went by. Just a born fighter, and tough beyond belief. He hasn't a heart. He's a piece of ice. And he never talked eleven words in a string since I know him. He saws wood and does his work.''

"I've seen 'm," the secretary said. "He's worked a lot for you."

"All the big little fellows has tried out on him," Roberts answered. "And he's learned from 'em. I've seen some of them he could lick. But his heart wasn't in it. I reckoned he never liked the game. He seemed to act that way."

"He's been fighting some before the little clubs the last few months," Kelly said.

"Sure. But I don't know what struck 'm. All of a sudden his heart got into it. He just went out like a streak and cleaned up all the little local fellows. Seemed to want the money, and he's won a bit, though his clothes don't look it. He's peculiar. Nobody knows his business. Nobody knows how he spends his time. Even when he's on the job, he plumb up and disappears most of each day soon as his work is done. Sometimes he just blows away for weeks at a time. But he don't take advice. There's a fortune in it for the fellow that gets the job of managin' him, only he won't consider it. And you watch him hold out for the cash money when you get down to terms."

It was at this stage that Danny Ward arrived. Quite a party it was. His manager and trainer were with him, and he breezed in like a gusty draught of geniality, good nature, and all-conqueringness. Greetings flew about, a joke here, a retort there, a smile or a laugh for everybody. Yet it was his way, and only partly sincere. He was a good actor, and he had found geniality a most valuable asset in the game of getting on in the world. But down underneath he was the deliberate, cold-blooded fighter and businessman. The rest was a mask. Those who knew him or trafficked with him said that when it came to brass tacks he was Danny on the Spot. He was invariably present at all business discussions, and it was urged by some that his manager was a blind whose only function was to serve as Danny's mouthpiece.

Rivera's way was different. Indian blood, as well as Spanish, was in his veins, and he sat back in a corner, silent, immobile, only his black eyes passing from face to face and noting everything.

"So that's the guy," Danny said, running an appraising eye over his proposed antagonist. "How de do, old chap?"

Rivera's eyes burned venomously, but he made no sign of acknowledgment. He disliked all gringos, but this gringo he hated with an immediacy that was unusual even in him.

"Gawd!" Danny protested facetiously to the promoter. "You ain't expectin' me to fight a deef mute." When the laughter subsided he made another hit. "Los Angeles must be on the dink when this is the best you can scare up. What kindergarten did you get 'm from?"

"He's a good little boy, Danny, take it from me," Roberts defended. "Not as easy as he looks."

"And half the house is sold already," Kelly pleaded. "You'll have to take 'm on, Danny. It's the best we can do."

Danny ran another careless and unflattering glance over Rivera and sighed.

"I gotta be easy with 'm, I guess. If only he don't blow up."

Roberts snorted.

"You gotta be careful," Danny's manager warned. "No taking chances with a dub that's likely to sneak a lucky one across."

"Oh, I'll be careful all right," Danny smiled. "I'll get 'm at the start an' nurse 'm along for the dear public's sake. What d'ye say to fifteen rounds, Kelly—an' then the hay for him?"

"That'll do," was the answer. "As long as you make it realistic."

"Then let's get down to biz." Danny paused and calculated. "Of course, sixty-five per cent of gate receipts, same as with Carthey. But the split'll be different. Eighty will just about suit me." And to his manager, "That right?"

The manager nodded.

"Here, you, did you get that?" Kelly asked Rivera.

Rivera shook his head.

"Well, it's this way," Kelly exposited. "The purse'll be sixty-five per cent of the gate receipts. You're a dub, and an unknown. You and Danny split, twenty per cent goin' to you, an' eighty to Danny. That's fair, isn't it, Roberts?"

"Very fair," Roberts agreed. "You see, you ain't got a reputation yet."

"What will sixty-five per cent of the gate receipts be?" Rivera demanded.

"Oh, maybe five thousand, maybe as high as eight thousand," Danny broke in to explain. "Something like that. Your share'll come to something like a thousand or sixteen hundred. Pretty good for takin' a licking from a guy with my reputation. What d'ye say?"

Then Rivera took their breaths away.

"Winner takes all," he said with finality.

A dead silence prevailed.

"It's like candy from a baby," Danny's manager proclaimed.

Danny shook his head.

"I've been in the game too long," he explained. "I'm not casting reflections on the referee or the present company. I'm not sayin' nothing about bookmakers an' frame-ups that sometimes happen. But what I do say is that it's poor business for a fighter like me. I play safe. There's no tellin'. Mebbe I break my arm, eh? Or some guy slips me a bunch of dope." He shook his head solemnly. "Win or lose, eighty is my split. What d'ye say, Mexican?"

Rivera shook his head.

Danny exploded. He was getting down to brass tacks now.

"Why, you dirty little greaser! I've a mind to knock your block off right now."

Roberts drawled his body to interposition between hostilities.

"Winner takes all," Rivera repeated sullenly.

"Why do you stand out that way?" Danny asked.

"I can lick you," was the straight answer.

Danny half started to take off his coat. But, as his manager knew, it was grandstand play. The coat did not come off, and Danny allowed himself to be placated by the group. Everybody sympathized with him. Rivera stood alone.

"Look here, you little fool," Kelly took up the argument. "You're nobody. We know what you've been doing the last few months—putting away little local fighters. But Danny is class. His next fight after this will be for the championship. And you're unknown. Nobody ever heard of you out of Los Angeles."

"They will," Rivera answered with a shrug, "after this fight."

"You think for a second you can lick me?" Danny blurted in.

Rivera nodded.

"Oh, come; listen to reason," Kelly pleaded. "Think of the advertising."

"I want the money," was Rivera's answer.

"You couldn't win from me in a thousand years," Danny assured him.

"Then what are you holding out for?" Rivera countered. "If the money's that easy, why don't you go after it?"

"I will, so help me!" Danny cried with abrupt conviction. "I'll beat you to death in the ring, my boy—you monkeyin' with me this way. Make out the articles, Kelly. Winner take all. Play it up in the sportin' columns. Tell 'em it's a grudge fight. I'll show this fresh kid a few."

Kelly's secretary had begun to write, when Danny interrupted.

"Hold on!" He turned to Rivera. "Weights?"

"Ringside," came the answer.

"Not on your life, fresh kid. If winner takes all, we weigh in at ten A.M."

"And winner takes all?" Rivera queried.

Danny nodded. That settled it. He would enter the ring in his full ripeness of strength.

"Weigh in at ten," Rivera said.

The secretary's pen went on scratching.

"It means five pounds," Roberts complained to Rivera. "You've given too much away. You've thrown the fight right there. Danny'll be as strong as a bull. You're a fool. He'll lick you sure. You ain't got the chance of a dewdrop in hell."

Rivera's answer was a calculated look of hatred. Even this gringo he despised, and him had he found the whitest gringo of them all.

IV

Barely noticed was Rivera as he entered the ring. Only a very slight and very scattering ripple of half-hearted hand-clapping greeted him. The house did not believe in him. He was the lamb led to slaughter at the hands of the great Danny. Besides, the house was disappointed. It had expected a rushing battle between Danny Ward and Billy Carthey and here it must put up with this poor little tyro. Still further, it had manifested its disapproval of the change by betting two, and even three, to one on Danny. And where a betting audience's money is, there is its heart.

The Mexican boy sat down in his corner and waited. The slow minutes lagged by. Danny was making him wait. It was an old trick, but ever it worked on the young, new fighters. They grew frightened, sitting thus and facing their own apprehensions and a callous, tobacco-smoking audience. But for once the trick failed. Roberts was right. Rivera had no goat. He, who was more delicately coordinated, more finely nerved and strung than any of them, had no nerves of this sort. The atmosphere of foredoomed defeat in his own corner had no effect on him. His handlers were gringos and strangers. Also they were scrubs—the dirty driftage of the fight game, without honor, without efficiency. And they were chilled, as well, with certitude that theirs was the losing corner.

"Now you gotta be careful," Spider Hagerty warned him. Spider was his chief second. "Make it last as long as you can—

them's my instructions from Kelly. If you don't, the papers'll call it another bum fight and give the game a bigger black eye in Los Angeles.''

All of which was not encouraging. But Rivera took no notice. He despised prize fighting. It was the hated game of the hated gringo. He had taken up with it, as a chopping block for others in the training quarters, solely because he was starving. The fact that he was marvelously made for it had meant nothing. He hated it. Not until he had come in to the Junta had he fought for money, and he had found the money easy. Not first among the sons of men had he been to find himself successful at a despised vocation.

He did not analyze. He merely knew that he must win this fight. There could be no other outcome. For behind him, nerving him to this belief, were profounder forces than any the crowded house dreamed. Danny Ward fought for money and for the easy ways of life that money would bring. But the things Rivera fought for burned in his brain—blazing and terrible visions, that, with eyes wide open, sitting lonely in the corner of the ring and waiting for his tricky antagonist, he saw as clearly as he had lived them.

He saw the white-walled, water-power factories of Rio Blanco. He saw the six thousand workers, starved and wan, and the little children, seven and eight years of age, who toiled long shifts for ten cents a day. He saw the perambulating corpses, the ghastly death's heads of men who labored in the dye rooms. He remembered that he had heard his father call the dye rooms the ''suicide holes,'' where a year was death. He saw the little patio, and his mother cooking and moiling at crude housekeeping and finding time to caress and love him. And his father he saw, large, big-mustached, and deep-chested, kindly above all men, who loved all men and whose heart was so large that there was love to overflowing still left for the mother and the little *muchacho* playing in the corner of the patio. In those days his name had not been Felipe Rivera. It had been Fernandez, his father's and mother's

name. Him had they called Juan. Later he had changed it himself, for he had found the name of Fernandez hated by prefects of police, *jefes políticos*, and *rurales*.

Big, hearty Joaquin Fernandez! A large place he occupied in Rivera's visions. He had not understood at the time, but, looking back, he could understand. He could see him setting type in the little printery, or scribbling endless hasty, nervous lines on the much-cluttered desk. And he could see the strange evenings, when workmen, coming secretly in the dark like men who did ill deeds, met with his father and talked long hours where he, the *muchacho*, lay not always asleep in the corner.

As from a remote distance he could hear Spider Hagerty saying to him: "No layin' down at the start. Them's instructions. Take a beatin' an' earn your dough."

Ten minutes had passed, and he still sat in his corner. There were no signs of Danny, who was evidently playing the trick to the limit.

But more visions burned before the eye of Rivera's memory. The strike, or, rather, the lock-out, because the workers of Rio Blanco had helped their striking brothers of Puebla. The hunger, the expeditions in the hills for berries, the roots and herbs that all ate and that twisted and pained the stomachs of all of them. And then the nightmare; the waste of ground before the company's store; the thousands of starving workers; General Rosalio Martinez and the soldiers of Porfirio Diaz; and the death-spitting rifles that seemed never to cease spitting, while the workers' wrongs were washed and washed again in their own blood. And that night! He saw the flat cars, piled high with the bodies of the slain, consigned to Vera Cruz, food for the sharks of the bay. Again he crawled over the grisly heaps, seeking and finding, stripped and mangled, his father and mother. His mother he especially remembered—only her face projecting, her body burdened by the weight of dozens of bodies. Again the rifles of the soldiers of Porfirio Diaz cracked, and again he dropped to the ground and slunk away like some hunted coyote of the hills.

To his ears came a great roar, as of the sea, and he saw Danny Ward, leading his retinue of trainers and seconds, coming down the center aisle. The house was in wild uproar for the popular hero who was bound to win. Everybody proclaimed him. Everybody was for him. Even Rivera's own seconds warmed to something akin to cheerfulness when Danny ducked jauntily through the ropes and entered the ring. His face continually spread to an unending succession of smiles, and when Danny smiled he smiled in every feature, even to the laughter wrinkles of the corners of the eyes and into the depths of the eyes themselves. Never was there so genial a fighter. His face was a running advertisement of good feeling, of good-fellowship. He knew everybody. He joked, and laughed, and greeted his friends through the ropes. Those farther away, unable to suppress their admiration, cried loudly: "Oh, you Danny!" It was a joyous ovation of affection that lasted a full five minutes.

Rivera was disregarded. For all that the audience noticed, he did not exist. Spider Hagerty's bloated face bent down close to his.

"No gettin' scared," the Spider warned. "An' remember instructions. You gotta last. No layin' down. If you lay down, we got instructions to beat you up in the dressing-rooms. Savvy? You just gotta fight."

The house began to applaud. Danny was crossing the ring to him. Danny bent over him, caught Rivera's right hand in both his own and shook it with impulsive heartiness. Danny's smile-wreathed face was close to his. The audience yelled its appreciation of Danny's display of sporting spirit. He was greeting his opponent with the fondness of a brother. Danny's lips moved, and the audience, interpreting the unheard words to be those of a kindly-natured sport, yelled again. Only Rivera heard the low words.

"You little Mexican rat," hissed from between Danny's gaily smiling lips, "I'll fetch the yellow outa you."

Rivera made no move. He did not rise. He merely hated with his eyes.

"Get up, you dog!" some man yelled through the ropes from behind.

The crowd began to hiss and boo him for his unsportsmanlike conduct, but he sat unmoved. Another great outburst of applause was Danny's as he walked back across the ring.

When Danny stripped, there were ohs! and ahs! of delight. His body was perfect, alive with easy suppleness and health and strength. The skin was white as a woman's, and as smooth. All grace, and resilience, and power resided therein. He had proved it in scores of battles. His photographs were in all the physical-culture magazines.

A groan went up as Spider Hagerty peeled Rivera's sweater over his head. His body seemed leaner because of the swarthiness of the skin. He had muscles, but they made no display like his opponent's. What the audience neglected to see was the deep chest. Nor could it guess the toughness of the fiber of the flesh, the instantaneousness of the cell explosions of the muscles, the fineness of the nerves that wired every part of him into a splendid fighting mechanism. All the audience saw was a brown-skinned boy of eighteen with what seemed the body of a boy. With Danny it was different. Danny was a man of twenty-four, and his body was a man's body. The contrast was still more striking as they stood together in the center of the ring receiving the referee's last instructions.

Rivera noticed Roberts sitting directly behind the newspaper-men. He was drunker than usual, and his speech was correspondingly slower.

"Take it easy, Rivera," Roberts drawled. "He can't kill you, remember that. He'll rush you at the go-off, but don't get rattled. You just cover up, and stall, and clinch. He can't hurt you much.

Just make believe to yourself that he's choppin' out on you at the trainin' quarters.''

Rivera made no sign that he had heard.

''Sullen little devil,'' Roberts muttered to the man next to him. ''He always was that way.''

But Rivera forgot to look his usual hatred. A vision of countless rifles blinded his eyes. Every face in the audience, as far as he could see, to the high dollar seats, was transformed into a rifle. And he saw the long Mexican border arid and sun-washed and aching, and along it he saw the ragged bands that delayed only for the guns.

Back in his corner he waited, standing up. His seconds had crawled out through the ropes, taking the canvas stool with them. Diagonally across the squared ring, Danny faced him. The gong struck, and the battle was on. The audience howled its delight. Never had it seen a battle open more convincingly. The papers were right. It was a grudge fight. Three-quarters of the distance Danny covered in the rush to get together, his intention to eat up the Mexican lad plainly advertised. He assailed with not one blow, nor two, nor a dozen. He was a gyroscope of blows, a whirlwind of destruction. Rivera was nowhere. He was overwhelmed, buried beneath avalanches of punches delivered from every angle and position by a past master in the art. He was overborne, swept back against the ropes, separated by the referee, and swept back against the ropes again.

It was not a fight. It was a slaughter, a massacre. Any audience, save a prize-fight one, would have exhausted its emotions in that first minute. Danny was certainly showing what he could do—a splendid exhibition. Such was the certainty of the audience, as well as its excitement and favoritism, that it failed to notice that the Mexican still stayed on his feet. It forgot Rivera. It rarely saw him, so closely was he enveloped in Danny's man-eating attack. A minute of this went by, and two minutes. Then, in a separation, it caught a clear glimpse of the Mexican. His lip was cut, his nose was bleeding. As he turned and staggered into a clinch the welts of oozing blood, from his contacts with the ropes, showed in red bars across his back. But what the audience did not notice was that his chest was not heaving and that his eyes were coldly burning as ever. Too many aspiring champions, in the cruel welter of the training camps, had practiced this man-eating attack on him. He had learned to live through for a compensation of from half a dollar a go up to fifteen dollars a week—a hard school, and he was schooled hard.

Then happened the amazing thing. The whirling, blurring mix-up ceased suddenly. Rivera stood alone. Danny, the redoubtable Danny, lay on his back. His body quivered as consciousness strove to return to it. He had not staggered and sunk down, nor had he gone over in a long slumping fall. The right hook of Rivera had dropped him in mid-air with the abruptness of death. The referee

shoved Rivera back with one hand and stood over the fallen glad-
iator counting the seconds. It is the custom of prize-fighting au-
diences to cheer a clean knock-down blow. But this audience did
not cheer. The thing had been too unexpected. It watched the
toll of the seconds in tense silence, and through this silence the
voice of Roberts rose exultantly:

"I told you he was a two-handed fighter!"

By the fifth second Danny was rolling on his face, and when
seven was counted he rested on one knee, ready to rise after the
count of nine and before the count of ten. If his knee still touched
the floor at "ten" he was considered "down" and also "out." The
instant his knee left the floor he was considered "up," and in
that instant it was Rivera's right to try and put him down again.
Rivera took no chances. The moment that knee left the floor he
would strike again. He circled around, but the referee circled in
between, and Rivera knew that the seconds he counted were very
slow. All gringos were against him, even the referee.

At "nine" the referee gave Rivera a sharp thrust back. It was
unfair, but it enabled Danny to rise, the smile back on his lips.
Doubled partly over, with arms wrapped about face and abdomen, he cleverly stumbled into a clinch. By all the rules of the
game the referee should have broken it, but he did not, and Danny
clung on like a surf-battered barnacle and moment by moment
recuperated. The last minute of the round was going fast. If he
could live to the end he would have a full minute in his corner
to revive. And live to the end he did, smiling through all desper-
ateness and extremity.

"The smile that won't come off!" somebody yelled, and the
audience laughed loudly in its relief.

"The kick that greaser's got is something God-awful," Danny
gasped in his corner to his adviser while his handlers worked
frantically over him.

The second and third rounds were tame. Danny, a tricky and
consummate ring general, stalled and blocked and held on, de-
voting himself to recovering from that dazing first-round blow.

In the fourth round he was himself again. Jarred and shaken, nevertheless his good condition had enabled him to regain his vigor. But he tried no man-eating tactics. The Mexican had proved a tartar. Instead he brought to bear his best fighting powers. In tricks and skill and experience he was the master, and though he could land nothing vital, he proceeded scientifically to chop and wear down his opponent. He landed three blows to Rivera's one, but they were punishing blows only, and not deadly. It was the sum of many of them that constituted deadliness. He was respectful of this two-handed dub with the amazing short-arm kicks in both his fists.

In defense Rivera developed a disconcerting straight left. Again and again, attack after attack he straight-lefted away from him with accumulated damage to Danny's mouth and nose. But Danny was protean. That was why he was the coming champion. He could change from style to style of fighting at will. He now devoted himself to in-fighting. In this he was particularly wicked, and it enabled him to avoid the other's straight left. Here he set the house wild repeatedly, capping it with a marvelous lock-break and lift of an inside uppercut that raised the Mexican in the air and dropped him to the mat. Rivera rested on one knee, making the most of the count, and in the soul of him knew the referee was counting short seconds on him.

Again, in the seventh, Danny achieved the diabolical inside uppercut. He succeeded only in staggering Rivera, but in the ensuing moment of defenseless helplessness he smashed him with another blow through the ropes. Rivera's body bounced on the heads of the newspapermen below, and they boosted him back to the edge of the platform outside the ropes. Here he rested on one knee, while the referee raced off the seconds. Inside the ropes, through which he must duck to enter the ring, Danny waited for him. Nor did the referee intervene or thrust Danny back.

The house was beside itself with delight.

"Kill 'm, Danny, kill 'm!" was the cry.

Scores of voices took it up until it was like a war chant of wolves.

Danny did his best, but Rivera, at the count of eight, instead of nine, came unexpectedly through the ropes and safely into a clinch. Now the referee worked, tearing him away so that he could be hit, giving Danny every advantage that an unfair referee can give.

But Rivera lived, and the daze cleared from his brain. It was all of a piece. They were the hated gringos and they were unfair. And in the worst of it visions continued to flash and sparkle in his brain—long lines of railroad track that simmered across the desert; *rurales* and American constables; prisons and calabooses; tramps at water tanks—all the squalid and painful panorama of his odyssey after Rio Blanco and the strike. And, resplendent and glorious, he saw the great red revolution sweeping across his land. The guns were there before him. Every hated face was a gun. It was for the guns he fought. He was the guns. He was the revolution. He fought for all Mexico.

The audience began to grow incensed with Rivera. Why didn't he take the licking that was appointed him? Of course he was going to be licked, but why should he be so obstinate about it? Very few were interested in him, and they were the certain, definite percentage of a gambling crowd that plays long shots. Believing Danny to be the winner, nevertheless they had put their money on the Mexican at four to ten and one to three. More than a trifle was up on the point of how many rounds Rivera could last. Wild money had appeared at the ringside proclaiming that he could not last seven rounds, or even six. The winners of this, now that their cash risk was happily settled, had joined in cheering on the favorite.

Rivera refused to be licked. Through the eighth round his opponent strove vainly to repeat the uppercut. In the ninth Rivera stunned the house again. In the midst of a clinch he broke the lock with a quick, lithe movement, and in the narrow space between their bodies his right lifted from the waist. Danny went to the floor and took the safety of the count. The crowd was appalled. He was being bested at his own game. His famous right uppercut had been worked back on him. Rivera made no attempt to catch him as he arose at "nine." The referee was openly blocking that play, though he stood clear when the situation was reversed and it was Rivera who was required to rise.

Twice in the tenth Rivera put through the right uppercut, lifted from waist to opponent's chin. Danny grew desperate. The smile never left his face, but he went back to his man-eating rushes. Whirlwind as he would, he could not damage Rivera, while Rivera, through the blur and whirl, dropped him to the mat three times in succession. Danny did not recuperate so quickly now, and by the eleventh round he was in a serious way. But from then till the fourteenth he put up the gamest exhibition of his career. He stalled and blocked, fought parsimoniously, and strove to gather strength. Also he fought as foully as a successful fighter knows how. Every trick and device he employed, butting in the clinches with the seeming of accident, pinioning Rivera's glove between arm and body, heeling his glove on Rivera's mouth to clog his breathing. Often, in the clinches, through his cut and smiling lips he snarled insults unspeakable and vile in Rivera's ear. Everybody, from the referee to the house, was with Danny and was helping Danny. And they knew what he had in mind. Bested by this surprise box of an unknown, he was pinning all on a single punch. He offered himself for punishment, fished, and feinted, and drew, for that one opening that would enable him to whip a blow through with all his strength and turn the tide. As another and greater fighter had done before him, he might do—a right and left, to solar plexus and across the jaw. He could do it, for he was noted for the strength of punch that remained in his arms as long as he could keep his feet.

Rivera's seconds were not half caring for him in the intervals between rounds. Their towels made a showing but drove little air into his panting lungs. Spider Hagerty talked advice to him, but

Rivera knew it was wrong advice. Everybody was against him. He was surrounded by treachery. In the fourteenth round he put Danny down again, and himself stood resting, hands dropped at side, while the referee counted. In the other corner Rivera had been noting suspicious whisperings. He saw Michael Kelly make his way to Roberts and bend and whisper. Rivera's ears were a cat's, desert-trained, and he caught snatches of what was said. He wanted to hear more, and when his opponent arose he maneuvered the fight into a clinch over against the ropes.

"Got to," he could hear Michael, while Roberts nodded. "Danny's got to win—I stand to lose a mint. I've got a ton of money covered—my own. If he lasts the fifteenth I'm bust. The boy'll mind you. Put something across."

And thereafter Rivera saw no more visions. They were trying to job him. Once again he dropped Danny and stood resting, his hands at his side. Roberts stood up.

"That settled him," he said. "Go to your corner."

He spoke with authority, as he had often spoken to Rivera at the training quarters. But Rivera looked hatred at him and waited for Danny to rise. Back in his corner in the minute interval, Kelly, the promoter, came and talked to Rivera.

"Throw it, damn you," he rasped in a harsh low voice. "You gotta lay down, Rivera. Stick with me and I'll make your future. I'll let you lick Danny next time. But here's where you lay down."

Rivera showed with his eyes that he heard, but he made neither sign of assent nor dissent.

"Why don't you speak?" Kelly demanded angrily.

"You lose anyway," Spider Hagerty supplemented. "The referee'll take it away from you. Listen to Kelly and lay down."

"Lay down, kid," Kelly pleaded, "and I'll help you to the championship."

Rivera did not answer.

"I will, so help me, kid."

At the strike of the gong Rivera sensed something impending. The house did not. Whatever it was, it was there inside the ring with him and very close. Danny's early surety seemed returned to him. The confidence of his advance frightened Rivera. Some trick was about to be worked. Danny rushed, but Rivera refused the encounter. He sidestepped away into safety. What the other wanted was a clinch. It was in some way necessary to the trick. Rivera backed and circled away, yet he knew, sooner or later, the clinch and the trick would come. Desperately he resolved to draw it. He made as if to effect the clinch with Danny's next rush. Instead, at the last instant, just as their bodies should have come together, Rivera darted nimbly back. And in the same instant Danny's corner raised a cry of foul. Rivera had fooled them. The referee paused irresolutely. The decision that trembled on his lips was never uttered, for a shrill, boy's voice from the gallery piped, "Raw work!"

Danny cursed Rivera openly and forced him, while Rivera danced away. Also Rivera made up his mind to strike no more blows at the body. In this he threw away half his chance of winning, but he knew if he was to win at all it was with the outfighting that remained to him. Given the least opportunity, they would lie a foul on him. Danny threw all caution to the winds. For two rounds he tore after and into the boy who dared not meet him at close quarters. Rivera was struck again and again; he took blows by the dozens to avoid the perilous clinch. During this supreme final rally of Danny's the audience rose to its feet and went mad. It did not understand. All it could see was that its favorite was winning after all.

"Why don't you fight?" it demanded wrathfully of Rivera. "You're yellow! You're yellow!" "Open up, you cur! Open up!" "Kill 'm, Danny! Kill 'm!" "You sure got 'm! Kill 'm!"

In all the house, bar none, Rivera was the only cold man. By temperament and blood he was the hottest-passioned there; but he had gone through such vastly greater heats that this collective passion of ten thousand throats, rising surge on surge, was to his brain no more than the velvet cool of a summer twilight.

Into the seventeenth round Danny carried his rally. Rivera,

under a heavy blow, dropped and sagged. His hands dropped helplessly as he reeled backwards. Danny thought it was his chance. The boy was at his mercy. Thus Rivera, feigning, caught him off his guard, lashing out a clean drive to the mouth. Danny went down. When he arose Rivera felled him with a down-chop of the right on neck and jaw. Three times he repeated this. It was impossible for any referee to call these blows foul.

"Oh, Bill! Bill!" Kelly pleaded to the referee.

"I can't," that official lamented back. "He won't give me a chance."

Danny, battered and heroic, still kept coming up. Kelly and others near to the ring began to cry out to the police to stop it, though Danny's corner refused to throw in the towel. Rivera saw the fat police captain starting awkwardly to climb through the ropes, and was not sure what it meant. There were so many ways of cheating in this game of the gringos. Danny, on his feet, tottered groggily and helplessly before him. The referee and the captain were both reaching for Rivera when he struck the last blow. There was no need to stop the fight, for Danny did not rise.

"Count!" Rivera cried hoarsely to the referee.

And when the count was finished Danny's seconds gathered him up and carried him to his corner.

"Who wins?" Rivera demanded.

Reluctantly the referee caught his gloved hand and held it aloft.

There were no congratulations for Rivera. He walked to his corner unattended, where his seconds had not yet placed his stool. He leaned backwards on the ropes and looked his hatred at them, swept it on and about him till the whole ten thousand gringos were included. His knees trembled under him, and he was sobbing from exhaustion. Before his eyes the hated faces swayed back and forth in the giddiness of nausea. Then he remembered they were the guns. The guns were his. The revolution could go on.

James D. Houston

PRUNEPICKER

*It takes a lot to make a dream come true—
especially if the dream isn't yours.*

It was the first day of pre-season practice and I was standing next to Buster, suiting up. We had lockers side by side but this happened to be the first time we had seen each other unclothed. He was watching me lace my hip pads. With what I took to be an appreciative little grin he said, "You're a husky sumbitch."

My laugh came out high, betraying me. I was seventeen, a very green and nervous and insecure freshman. He was twenty-four. He had served in World War Two and he was still in college, playing out his final year of eligibility. Next to Buster Budlong I did not feel very husky at all. I weighed around one seventy in those days, a lean and lanky six foot two. He was taller by a couple of inches, and much thicker. He had thick bones covered with leathery muscular skin, and on his head a cap of brown hair made of bristles that in my memory were so short and stiff he could easily have played without a helmet.

"You must of been a tackle in high school," he said.

"Fullback," I said. "Blocking back most of the time."

"Out there in prunepicker country?"

His eyes challenged mine. His mouth curved in a self-satisfied grin. I tried to match it with a grin of my own. I had been in west Texas about a week, and I was already weary of these cornball jokes about California. But I wasn't saying anything yet, still uncertain where to draw the line between kidding around and insult.

When all the laces were tight, I followed him to the door. The sky was rosy with a dawn cloud cover. The air was heavy. It was so hot, in mid-August, we had to get up at 4:30 and practice from 5:30 to 7:30, then sweat somewhere until sundown when we would practice again. We stepped out into the heat and walked together across the cinder track toward the field. It was patched here and there with pale green, but most of what had once been grass was as dry and bristled as the short hair on Buster's head.

A blocking sled stood at the edge of the field. Just for the hell of it, he dipped and ran at the sled and threw a shoulder into the raggedy pad, more metal backing now than stuffed canvas. He began shoving it across the field, making the whole weighted sled jump with each punch of his enormous shoulder.

"Hyah!" he would shout as he lunged. "Hyah! Hyah! Hyah!"

"Hey, look at ol Buster," one of the backs called out. "What'd you have for breakfast this mornin, Buster?"

"I aint had breakfast yet. Gonna have me a prunepicker for breakfast."

The back laughed, swinging his arms. Waiting for the coach to call us together, he had a few moments to play Buster's straight man. "Well now, just how do you recognize a prunepicker when you see one?"

Buster pushed away from the sled and stood up with his hands on his hips. "You look at the eyes," he said. "There's only two kinds of people from California—prunepickers and movie stars. And movie stars always wear dark glasses."

This line, which I had already heard four or five times, drew some chuckles from players moving past us toward midfield, where the head coach now stood, in his T-shirt and his sweatpants and his billcap. We jogged over there and ganged around to listen to the morning's agenda—warm-ups, wind sprints, blocking sled for the linemen, pass drill for the backs and ends, with thirty minutes of light scrimmage to run through some plays we had seen last night on the chalkboard.

This was Abilene Christian College in the early 1950s. There was no freshman squad, no junior varsity. We all worked out together, and you were either on the varsity or you were not. In this league I was too slow to do what I had done in high school in San Jose the previous season, although I did not know this until the day I arrived, until I stepped out of the Trailways bus that had carried me across Arizona and New Mexico, to meet the coach and meet his eyes as he sized me up. Someone had sent him my best times in the fifty- and the hundred-yard dash. He was already thinking tackle, maybe defensive end. "You got the height for it, son," the coach had said, steady-eyed and fatherly. "You start puttin away enough a this good Texas food, maybe we can beef you up some by the time the season starts."

From the way I began to sweat I would have to eat and drink six times a day just to stay even. Before the warm-up calisthenics were done, I was telling myself I had better take it easy until my blood thinned out. In this kind of climate you could drop from heat exhaustion by sunrise. That was my rationale for holding back in the linemen's drills, which I didn't much like. Maybe I still thought of myself as a fullback, who should not have to be doing this kind of donkey-work. Maybe a little arrogance showed as I approached the sled. Maybe that had something to do with why Buster did what he did.

When it came time for the scrimmage that ended the workout, I was crouched across from him, trying to see his eyes underneath the helmet-edge and the bushy blond brows that bunched out like awnings of solidified flesh. The first string had a new series of plays to run through. I had been put into the defensive line. As I understood it, we were there mainly to remind the offense where enemy bodies would be located. This, in my experience, had been the meaning of "run-through." Buster saw it differently.

The first play was a simple handoff that would send a running back between guard and tackle. His job was to move me out of the way, which I fully intended to allow him to do. When the ball was snapped, I stepped toward him, hands out, expecting his shoulder to come at my belt in a half-speed block. But that huge shoulder rose over my hands with a ferocious thrust, followed by his elbow, which cracked into the side of my chin. It lifted me and sent me sprawling backward onto the stubble.

Tears sprang to my eyes from the shock and from the rising dust. I blinked them away and looked around. No one seemed to have noticed this. It was between me and Buster, and he too seemed oblivious, standing again with his hands on his hips, gazing downfield as if to follow the ball-carrier's path. I touched my jaw, expecting blood. It felt broken, though it wasn't. Afraid to move it, I spoke through clenched teeth.

"Buster."

He looked down, as if he had forgotten I was there.

"Buster, you know you elbowed me right in the face."

The way he was squinting I still could not see his eyes. But I could see his mouth curve into the same self-satisfied grin. "That's right, prunepicker. That's the way we play ball down here in Texas."

It had not occurred to me that the blow was deliberate. As he said this my limbs went hollow. In that oppressive heat they were instantly filled with the cold wind of absolute fear. His eyes were ball bearings. He was made of solid rock. He outweighed me by about sixty pounds. And sometime within the next couple of minutes I was going to have to get to my feet, line up across from him again, assume the stance and take another blow like that or try to deliver one, which seemed futile, or turn tail and walk off the field, which was not really an option, though it was a fantasy

I clung to for about fifteen seconds, until my saviour appeared, an angel in the form of the head coach. He evidently had witnessed this scene from the sidelines.

Buster had just taken his first step back toward the huddle when the coach threw an arm around his vast shoulder and said softly as they walked together, "We got some money invested in this boy, Buster. We'd like him to last at least halfway through the season."

Then the coach was calling out to his backs to try that same play one more time, a little differently, pulling them toward him with a double-armed wave, like a reversed butterfly stroke. This gave me an extra moment to sit in the dirt and feel the numbness of my jaw begin to swell and become a throb of emerging pain and ponder how the hell I had ended up on my butt in disgrace in the dry wind and stubble of a practice field fifteen hundred miles from home.

At age seventeen I had a lot of fear and confusion, but I had no answer to that question. Many years would pass before I saw how far back it went, that it was both cultural and genetic. In the America of my youth the curse of being too small was that you could not go out for football. The curse of being six foot two was that you could not avoid going out for football, for fear your very manhood would be questioned. In my case there was also the influence, perhaps I should say the deep longing, of an uncle, my favorite uncle, who in two important ways was much like Buster. He was not nearly as mean, but he too had grown up in a small west Texas town, and he too believed in football.

His friends called him J.C. I always called him Jay. When he was very young, his father had run off, leaving my grandmother with two kids to raise. By the time Jay started high school, in the late 1920s, she was still alone and trying to manage a quarter-section of land. Money was scarce, and the soil in their part of Texas had never been generous. Cotton was her main crop. It took a terrible amount of work to make it pay anything at all.

Jay collected football photographs and dreamed of the day when he would be a starting player. In his spare time he lifted weights, hoping for bulk, and he would run fantasy plays in the yard in the waning dusk. He spent his freshman and sophomore seasons on the bench. The year he had a shot at making first string, as a junior, he didn't enroll. There was just too much work at home. Grandma couldn't handle it all. At sixteen he had to drop out of high school, give up his football dreams and be the man of the family, helping her tend that quarter-section.

Later on, after they had all found their way out to the West Coast and San Francisco, Jay married and had a daughter, but no sons. When I came along I was the one young male in our transplanted west Texas clan. All his hopes for gridiron glory were transferred to me. Every New Years Day he would take me to the East-West game at Kezar Stadium. When I stayed overnight at his house, he would stuff me with syrupy, butter-soaked hotcakes and tell me how good this was for putting power in the legs and zip in the throwing arm.

The summer before I started high school we took off on a fishing trip—my dad, my uncle Jay, and a couple of the journeyman painters dad would hire whenever he had a big job in the city. Clear Lake was where they did most of their fishing, two hours north of San Francisco. They would rent a couple of motel cabins and rent a boat or two, and we would motor out onto the lake in search of bass and catfish. At night we would eat in a restaurant, then sit around one of the cabins and talk and get to bed early so we could get up early and back out onto the lake.

One of these nights after dinner Jay had had a few beers, which made his eyes get sentimental. He sat down next to me, talking about starting high school in the fall, what a great opportunity that would be and not to let it slip past me. He was talking of course about the opportunity to play football.

"What position you going to go out for?" he said.

We were lounging on two single beds. I was bored out of my thirteen-year-old skull watching the four of them drink beer. There was nothing else to do but listen or sleep, and it was too early to sleep. This was before television. There was a table-model radio between the beds, two chairs, a desk with a Bible in the drawer.

"Halfback," I said, knowing that's what he wanted to hear.

Driving up there he had talked about Glenn Davis, the all-American halfback from West Point. For three years in the mid-1940s Davis and his running mate, Doc Blanchard—Mr. Outside and Mr. Inside—had dominated the sports pages. They were still talked about, living legends you measured other players against. "Shoot, son," Jay said, "if you go out for halfback, we'll never hear about Glenn Davis again. You'll just leave him in the shade."

He took a long sip and said to my father, who was eased back on one elbow on the other bed, "Hey, Dudley, this boy here is gonna give em a run for their money. He just might leave ol Glenn Davis in the shade."

My father didn't care much about football one way or the other, but he went along with most of what Jay said. It was not his style to disagree out loud. When he did not react, Jay escalated the prediction. "You know, Dudley, this boy here is not gonna be just any old halfback. He might turn out to be an all-American. Wouldn't that be something now? If he made the all-American team one a these days?"

My father nodded and smiled. "It sure would be something."

With a little shoulder punch Jay said to me, "Hey now, that really *would* be something. All-American halfback. Huh? Waddya say to that!"

I looked at him. His face was turning red with more than the flush that comes from drinking. His eyes were wet, brimming. "Dammit . . ." he said, and cleared his throat, his voice filled with sudden emotion he could not control. "Dammit, son, if you made the all-American team, you know what I'd do?"

Tears had started dripping down his florid cheeks. He gripped my arm. "I'd give you a gold watch! I swear it!"

His eyes were pleading, begging me to undertake this task.

At the same time his weeping eyes were proud, as if I had already done it and he had the watch in his pocket, and was ready to pull it out and surprise me with the gift that would validate the great honor I had brought to the family.

"You hear me, son? The day you make the all-American team, I am gonna give you a two-hundred-dollar gold watch and have it engraved and it's gonna say To My One and Only Nephew, with Pride from his Uncle Jay!"

I looked down at the flimsy bedspread, unable to reply. At age thirteen I had many fantasies, but that was not among them. Even as he spoke I knew it wasn't possible. Yet his belief ran so deep, or seemed to, another part of me wanted his prediction to come true, at least be probable. For his sake. Jay had created a future that had not occurred to me before. For his sake I let it live awhile.

Working out with the freshman team at Lowell High School in San Francisco, I would sometimes see myself standing in that great lineup in the sky. Dreaming of the backfield, I played guard and tackle for two seasons at Lowell. I was never very good, didn't make varsity, but I knew I would get better, I would get bigger and stronger, and with size would come miraculous new levels of ability and courage. When I was fifteen we moved from San Francisco south to Santa Clara Valley, and there my football fortunes took a lucky turn. In a school half the size, with a smaller team, I finally moved from guard to fullback, and in my senior year made first string, threw a few passable downfield blocks, and scored a couple of touchdowns, the most significant being a three-yard run against San Jose High, our arch-rival, on Thanksgiving Day, before five thousand fans.

I remember lying facedown in the grass, and the blades of grass tickling my nostrils, and the rich smell of autumn grass and damp earth as I opened my eyes when the play was over. So many bodies were layered above me I could only move my head and my neck. I turned and saw the merry eyes of Roy Krickeberg right next to me. He was our powerhouse guard. He had opened the hole I had just plunged through, and we had a few seconds of comradeship and intimacy there, pressed into the grass while the bodies above us peeled away.

I said to Roy, "How far did we get?"

He said, "Your nuts are on the goal line, amigo. We just won the game."

That little moment, I realize now, was the high point of my football career. I should have quit right then. But you never know these things at the time. I had already received a letter from the athletic department at Abilene, offering me room, board and tuition. This three-yard rush, coming at the end of a season in which I had started every game, seemed to confirm the wisdom and the rightness of accepting the offer. It was, I should point out, the only such offer I received and had less to do with my ability than with the fact that my family belonged to the Church of Christ, which supported the college. I was not very brave, and I was not very fast, but in the small-town world of Santa Clara Valley my picture had appeared once or twice in the paper. Since a cousin of ours back in Texas knew someone who knew someone, wheels were greased and doors were opened. One morning I climbed onto a bus heading south from San Jose toward Los Angeles, where I caught another bus heading inland. Two days went by, during which the world turned drier and flatter and hotter. A week later I found myself sitting in the dust at 7 A.M., gingerly touching my injured jaw to gauge its tenderness while I watched Buster and the head coach walk back toward the offensive huddle.

Claiming to believe in Jesus, by the way, was not the only qualification for playing on this team. Being from Texas was equally important, or having relatives there. Most of the players came from church families in other nearby towns and cities. In the case of good ol boys like Buster, whose Christian traits were sometimes hard to identify, other virtues were carefully considered.

Many sins were forgiven if you weighed over two twenty-five or could run the hundred in ten seconds, or both.

After we had trooped into the locker room to change, then to the chow hall to shovel in the hotcakes and scrambled eggs and sausages, I wandered back to my dorm room and lay down on the bed, sweating and thinking. I lay there most of the day feeling sorry for myself, feeling exiled and excluded. I wanted to climb back on the bus that very afternoon and leave west Texas behind. But I couldn't. It would seem too cowardly. Something else was required, though I didn't know quite what. Short of picking him off with a deer rifle from a moving car, there was no way I could imagine getting even with Buster. He was too large and thick and thick-skinned, with the brute strength to break my arms into tiny pieces.

I was lucky, I suppose. If he were closer to my own size and age I would have had to challenge him immediately. No one really expected me to. But I didn't understand that yet. I was in turmoil, and prickly with the day's rising heat. It made me sullen, and this became my mood for the next week or so, bringing me a nickname. Prunepicker became Pruney, which just fed my sense of alienation, particularly when it came from Buster. Warned by the coach to keep his elbows under control, he continued rabbit-punching with his voice.

"Hey, Pruney," he would call as we lined up for a charging drill, "you crouch that low so you can scoop up more prunes?"

Around the middle of the second week something happened. Call it the lighting of a slow-burning fuse. Call it anger. Call it pride. One morning I hit the practice field fifteen minutes early, imitating his crazy lunge at the sled, half hoping I would dislocate a shoulder. I began pushing myself in every drill, every play. On wind sprints I would drive my legs until they burned, until my stomach burned with nausea, and I would vomit clear water into the dry grass. Some days we would be working out in 85 and 90 degrees. It was a badge of honor to be seen throwing up, a way to let the world know how much you cared. I began to look forward to the vomiting. I was in a kind of fever, fired by salt pills and hot, dry wind. It propelled me right into our first pre-season game, officially called a scrimmage, though that was an understatement. Our opponents came from Hardin-Simmons, a crosstown rival. The main difference between this game and later games was that the coach gave everyone a chance to play.

Mine came in the second quarter. I went in on defense to replace a tackle whose shoelace had inexplicably unraveled. I was positioned just inside their left end, a fellow about my size and weight, maybe a year older, lean and wiry and looking as weathered as a Texas fence post. I was ready to overpower someone. I had reached a point of pure recklessness, and it must have shown. The moment we made eye contact I knew I had the advantage.

Their quarterback was calling signals. When the ball was snapped, this rangy end came at me low, to move me farther inside, but he was not low enough. I got in under him, my legs pumping. He seemed to have no weight. With my hands and a shoulder I lifted him and threw him aside like a sack of kindling, then saw nothing but open space between me and the ball-carrier, a broad, squat running back with piston legs. He had just taken a handoff on some kind of tricky reverse that was supposed to send him skirting my end of the line. When he saw me coming, a ripple of fear crossed his chunky face. It gave me speed. By that time I was eager to hurt someone or die in the attempt. I took a bead on his belt, drove my shoulder in, and we both went down in that lovers' roll they call a tackle. It was the one perfect tackle of my life. If Ernest Hemingway had been reporting this game he would have described it that way: "He went in well, right under the ball-carrier's elbows, and tackled perfectly."

The back lay there for a second as if dead. Then I heard him slam the ball at the grass and curse in self-disgust.

It was a crucial play, a fourth down on our thirty with two

yards to go for a first. They had tried for the yardage. Instead of gaining two they lost ten, giving us a first down with fine midfield position.

Jogging toward the sidelines I heard a chorus of shouts I thought at first were jeers. But they were shouts and hoots of praise. "Whoo-ee!" they cried, and "Attaboy!"

Someone slapped me on the pads. "You about cut that sucker half in two!"

"Lord have mercy," said someone else. "He went and turned this whole game right around."

I could only stand there and grin, my adrenaline running, until Buster appeared, looming up next to me with a wink. He patted me on the butt and said, "Son, you done real good out there. You aint gonna be a prunepicker anymore."

I was floating. I was an unknown actor suddenly surrounded with microphones, getting an Academy Award and shaking hands with John Wayne. Then Buster passed by me, moving along the sidelines. My exhilaration passed too, replaced by a deep and lonesome sadness I had no words for. I looked at his broad back and at the faces, the helmeted profiles of the others, whose eyes had turned toward the midfield action. If I had been able to put into words what I felt at that moment, it would have gone something like this: "Is that it? Is that all? To pass the test and be admitted into the lobby of this club, is that really what's required?"

I did not know what to do with this feeling. I had no place to put it. I had never seen it expressed or heard it talked about. You were supposed to exult in conquest, not feel short-changed. That evening at the dinner table in the chow hall, as we celebrated our performance, I added my voice to the rounds of congratulations, even though that other voice was right behind it, the voice with no words.

At practice I kept pushing. On the day I made it through two hours without having to force down waves of nausea, I told myself I was finally in shape. I told myself I was ready to reenact the same bold play in a stadium filled with cheering fans. If something like that had happened, things might have turned out differently. A few scraps of glory might have silenced the voice of the nonbeliever, or put it on hold for a season or two. But this was a team of seniors who had eyes on the championship and finishing out their college years together in a blaze of victory. With no JV squad it was unlikely I would log any game time at all, even at tackle.

By midseason I had brooded myself to a standstill. I should say, to a sit-still. What a pointless waste, I told myself, to be in this kind of shape and spend game after game on the bench. Yet each game spent sitting left me more inert, less inclined to move.

I was in the darkest grip of fourth-string inertia when we came up against Carswell Air Force Base, which I remember as an entire team of men like Buster, grown men in their twenties who had reenlisted after World War Two. They were known to play a vicious brand of street-fighter football. Maybe it wasn't football. From the bench it looked like hand-to-hand combat. At halftime they were leading 20–12, and everyone who had seen action was hurting somewhere. The ghastly silence in our locker room was broken only by the coach's announcement that, since this was a nonleague game, he might soon be giving some freshman a chance to play.

During the third quarter he started glancing toward the low end of the bench. This was a night game, which made it easier to avoid his glaze. I was trying to appear intent upon the midfield carnage, watching yet not watching, when into my range of vision came Buster, limping toward us. The front of his jersey was wet with blood. His nose had turned purple. His shins were cut. From his ankles to his eyes he looked more than battered, he looked stunned. That was what hit me, the shock in his eyes.

I admired Buster, in spite of what he had done to me, perhaps because of it. He was the most formidable man I had ever spoken to. He was indestructible. Yet somewhere in that murky realm where huge bodies crash together play after play after play, he had come up against someone or something that could make his flinty eyes go hollow. If they could do this to Buster's face, what could they do to mine?

He fell onto the bench, with his feet spread and his head back while a trainer tried to stop the bleeding. I watched him staring at the key, a wounded Goliath. And this was the moment, as terror and doubt swirled together, when my heart went out of the game. Whatever I felt I owed my uncle Jay just floated right out of me and up into the same sky Buster was gazing at, the big nighttime sky above west Texas.

After that I dreaded the workouts. Pure drudgery. I kept going through the motions because I was still on the team and they were paying my way, and I could not see beyond this. I could have quit, and probably should have, but it did not occur to me to quit. I was stuck. I was a football prisoner, waiting for another kind of angel to come along and rescue me the way the coach had rescued me from Buster.

When he first appeared, in the newspapers, and then on posters all over town, I did not see him as an angel. He was too familiar. He was famous. His name was Horace Heidt. He hosted a national radio show, an amateur hour known for its accordion players, Swiss bell ringers, harmonica wizards. He also lent his name to a troupe that moved around the country making weekly stops, a touring vaudeville show. The best of his radio acts would appear on a variety program along with local amateur performers who had been selected in advance. By a miracle of uncanny timing Horace Heidt's traveling show came to town just when I needed it most.

In Abilene I had a shadow life, a second life, totally unconnected to football. Three nights a week I was rehearsing songs with a couple of newfound musical buddies. They happened to be Bible students, but not the somber and self-righteous kind. They liked to tell obscene stories, and they liked to sing jazzy two-beat and swing tunes from the 20s and 30s, a taste I had picked up in high school, soon after I started fooling around with stringed instruments—bass, guitar and the ukulele, which in those days was making the first of several comebacks. Our little trio had roughed out maybe half a dozen songs when we saw the posters bearing the name and face of the smiling impresario, and beneath the face the beguiling phrase TALENT SEARCH.

On audition day the basement of Abilene High School was mobbed with sopranos and barbershop quartets and young girls who sang hymns and young men prepared to recite the Gettysburg Address. We were there for the hell of it, we told ourselves, on the chance that we might see Horace himself. With such a crowd of hopefuls we did not really expect to make the final cut.

But we did. Three acts were chosen to perform at the civic auditorium one Saturday night in November, and suddenly I was faced with what appeared to be a painful choice. It was also the night of our Homecoming Game when, by tradition, Abilene Christian met its arch-enemy, McMurry, another local college. In this contest, more than football was at stake. McMurry was Baptist. Since their reading of the New Testament differed from ours on several key points of doctrine, the pre-game excitement was always flavored with a fierce evangelical zeal. Most of this was lost on me. I had not been around long enough to take the rivalry seriously, nor did I have strong feelings about Baptists, one way or the other, nor did I see how my presence on the sidelines could possibly affect the outcome of the game. Though I pretended to be torn, I was not.

At the civic that Saturday night we were ushered backstage to mingle with the chorus girls who sang and danced high-stepping routines between the main acts, changing costumes before our very eyes. We met a rotund and untutored baritone who was blind and wore overalls and had to be led to the microphone to sing the Lord's Prayer. We heard a trumpet virtuoso play ''Caravan'' and watched a bald-headed man imitate the voices of Humphrey Bogart and Harry S. Truman. Then we were out there,

under the blinding lights. Calling ourselves "The Jazzberries"—
guitar, ukulele and washtub bass—we gave them our smoothest
numbers, "Sweet Georgia Brown," "Minnie the Mermaid," "Please
Don't Talk About Me When I'm Gone."

At the end of the show the audience was asked to applaud
again for each of the three local acts. We walked off with fifteen
dollars, coming in third, after a cowgirl singer and a French horn
soloist who won the hearts of the crowd playing "The Stars and
Stripes Forever."

The following Monday I was back in the locker room suiting
up, as if nothing unusual had happened over the weekend. One
part of me actually believed I could get away with this, could
appear on the practice field with no questions asked. Another
part of me must have known what I had created for myself and
thus arranged for me to step alone into the sunlight just as the
coach came around the corner of the gym.

I heard his voice before I saw him, as flat and uncompromis-
ing as the voice of a traffic cop asking to see your license and
your registration. He spoke my name.

I froze, waiting.

"We missed you Saturday night."

"Yes sir. I was . . ."

"I know where you were. I saw your name in the paper."

This pleased me. I thought I heard a hint of forgiveness there.
I was wrong. He was standing close, but not looking at me. He
was studying the dirt, as if some explanation for my behavior
might crawl out from under the broken concrete path. The coach,
it should be pointed out, was an honorable man. In his world he
was successful and highly regarded, a man who had played well
in high school and in college and had coached well ever since,
winning more games than he had lost. He was fair and just and
direct and single-minded. On that Monday he had one goal in
life, which was to bring in another championship team. In this
world I had committed an unpardonable sin. Failing to suit up
for the Homecoming Game? I may as well have taken a flatbed

truck with loudspeakers down the main street of Abilene blaspheming the name of the Lord and all twelve Apostles.

Gazing at the ground he said, "Looks to me like you might have other things in life more important to you than football."

I considered lying, or inventing an elaborate alibi. I thought of pleading for a second chance. That is what the moment called for. But my mind went blank.

I said, "I guess it does look that way, yes."

His eyes turned toward me, cold, disappointed. "Then I suppose that's all you and I have to say to each other."

It was. I never saw him again, nor do I remember seeing Buster again after that day, except in dreams.

The coach walked on toward the field. I walked back to an empty locker room and took the pads and cleats off for the final time and changed into my street clothes. I had just been excommunicated. I should have felt guilt, or shame, or failure. But I didn't. For a few hours I felt nothing. I was numb, in shock. Distantly I worried about money, about how to break this news to my family, to Uncle Jay, to the cousin who had wangled the scholarship. It took me three full days to realize, to admit what a burden had been lifted from my shoulders, a nine-hundred-pound anvil I had been carrying around for half my life. It was a form of weight loss, almost an out-of-body experience. I was airborne. I was freed from something I did not even suspect had been holding me captive. I had been released.

This is a story that has no end. One Sunday afternoon about thirty years later, long after I had returned to California, my wife and I were watching the playoffs. She said, "Why are we doing this?"

I said, "Wait a minute, they're getting ready to score."

At the next time-out she went over and turned the sound down. "It's a very male thing, isn't it."

"What is?"

"Watching football."

"Women watch football."

"Not very many. Not the way men do. What's going on? Is it the violence?"

"This isn't violent," I said. *"The Godfather* is violent. The ten o'clock news is violent."

"Well, what's the big attraction? A bunch of grown men throwing a ball around. You see something I don't see?"

"I see what everybody sees. It's right there on the screen. I'm turning the sound up now, okay? They're going for a field goal."

This was January 1982. The San Francisco 49ers were playing the Dallas Cowboys for the conference championship. The winner would go to the Super Bowl. Ray Wersching, the great 49ers placekicker, was trying for a score from thirty yards out. I remember that later in the day Joe Montana's final pass seemed too high above the end zone for anyone to catch and Dwight Clark, who is six foot four, made a superhuman effort, leaped and caught the ball landing in bounds and on his feet in the last seconds of the fourth quarter, to clinch both the game and the bowl trip. But I have no memory of Wersching and this midgame field goal attempt. As the teams lined up, a recurring dream began to roll across my inner screen. Though I had dreamed it many times, I had never before recalled it during my waking hours.

In this dream I am back in west Texas, and I am suiting up again. The time is now. I have not played in thirty years. I am out of shape, and I am scared. I am wearing pads and cleats, and we are warming up before the Homecoming Game. I am here as a returning alumnus. They have asked me to play in this game, hoping my presence on the field will draw a large crowd. I like this part of it. I too am hoping my presence will draw a crowd. This is the only reason I have agreed to suit up. I am feverish with heat and squirming against the rub of the unfamiliar pads and giddy with terror. I know that if I have to carry the ball, or mix it up in any way, I will get badly injured. I mention to the quarterback that I am not as young as I used to be. When he looks at me I see that he is the same quarterback, and he is still the same age. I look around. It is the same team. I am older. They are not. The quarterback grins cryptically. "Take it easy, prunepicker, don't worry, we have thought of that."

The plays they have worked out for me, he says, are end sweeps, which will give our blockers plenty of time to cut down the defense, or tire them out, so that by the time they get to me they won't be so energetic, they won't be hitting that hard. "It won't be too bad," he says. I know I could live with this strategy, but I do not trust the quarterback. In the old days he and I were once interested in the same girl. Maybe we still are. No matter what he says, I know he is going to send me over center, or off tackle, and I can already feel the armored bodies of the hulking Texas linemen who recognize me and will be waiting with knees and fists.

I was not surprised that such a dream should come to the surface during the 49ers–Dallas game. In my inner history Texas and football are always linked. The surprise was discovering that whenever I watch a football game, college or pro, part of me returns to Abilene, has been returning, time and time again. Like the dream figure, a man of my age returns to the field of thirty-five years ago. For a few seconds they merge, they are one, the dream and the figures on the screen. This never lasts long. Soon after kickoff the dream players dissolve, and with them all memory of fear. Then I am a fan again, one among millions, watching a game. My wife wants to know why, and she would prefer a general answer. I don't have a general answer. I can only speak for myself. I watch with wonder now, true wonder at what men will pursue and believe in—Dwight Clark's catch: an act of faith—and I watch on behalf of my uncle Jay, who has already been gone a dozen years. I suppose the watching is one way of paying tribute to this man, my favorite and most influential uncle, who loved the game as only Texans can, who believed in football with all his heart and never had the chance to play.

Jay Neugeboren

EBBETS FIELD

He was a born athlete, grappling with the games grownups play.

Eddie Gottlieb moved into my neighborhood in the fall of 1955 and I knew right away we were going to become pretty good friends. I was in the eighth grade then, at P.S. 92, and Eddie was brought into my official class about two weeks after school had started. At that time I was going through what my parents called one of my "growing periods"—always talking out in class, making some wiseacre remark, or doing something stupid to get attention, and for this I'd been rewarded with a seat right in front of the teacher's desk, with nobody allowed to sit next to me.

There were no other empty seats in the room, so when our teacher Mrs. Demetri told us that we were going to get a new boy in our class, I figured he'd be sitting next to me. Our official class hadn't changed much since first grade and it was always a pretty big event when somebody new came into it. When I saw Eddie walk through the door behind Mr. Weiner, the Assistant Principal, though, my heart really jumped. I could tell right away he was a good ballplayer. He was very tall and lanky—about six-two then—with thick curly hair that reached down into the collar of his shirt. He sort of shuffled into the room, moving very slowly, his body swaying from side to side, his arms swinging freely. They were really long, coming down just about to his knee-caps. He kept staring at the floor, and when we all started laughing and giggling he must have thought we were laughing at him, because he blushed and fidgeted with his hands and feet a lot; what we were laughing at, though, was not the way Eddie looked, but at the way he looked coming in *behind* Mr. Weiner, and I think Mr. Weiner knew it, because his face got all red and angry. He was only about five-foot-one or two and when he walked he always took these huge steps, almost as if he were goose-stepping. At lunchtime we would always prance around the school-yard or the lunchroom, mimicking him, and the teachers would never try very hard to make us stop. He was already at Mrs. Demetri's desk, right in front of me, and Eddie was only a couple of steps away from the door, when he whirled around and glared at him.

"What's taking you so long?" he demanded. "Come here!"

Then, I remember, Eddie grinned broadly and in two giant steps he was in front of Mr. Weiner, towering over him, standing at attention, still grinning. We broke into hysterics. Mr. Weiner glared at us and we stopped. "Now, young man," he said to Eddie, "wipe that grin off your face. What are you—some kind of gangling idiot?"

Eddie shrugged. "I don't know," he said.

We laughed again and Mr. Weiner turned on us. "All right then. Who wants to be the first to have a private conference in my office today?" he asked.

We all shut up. Eddie was staring at the floor again. I could tell that he knew he had done something wrong—but it was obvious he didn't know what it was.

"What's that in your pocket?" Mr. Weiner asked him, pointing.

"A baseball."

"Let me see it."

Eddie put his lunchbag on my desk and twisted the ball

out of his side-pocket. He showed it to Mr. Weiner. When Mr. Weiner reached for it, though, he pulled his hand away.

"Let me have it," Mr. Weiner demanded.

"No," Eddie said, and he put his hand behind his back, gripping the ball tightly. I could tell from the printing that it was an Official National League ball. It was really beautiful!

"I said let me have it!"

Eddie shook his head sideways. "It's mine," he said. Everybody was perfectly quiet. I glanced across the room at Izzie and Corky and Louie. They were on the edges of their seats.

"Young man, you will let me have it by the time I count three or I will know the reason why!"

"Do you promise you'll give it back?" Eddie asked.

Mr. Weiner blinked. "Do I *what*—?"

Eddie was looking at Mr. Weiner now, intently. "I gotta have it," he said. "I just *gotta!* I never go anywhere without it."

"We do not allow hardball playing in this school."

Eddie grinned then, as if everything was okay, and brought the ball out from behind his back. "I didn't know that," he said. "I'm sorry." He pushed the ball right in front of Mr. Weiner's face. We all gasped and Mrs. Demetri took a step toward them. "See—?" Eddie said, smiling. "It's got Campy's signature on it."

"Who?"

"*Campy!*" Eddie said.

"Who, may I ask, is Campy?"

"Campy—Roy Campanella—he catches for the Dodgers!" Eddie was excited now. "You know—"

"Of course," Mr. Weiner said. Then he smiled, awkwardly. There was something about Eddie that had him mystified. You could tell. "Well, put that ball away and don't bring it to school again," he said. "This is your first day here, so I'll excuse you. But there are no second chances with me. Remember that."

When he left, Mrs. Demetri introduced Eddie to us. I applauded and most of the guys followed my lead. Mrs. Demetri didn't get too angry at me, though—in fact, after she gave Eddie the seat next to me, she put me in charge of getting him his books and making sure he knew where things were. Maybe she figured I'd be less trouble that way. At any rate, I was glad. The first thing I did was to ask him where he'd gotten the baseball.

"I won it," he said.

"Where?"

"On Happy Felton's Knothole Gang."

"Really?"

Eddie nodded and I nearly exploded out of my seat, wanting to tell all the guys. The Knothole Gang was this show they had on television then, that came on before all the Dodger games. Three or four guys who played the same position would get together with Happy Felton and one of the Dodgers down the right field line and they'd be tested on different things. Then, at the end, the Dodger would pick one of the guys as a winner, and give the reasons he'd picked him.

I asked Eddie a few more questions and then I began telling him about our baseball team, The Zodiacs. He said he'd read about us in Jimmy O'Brien's column in the *Brooklyn Eagle*.

"You got that good pitcher, don't you—and that crazy kid who brings an old victrola to the games and plays the Star-Spangled Banner on it—right?"

"That's Louie," I said, pointing across the room. "He lives in my building. But we don't have the pitcher any more. He's in high school now. Izzie pitches for us most of the time this year."

We talked some more and I asked him if he wanted to play with us, as long as he was in our class now, and he said he'd love to, if we'd let him. Then I wrote out a note, telling all the guys that Eddie had won the baseball on Happy Felton's show and that he'd agreed to play on our team, and I passed it across the room to Louie. His face lit up, and he passed it on to Corky. By the time we got into the yard for lunch that day, Eddie was a hero, and all the guys crowded around him, asking about what Campy had said to him and about what team he had played on before and things like that.

I got to know Eddie pretty well during the next few weeks. He wasn't very bright—this was pretty obvious the first time Mrs. Demetri called on him to read something—and he was very quiet, but he would have done anything for you if you were his friend. All the guys liked him and we were pretty happy he had moved into our neighborhood. He was the kind of guy you wished you had for a brother. His father had died a couple of years before and until he moved, he'd been living in Boro Park with his mother. He never talked a lot about her or his home or what it had been like living in Boro Park, but we all knew the most important thing—that his family was Orthodox. The first time one of us said something to him about making the big leagues someday, he shook his head and said that he didn't think he ever would because he couldn't play or travel on Saturdays. When we brought up the names of other Jewish ballplayers who had played—Hank Greenberg, Cal Abrams, Sol Rogovin, Sid Gordon, Al Rosen—he said that they hadn't come from families like his. He said it would kill his mother if any of his relatives ever found out about the things he did on Saturday—that he could hide most things as long as he wasn't living near them, but that if he ever got his picture in the papers for doing something on Saturday, they'd know about it.

Eddie himself wasn't very religious—he played ball with us at the Parade Grounds on Saturdays—but he was determined not to hurt his mother, and I guess I could understand why at the time. I knew she worked to support the two of them, and that Eddie felt pretty bad toward her about moving from their old neighborhood. I guess he felt she had moved because of him. At any rate, even though he may have felt obligated to her in a lot of ways, she didn't stop him from really wanting to be a big league ballplayer. That was pretty obvious.

1955 was the year the Dodgers beat the Yankees in the World Series, and Eddie came over to my house to watch the games on television. I don't think I've ever seen a guy get more excited than he did during the last game of that series. The Dodgers had one of their great teams then—Campy, Furillo, Robinson, Reese, Snider, Hodges, Newcombe, Erskine—but the heroes of that last game were two other guys, Sandy Amoros and Johnny Podres. When Amoros made his famous catch of Yogi Berra's fly ball in the sixth inning, and without hesitating turned and threw to Reese who doubled-up McDougald at first base, Eddie went wild. He couldn't sit down after that. He just kept walking around the room, pounding guys on the back, shaking our hands, and repeating again and again: "Did you see that catch? Boy, did you see that catch?"

We must have relived each inning of that series a hundred times during the rest of that year. I kept telling Eddie that since Podres—who had won the third and last games of the series—was only 23 years old, he'd still have plenty of years to pitch to Eddie when Eddie got to the Dodgers. Eddie always insisted it was an impossibility, but then Louie came up with another one of his bright ideas—if Eddie changed his name and grew a moustache someday, how would his relatives ever find out? Eddie liked the idea and that spring, for practice, Eddie used the name of Johnny Campy when he played with our team.

We played in the Ice Cream League at the Parade Grounds and we did pretty well, even though we didn't win the championship. Eddie was fantastic. He batted over .400, was lightning on the bases, only made about two or three errors, threw out ten guys stealing and did the one thing he did in no other place—he talked all the time. He'd be quiet until we got to the field, but the minute he put his shin guards, protector and mask on, his mouth began moving a mile-a-minute, and he'd keep up the chatter the whole game. I loved to listen to him. "C'mon, Izzie babe," he'd yell, crouched behind the plate. "Chuck it here, chuck it here. Plunk it home to Campy, honeybabe. Show 'em how, show 'em how. Plunk it home to Campy! This batter's just posin' for pictures. Let's go babe. Plunk it home to Campy . . ."

He was one of the greatest natural athletes I've ever seen—and not just in baseball, as we soon found out. Until he came to our school I was generally considered the best basketball player of all the guys, but Eddie made me look like an amateur. He was incredible! We were only in the eighth grade then, but when we'd play in the schoolyard on weekends Eddie could hold his own with the high school and college boys.

He was skinny and got banged around a lot under the boards, but he was still the most fantastic leaper I've ever seen. Lots of times, even when he was boxed out, he'd just glide up in the air, over everybody else, and pluck the ball out of the sky with those big hands of his. He could dunk the ball with either hand, too!

My parents knew how much I loved basketball and that summer, for the second straight year, they sent me to Camp Wanatoo, where Abe Goldstein, the Erasmus coach, was head counselor. I remember he got pretty upset when I told him that Eddie was supposed to go to Westinghouse—a vocational high school—instead of to Erasmus. Schoolyard reputations spread pretty fast in our neighborhood and he'd already heard about Eddie from a lot of the guys on his team. I explained to him about how Eddie's grades weren't too good, and about his mother and everything.

When I got back from camp and saw Eddie, the first thing he said to me was that he'd decided to go to Erasmus. He said that Mr. Goldstein had visited him and promised him and his mother that Eddie would get through high school—and that he could get him a scholarship to college. I was really happy. We spent a lot of time that fall playing in the schoolyard together, and Eddie got better and better. He had spent the summer in the city, working as a delivery boy and helper in his uncle's butcher shop in Boro Park, and he had developed a gorgeous fade-away jump shot that was impossible to stop. When we weren't playing, we'd sit by the fence in the schoolyard and talk about the guys on the Erasmus team or about the Dodgers—and we'd have long debates on whether it was better to get a college education and then play pro basketball, or to forget about college and take a big bonus from a major league baseball team.

That winter we played on a basketball team together in the *Daily Mirror* tournament and we probably would have won the championship, only in the big game for the Brooklyn title Eddie didn't show up until the last quarter. He went wild then, putting in shots from crazy angles, rebounding like a madman, stealing the ball and playing his heart out—but we were fifteen points behind when he arrived, and when the clock ran out were still down by four. For weeks afterwards you could hardly talk to him, he was so upset. All of us told him to forget it, that we understood about his mother getting sick and him having to stay with her until the doctor came, but he still felt he had let us down.

His mother got better, spring came, the baseball season started and Eddie stopped coming to school almost completely. Anytime the Dodgers were in town—except for the days our baseball team had a game or the afternoons that he worked as a delivery boy for his uncle—Eddie would be at Ebbets Field. He was always trying to get me to come along with him, but I usually found one excuse or another not to. He kept telling me there was nothing to worry about. He said he knew somebody in the attendance office and that all we had to do was give him our programs and show up for home-room period in the morning—the guy in the office would write in our names as absent on the sheets that went to the teachers whose classes we'd be cutting. He never seemed to get into any trouble and finally, in the middle of June, I told him I'd go with him.

We made up to meet in front of Garfield's Cafeteria, at the corner of Flatbush and Church, at 10:30, right after second period. Eddie was there ahead of me and we got on the Flatbush Avenue bus and paid our fares. I kept looking around, expecting to see a teacher or a cop.

"Just act normal," Eddie told me. "And if anybody stops us, just put one of these on your head"—he reached into a pocket and pulled out two *yamalkahs*—"and tell whoever asks you it's a Jewish holiday and that we go to Yeshiva. That always works."

When we got off the bus at Empire Boulevard, where the Botanic Gardens begin, we still had a couple of hours until the game started and I asked Eddie what we were going to do until then.

He smiled. "Follow me," he said.

I followed. I saw a few cops along the street, but none of them bothered us. Some old men were getting their boards ready, with buttons and pennants and souvenirs, and when we got to McKeever and Sullivan Place, where the main entrance was, a few guys were selling programs and yearbooks. We walked along Sullivan Place and Eddie stopped about halfway down the block, where the players' entrance was.

A minute later a taxi stopped at the curb and two big guys got out—I recognized them right away as Gil Hodges and Duke Snider. It really surprised me, I remember, to discover that we were as tall as both of them—taller than Snider.

"Any extra tickets?" Eddie asked.

"Sorry—not today, Eddie," the Duke said, and the two of them disappeared into the clubhouse.

I nearly died. "You mean you actually *know* them?" I asked.

"Sure," Eddie said. "Hell—I've been out here like this for three years now." He scratched at his cheek and tried to act nonchalant, but I could tell he was as proud as he could be that a Dodger had called him by name with me there. "I don't think they'll have any extras today, though—Milwaukee has a good team this year and there were probably lots of their friends wanting tickets."

"It's okay," I said, still flabbergasted. "I got a couple of bucks for tickets."

"We won't need 'em, I hope," he said. "If nobody has extras we can try waiting in the gas station on Bedford Avenue. There's always a bunch of kids there, hoping to catch a ball, but they usually hit four or five out in batting practice. If we can get just one the guy at the gate will let us both in—he knows me."

"If not?"

He shrugged. "The bleachers. It's only 75 cents, and after about the second inning you can sneak into the grandstands."

In a few minutes some more Dodgers came by and they all smiled and said hello to Eddie, but none of them had any extra tickets. It didn't bother me! After a while, I just followed Eddie's lead and said hello to the players too, saying things like, "How're you doing, Carl?—We're rooting for you!" to Furillo, or "How're you feeling today, Campy?" and I hardly believed it when some of the players would actually answer me! As I got more confidence I got braver—telling Pee Wee to watch out for guys sliding into second base, telling Karl Spooner that if he pitched he should keep the ball low and outside to Aaron—and after each group of guys would go into the clubhouse, I'd slam Eddie on the back and punch him in the arm. "C'mon," I'd say to him, "pinch me right on the ass, buddy. Then I'll know it's true!" And Eddie, he just kept grinning and telling me how stupid I'd been to wait this long to come to a game with him.

By 11:30, though, we still didn't have any tickets.

"We should of waited by the visiting team's entrance," Eddie said. "They hardly ever use up their passes—"

Then, as we started to walk toward Bedford Avenue, we saw this little guy come trotting up the street toward us. Eddie squinted.

"It's Amoros," he said. "Hey Sandy—any tickets?" he called.

"Oh man, I late today," Amoros said, when he got to us, shaking his head back and forth. He reached into his wallet, handed us two tickets and we wished him luck. Then he continued toward the players' entrance, running.

"Whooppee!" I shouted as soon as he was gone. "Amoros for Most Valuable Player!" I threw my arm around Eddie's shoulder and we ran down the street together, half-dragging each other, until we got to the turnstile entrance. Then we stopped and strutted inside together, handing the guard the tickets as if it was something we did every day of the week. As soon as we were inside Eddie yelled "Let's go!" and we raced under the arcade, laughing and giggling. The instant we saw the field, though, we stopped. The groundskeepers had just finished hosing down the basepaths and the visiting team hadn't come out yet for batting practice. There was hardly anybody in the stands and the sight of the empty ballpark seemed to sober us both up. To this day I don't think there's any sight that's prettier than a ballpark before a game's been played. Watching on television all the time, you forget how green and peaceful the field looks.

We had great seats that day, right over the Dodger dugout. They blasted the Braves, 9-1, with 14 or 15 hits, and we cheered and shouted like mad, especially when Amoros came up to bat. I remember everything about the ballpark that day, and I think I remember the things that happened off the field more than I do the actual game. I remember the Dodger Symphony marching around the stands, and Mabel swinging her cowbell, and Gladys Gooding singing the national anthem and playing "Follow the Dodgers" on the organ, and the groundskeepers wheeling the batting cage back out to center field, and the people across Bedford Avenue watching from their roofs. I remember being surprised at how many guys our age—and even younger—had come to the game, and I remember feeling really great when I heard somebody calling my name and I turned around and saw Mr. Hager wave to me. I waved back at him and then told Eddie about him. Mr. Hager was a retired fireman who lived on my block. He went to every Dodger game and when they lost he always wore a black armband. When the Giants beat the Dodgers in the playoff in '51, nobody saw him for weeks afterwards, and then he wore the same black suit day in and day out until they won the pennant back in '52. Everybody in our neighborhood knew him and it was said that he got into at least two or three fights a week at Hugh Casey's bar on Flatbush Avenue. There were a lot of Dodger fans like him in those days.

Most of all, though, I remember how *good* I felt that day—just sitting with Eddie, eating peanuts and cheering and talking baseball. As it turned out, that was the last time I ever got to see a Dodger game. At the end of the season they announced they were moving to Los Angeles.

I went to Camp Wanatoo again that summer and Eddie stayed in the city. His uncle had gotten him a job loading sides of beef into refrigerator cars and this really built up his chest and shoulders and arms. In the fall everybody was predicting he'd be the next great basketball star at Erasmus—maybe even All-City in his sophomore year.

When the time came for varsity try-outs, though, he didn't show up. Nobody could figure it out. Two days later he stopped by my house at night and asked if I wanted to go for a walk. He looked terrible—his face was long and he seemed to have lost a lot of weight. At first I figured it had something to do with his mother, but when I asked him he shook his head.

"Nah," he said, when we were downstairs. He sighed. "I guess you were wondering why I didn't try out for the team, huh?"

"Everybody was—" I said.

"I know. Mr. Goldstein called my house tonight and I had to tell him—that's why I came by your house. I wanted you to know before the other guys. Maybe you could tell them so I don't have to keep repeating the story."

"Sure," I said. "What is it?"

"It's my damn heart," he said. I looked at him and he was biting the corner of his lower lip, I remember. Then he shook his head back and forth and cursed. "I can't play anymore," he said. "The doctor said so." He stopped. "Jesus, Howie, what am I gonna do? What am I gonna do?" he pleaded. I didn't know what to say. "Shit," he said. "Just shit!" Then his body seemed to go limp. "C'mon, let's walk."

"How'd you find out?" I asked.

"Ah, since the summer I've had this pain in my chest and when it didn't go away I went to our family doctor. My mother telephoned him about a week ago and he told her. It's only a murmur—nothing really dangerous—but it means no varsity."

"Can't you play at all?"

"Oh yeah—as long as I take it easy. I just have to get a lot of sleep, and whenever I feel any of this pressure building up in my chest I have to be sure to stop."

We walked for a long time that night—up Bedford Avenue all the way past Ebbets Field to Eastern Parkway, then back home along Flatbush Avenue, and most of the time neither of us said anything. What could you say?

I made the varsity that year and Eddie came to all the games, home and away. He worked five afternoons a week at his uncle's butcher shop now, but on Saturdays, when it was closed, he'd come down to the schoolyard and play a few games. He kidded around a lot, telling everybody to take it easy against him because of his heart, but he was still tremendous. I was already about an inch taller than he was, and a pretty good jumper, but he'd go up over me as if I had lead in my sneakers.

In about the middle of our junior year he quit school and went to work full-time as an assistant to his uncle. He kept coming to all the Friday night games, though, and sometimes when I didn't have a date, we'd go to Garfield's afterwards and then walk home together.

Eddie and I lost touch with each other during my first two years of college—I don't think I even saw him once—but when I was home for spring vacation during my junior year my mother told me he'd bought a half-interest in Mr. Klein's kosher butcher shop on Rogers Avenue. I went over to see him the next morning and there he was, behind the counter. I stood outside for a while, watching him wait on customers, and then when the store was empty, I went inside.

"Hey, Campy—!" I called. He was at the far end of the counter, cutting up some meat.

He turned around. "Jesus—Howie!" He wiped his hands on his apron and then we shook hands and pounded each other on the back for a while. "Boy, it's good to see you—how've you been?"

"Pretty good," I said. "When did all this happen?" I asked, motioning around the store.

"C'mon next door to the candy store," he said, taking off his apron. "I'll get you a Coke—boy, it's been a long time!"

He got Mr. Klein out of the big walk-in freezer in the back and then we went next door and Eddie told me about how he had saved up money while he was working for his uncle—with that and some insurance money his mother had put away after his father's death, he was able to buy a half-interest from Mr. Klein, who was getting old and wanted to retire soon. By then Eddie could buy out the other half and the store would be his.

"How about you?" he asked. "How do you like college?"

"It's okay," I said.

"What're you studying?"

"Liberal arts."

"Oh yeah?—What subjects?"

I laughed. "You don't have to sound interested," I said.

He shrugged, embarrassed. "Anyway I follow your team in the papers all the time—the *Times* always prints box scores of your games. You did real well this year—second high scorer on your team, weren't you?" When I didn't answer, he punched me in the arm. "Ah, don't be modest—you're a good ballplayer, Howie. Bet you got all those pretty girls running after you, too—"

"We'll be playing in the Garden against N.Y.U. next year," I said. "I'll get you some tickets—you can bring a girl and maybe we'll double after or something—"

"Sure," he said. "I'm going with a girl now—real nice, you'd like her." He shrugged, then grinned. "I'll probably be a married man by this time next year—"

When we played in the Garden the next year I sent him two passes, but I had to leave right after the game in order to get the bus that was taking us back to school that night. I got an invitation to his wedding right after that. It was scheduled for Christmas week but I couldn't go because of a holiday tournament our team was playing in at Evansville, Indiana. I called him when I came in for spring vacation and told him how sorry I was that I hadn't been there.

"Jesus, Howie," he said. "Forget it. How could you have been? You were in that tournament in Indiana. I followed the whole thing." He laughed. "My wife nearly slammed me because on the first day of our honeymoon I rushed out in the morning to get the papers to see how many points you'd scored."

We talked some more and then he asked me over to dinner. I accepted the invitation, but I felt kind of funny about it. I suppose I was afraid we wouldn't have anything to talk about—or, what seemed worse, that we'd spend the entire evening reminiscing about things we'd done when we were thirteen or fourteen.

I was partially right—we did spend a lot of time reminiscing, but I didn't mind at all. Eddie and I filled each other in on what had happened to guys we'd grown up with—who was getting married, who had finished college, who had moved out of the neighborhood—and I had a good time. Susie was, as Eddie had promised, a terrific cook. She had graduated from high school and was in her last year of nurse's training—perfect for Eddie, I thought. After supper, while she did the dishes, Eddie and I sat in the living room and talked. I told him how much I liked her and he smiled.

"She's good for me," he said, nodding. "I'll tell you something—because of her I'm even thinking of going back to high school evenings to finish up."

"Does she want you to?"

"She'd never say so, even if she did—she lets me make up my own mind. But I think she'd like it."

"Sounds like a good idea," I offered.

"Yeah—but when do I have time? Running the store by myself now there's a lot of work—books—I have to bring home, and then I'm so tired after being on my feet all day, about all I can do in the evening is turn on the TV and watch the Yanks or the Mets." He sighed. "But we'll see. I'd like to finish up."

"How's your health been?" I asked.

"Fine," he said, shrugging. Then his eyes opened wide. "Jesus!" he exclaimed. "You don't know, do you?"

"Know what?"

"About my heart—" I must have looked scared then, because he started laughing at me. "Thank God Kennedy put through that draft-exemption for married men," he said, "otherwise I'd be carrying a rifle—"

"I don't understand. I thought—"

"It's a long story," he said, "but the short of it is there was never anything wrong with my heart." He stood up and paced around the room. "When I went for my Army physical about a year and a half ago, they didn't find anything wrong with me. That's how I found out."

"But what about—?"

"Ah, that was just a thing my mother told me that the family doctor went along with," he said, stopping my question. "He was religious or something I guess. I don't know. What's the difference now? Thinking back, I guess he *himself* never really told me outright I had a murmur—"

Susie came back into the room and I could tell she knew what Eddie had been telling me. She put her arms around his waist and hugged him.

"My God!" I exclaimed. "How could she—?"

He was about to say something, but then Susie looked at him and he changed his mind. "That's the way the ball bounces, I guess," he said, shrugging his shoulders, and I could tell that he had used the same expression before in similar situations. He kissed Susie on the forehead and held her close to him. "Anyway," he laughed, "if you're in pro ball you got to be away from your wife and kids half the year."

"But Christ, Eddie," I began; Susie glared at me and I stopped. Eddie sat down and nobody said anything for a while—then suddenly, he started talking. "You know something," he said. "My business is pretty good. I mean, I'm making a good living and at least I'm not working for somebody else—but you know what I'd *really* like to do?" He leaned forward and rubbed his hands together. He looked at Susie and she smiled. "I'd like to coach kids. No kidding."

"He's terrific with them, Howie," Susie said. "Really terrific."

"I love it—I help out at the center sometimes, and with this team of kids from our block. Guess what they call themselves?— The Zodiacs!" We both laughed. "It's something how these things get passed down—"

We began reminiscing again and soon we were both telling Susie about the day we'd played hooky together and gone to Ebbets Field.

"Have you seen it since it's torn down?" Eddie asked. "They got these big apartment houses—"

"I've been there," I said.

"I have a girlfriend who lives in right field," Susie said. I glanced at her, puzzled. "The people all give their section of the development names according to the way the field used to be laid out," she explained. Then she laughed, but the laugh was forced and we all knew it. Eddie and I tried to get up a conversation about the old ballplayers and what they were doing then—Hodges managing the Senators, the Duke still hanging on as a pinch hitter, poor Campy in a wheelchair since his crash, conducting interviews on TV between Yankee doubleheaders—but our hearts weren't in it anymore and there were a lot of big silences. After a while I said I had to get up early the next morning for an interview. It wasn't even midnight. I thanked them for the dinner and I said I'd be in touch when I got back from school in June. Then, when I was at the door, Eddie put his arm around my shoulder.

"I been thinking," he said. "How about you playing some three-man ball with an old married man before you go back to school?"

"Sure," I said.

I met Eddie at the schoolyard on Saturday morning and we played for a couple of hours. He wasn't as graceful as I'd remembered him, but he could still jump—only now he knew how to throw his weight around and use his elbows and body and shoulders. He was murder under the boards and deadly with his jump shot and rough on defense. We played against some pretty tough high school and college and ex-college ballplayers that day and Eddie was the best of us all. Between games, we'd rest next to the fence together and Eddie would talk and joke and kid about the pot-belly he was putting on. When we played, though, he didn't smile and he didn't talk. He played hard and he played to win.

John Updike

MAN AND DAUGHTER IN THE COLD

*Parents have a lot to teach their kids —
and a lot to learn.*

"Look at that girl ski!" The exclamation arose at Ethan's side as if, in the disconnecting cold, a rib of his had cried out; but it was his friend, friend and fellow-teacher, an inferior teacher but superior skier, Matt Langley, admiring Becky, Ethan's own daughter. It took an effort, in this air like slices of transparent metal interposed everywhere, to make these connections and to relate the young girl, her round face red with windburn as she skimmed down the run-out slope, to himself. She was his daughter, age thirteen. Ethan had twin sons, two years younger, and his attention had always been focussed on their skiing, on the irksome comedy of their double needs—the four boots to lace, the four mittens to find—and then their cute yet grim competition as now one and now the other gained the edge in the expertise of gelän-desprungs and slalom form. On their trips north into the mountains, Becky had come along for the ride. "Look how solid she is," Matt went on. "She doesn't cheat on it like your boys—those feet are absolutely together." The girl, grinning as if she could hear herself praised, wiggle-waggled to a flashy stop that sprayed snow over the men's ski tips.

210

"Where's Mommy?" she asked.

Ethan answered, "She went with the boys into the lodge. They couldn't take it." Their sinewy little male bodies had no insulation; weeping and shivering, they had begged to go in after a single T-bar run.

"What sissies," Becky said.

Matt said, "This wind is wicked. And it's picking up. You should have been here at nine; Lord, it was lovely. All that fresh powder, and not a stir of wind."

Becky told him, "Dumb Tommy couldn't find his mittens, we spent an *hour* looking, and then Daddy got the Jeep stuck." Ethan, alerted now for signs of the wonderful in his daughter, was struck by the strange fact that she was making conversation. Unafraid, she was talking to Matt without her father's intercession.

"Mr. Langley was saying how nicely you were skiing."

"You're Olympic material, Becky."

The girl perhaps blushed; but her cheeks could get no redder. Her eyes, which, were she a child, she would have instantly averted, remained a second on Matt's face, as if to estimate how much he meant it. "It's easy down here," Becky said. "It's babyish."

Ethan asked, "Do you want to go up to the top?" He was freezing standing still, and the gondola would be sheltered from the wind.

Her eyes shifted to his, with another unconsciously thoughtful hesitation. "Sure. If you want to."

"Come along, Matt?"

"Thanks, no. It's too rough for me; I've had enough runs. This is the trouble with January—once it stops snowing, the wind comes up. I'll keep Elaine company in the lodge." Matt himself had no wife, no children. At thirty-eight, he was as free as his students, as light on his skis and as full of brave know-how. "In case of frostbite," he shouted after them, "rub snow on it."

Becky effortlessly skated ahead to the lift shed. The encumbered motion of walking on skis, not natural to him, made Ethan feel asthmatic: a fish out of water. He touched his parka pocket, to check that the inhalator was there. As a child he had imagined death as something attacking from outside, but now he saw that it was carried within; we nurse it for years, and it grows. The clock on the lodge wall said a quarter to noon. The giant thermometer read two degrees above zero. The racks outside were dense as hedges with idle skis. Crowds, any sensation of crowding or delay, quickened his asthma; as therapy he imagined the emptiness, the blue freedom, at the top of the mountain. The clatter of machinery inside the shed was comforting, and enough teen-age boys were boarding gondolas to make the ascent seem normal and safe. Ethan's breathing eased. Becky proficiently handed her poles to the loader points up; her father was always caught by surprise, and often as not fumbled the little maneuver of letting his skis be taken from him. Until, five years ago, he had become an assistant professor at a New Hampshire college an hour to the south, he had never skied; he had lived in those Middle Atlantic cities where snow, its moment of virgin beauty by, is only an encumbering nuisance, a threat of suffocation. Whereas his children had grown up on skis.

Alone with his daughter in the rumbling isolation of the gondola, he wanted to explore her, and found her strange—strange in her uninquisitive child's silence, her accustomed poise in this ascending egg of metal. A dark figure with spreading legs veered out of control beneath them, fell forward, and vanished. Ethan cried out, astonished, scandalized; he imagined the man had buried himself alive. Becky was barely amused, and looked away before the dark spots struggling in the drift were lost from sight. As if she might know, Ethan asked, "Who was that?"

"Some kid." Kids, her tone suggested, were in plentiful supply; one could be spared.

He offered to dramatize the adventure ahead of them: "Do you think we'll freeze at the top?"

"Not exactly."

"What do you think it'll be like?"

"Miserable."

"Why are we doing this, do you think?"

"Because we paid the money for the all-day lift ticket."

"Becky, you think you're pretty smart, don't you?"

"Not really."

The gondola rumbled and lurched into the shed at the top; an attendant opened the door, and there was a howling mixed of wind and of boys whooping to keep warm. He was roughly handed two pairs of skis, and the handler, muffled to the eyes with a scarf, stared as if amazed that Ethan was so old. All the others struggling into skis in the lee of the shed were adolescent boys. Students: after fifteen years of teaching, Ethan tended to flinch from youth—its harsh noises, its cheerful rapacity, its cruel onward flow as one class replaced another, ate a year of his life, and was replaced by another.

Away from the shelter of the shed, the wind was a high monotonous pitch of pain. His cheeks instantly ached, and the hinges linking the elements of his face seemed exposed. His septum tingled like glass—the rim of a glass being rubbed by a moist finger to produce a note. Drifts ribbed the trail, obscuring Becky's ski tracks seconds after she made them, and at each push through the heaped snow his scope of breathing narrowed. By the time he reached the first steep section, the left half of his back hurt as it did only in the panic of a full asthmatic attack, and his skis, ignored, too heavy to manage, spread and swept him toward a snowbank at the side of the trail. He was bent far forward but kept his balance; the snow kissed his face lightly, instantly, all over; he straightened up, refreshed by the shock, thankful not to have lost a ski. Down the slope Becky had halted and was staring upward at him, worried. A huge blowing feather, a partition of snow, came between them. The cold, unprecedented in his experience, shone through his clothes like furious light, and as he rummaged through his parka for the inhalator he seemed to be searching glass shelves backed by a black wall. He found it, its icy plastic the touch of life, a clumsy key to his insides. Gasping,

he exhaled, put it into his mouth, and inhaled; the isoproterenol spray, chilled into drops, opened his lungs enough for him to call to his daughter, "Keep moving! I'll catch up!"

Solid on her skis, she swung down among the moguls and wind-bared ice, and became small, and again waited. The moderate slope seemed a cliff; if he fell and sprained anything, he would freeze. His entire body would become locked tight against air and light and thought. His legs trembled; his breath moved in and out of a narrow slot beneath the pain in his back. The cold and blowing snow all around him constituted an immense crowding, but there was no way out of this white cave but to slide downward toward the dark spot that was his daughter. He had forgotten all his lessons. Leaning backward in an infant's tense snowplow, he floundered through alternating powder and ice.

"You O.K., Daddy?" Her stare was wide, its fright underlined by a pale patch on her cheek.

He used the inhalator again and gave himself breath to tell her, "I'm fine. Let's get down."

In this way, in steps of her leading and waiting, they worked down the mountain, out of the worst wind, into the lower trail that ran between birches and hemlocks. The cold had the quality not of absence but of force: an inverted burning. The last time Becky stopped and waited, the colorless crescent on her scarlet cheek disturbed him, reminded him of some injunction, but he could find in his brain, whittled to a dim determination to persist, only the advice to keep going, toward shelter and warmth. She told him, at a division of trails, "This is the easier way."

"Let's go the quicker way," he said, and in this last descent recovered the rhythm—knees together, shoulders facing the valley, weight forward as if in the moment of release from a diving board—not a resistance but a joyous acceptance of falling. They reached the base lodge, and with unfeeling hands removed their skis. Pushing into the cafeteria, Ethan saw in the momentary mirror of the door window that his face was a spectre's; chin, nose, and eyebrows had retained the snow from that near-fall near the top. "Becky, look," he said, turning in the crowded warmth and clatter inside the door. "I'm a monster."

"I know, your face was absolutely white, I didn't know whether to tell you or not. I thought it might scare you."

He touched the pale patch on her cheek. "Feel anything?"

"No."

"Damn. I should have rubbed snow on it."

Matt and Elaine and the twins, flushed and stripped of their parkas, had eaten lunch; shouting and laughing with a strange guilty shrillness, they said that there had been repeated loud-speaker announcements not to go up to the top without face masks, because of frostbite. They had expected Ethan and Becky to come back down on the gondola, as others had, after tasting the top. "It never occurred to us," Ethan said. He took the blame upon himself by adding, "I wanted to see the girl ski."

Their common adventure, and the guilt of his having given her frostbite, bound Becky and Ethan together in complicity for the rest of the day. They arrived home as sun was leaving even the tips of the hills; Elaine had invited Matt to supper, and while the windows of the house burned golden Ethan shovelled out the Jeep. The house was a typical New Hampshire farmhouse, less than two miles from the college, on the side of a hill, overlooking what had been a pasture, with the usual capacious porch running around three sides, cluttered with cordwood and last summer's lawn furniture. The woodsy sheltered scent of these porches, the sense of rural waste space, never failed to please Ethan, who had been raised in a Newark half-house, then a West Side apartment, and just before college a row house in Baltimore, with his grand-parents. The wind had been left behind in the mountains. The air was as still as the stars. Shovelling the light dry snow became a lazy dance. But when he bent suddenly, his knees creaked, and his breathing shortened so that he paused. A sudden rectangle of light was flung from the shadows of the porch. Becky came out into the cold with him. She was carrying a lawn rake.

He asked her, "Should you be out again? How's your frost-bite?" Though she was a distance away, there was no need, in the immaculate air, to raise his voice.

"It's O.K. It kind of tingles. And under my chin. Mommy made me put on a scarf."

"What's the lawn rake for?"

"It's a way you can make a path. It really works."

"O.K., you make a path to the garage and after I get my breath I'll see if I can get the Jeep back in."

"Are you having asthma?"

"A little."

"We were reading about it in biology. Dad, see, it's kind of a tree inside you, and every branch has a little ring of muscle around it, and they tighten." From her gestures in the dark she was demonstrating, with mittens on.

What she described, of course, was classic unalloyed asthma, whereas his was shading into emphysema, which could only worsen. But he liked being lectured to—preferred it, indeed, to lecturing—and as the minutes of companionable silence with his daughter passed he took inward notes on the bright quick impressions flowing over him like a continuous voice. The silent cold. The stars. Orion behind an elm. Minute scintillae in the snow at his feet. His daughter's strange black bulk against the white; the solid grace that had stolen upon her. The conspiracy of love. His father and he shovelling the car free from a sudden unwelcome storm in Newark, instantly gray with soot, the un-dercurrent of desperation, his father a salesman and must get to Camden. Got to get to Camden, boy, get to Camden or bust. Dead of a heart attack at forty-seven. Ethan tossed a shovelful into the air so the scintillae flashed in the steady golden chord from the house windows. Elaine and Matt sitting flushed at the lodge table, parkas off, in deshabille, as if sitting up in bed. Matt's way of turning a half circle on the top of a mogul, light as a diver. The cancerous unwieldiness of Ethan's own skis. His jealousy of his students, the many-headed immortality of their annual renewal. The flawless tall cruelty of the stars. Orion intertwined with the silhouetted elm. A black tree inside him. His daughter, busily sweeping with the rake, childish yet lithe, so curiously demonstrating this preference for his company. Feminine of her to forgive him her frostbite. Perhaps, flattered on skis, felt the cold her element. Her womanhood soon enough to be smothered in warmth. A plow a mile away painstakingly scraped. He was missing the point of the lecture. The point was unstated: an absence. He was looking upon his daughter as a woman but without lust. The music around him was being produced, in the zero air, like a finger on crystal, by this hollowness, this generosity of negation. Without lust, without jealousy. Space seemed love, bestowed to be free in, and coldness the price. He felt joined to the great dead whose words it was his duty to teach.

The Jeep came up unprotestingly from the fluffy snow. It looked happy to be penned in the garage with Elaine's station wagon, and the skis, and the oiled chain saw, and the power mower dreamlessly waiting for spring. Ethan was happy, precariously so, so that rather than break he uttered a sound: "Becky?"

"Yeah?"

"You want to know what else Mr. Langley said?"

"What?" They trudged toward the porch, up the path the gentle rake had cleared.

"He said you ski better than the boys."

"I bet," she said, and raced to the porch, and in the precipitate way, evasive and female and pleased, that she flung herself to the top step he glimpsed something generic and joyous, a pageant that would leave him behind.

William Saroyan

THE FIFTY-YARD DASH

Winning looks so easy — until the
starter's gun shatters the dream.

After a certain letter came to me from New York the year I was twelve, I made up my mind to become the most powerful man in my neighborhood. The letter was from my friend Lionel Strongfort. I had clipped a coupon from *Argosy All-Story Magazine,* signed it, placed it in an envelope, and mailed it to him. He had written back promptly, with an enthusiasm bordering on pure delight, saying I was undoubtedly a man of uncommon intelligence, potentially a giant, and—unlike the average run-of-the-mill people of the world who were, in a manner of speaking, dreamwalkers and daydreamers—a person who would some day be somebody.

His opinion of me was very much like my own. It was pleasant, however, to have the opinion so emphatically corroborated, particularly by a man in New York—and a man with the greatest chest expansion in the world. With the letter came several photographic reproductions of Mr. Strongfort wearing nothing but a little bit of leopard skin. He was a tremendous man and claimed that at one time he had been puny. He was loaded all over with

muscle and appeared to be somebody who could lift a 1920 Ford roadster and tip it over.

It was an honor to have him for a friend.

The only trouble was—I didn't have the money. I forget how much the exact figure was at the beginning of our acquaintance-ship, but I haven't forgotten that it was an amount completely out of the question. While I was eager to be grateful to Mr. Strongfort for his enthusiasm, I didn't seem to be able to find words with which to explain about not having the money, without immediately appearing to be a dreamwalker and a day-dreamer myself. So, while waiting from one day to another, looking everywhere for words that would not blight our friendship and degrade me to commonness, I talked the matter over with my uncle Gyko, who was studying Oriental philosophy at the time. He was amazed at my curious ambition, but quite pleased. He said the secret of greatness, according to Yoga, was the re-leasing within one's self of those mysterious vital forces which are in all men.

These strength, he said in English which he liked to affect when speaking to me, ease from God. I tell you, Aram, eat ease wonderful.

I told him I couldn't begin to become the powerful man I had decided to become until I sent Mr. Strongfort some money.

Mohney! my uncle said with contempt. I tell you, Aram, moh-ney is nawthing. You cannot bribe God.

Although my uncle Gyko wasn't exactly a puny man, he was certainly not the man Lionel Strongfort was. In a wrestling match I felt certain Mr. Strongfort would get a headlock or a half-nelson or a toe hold on my uncle and either make him give up or squeeze him to death. And then again, on the other hand, I wondered. My uncle was nowhere near as big as Mr. Strongfort, but neither was Mr. Strongfort as dynamically furious as my uncle. It seemed to me that, at best, Mr. Strongfort, in a match with my uncle, would have a great deal of unfamiliar trouble—I mean with the mysterious vital forces that were always getting released in my uncle, so that very often a swift glance from him would make a big man quail and turn away, or, if he had been speaking, stop quickly.

Long before I had discovered words with which to explain to Mr. Strongfort about money, another letter came from him. It was as cordial as the first, and as a matter of fact, if anything, a little more cordial. I was delighted and ran about, releasing mysterious vital forces, turning handsprings, scrambling up trees, turning somersaults, trying to tip over 1920 Ford roadsters, challenging all comers to wrestle, and in many other ways alarming my relatives and irritating the neighbors.

Not only was Mr. Strongfort not sore at me, he had reduced the cost of the course. Even so, the money necessary was still more than I could get hold of. I was selling papers every day, but *that* money was for bread and stuff like that. For a while I got up very early every morning and went around town looking for a small satchel full of money. During six days of this adventuring I found a nickel and two pennies. I found also a woman's purse containing several foul-smelling cosmetic items, no money, and a slip of paper on which was written in an ignorant hand: Steve Hertwig, 3764 Ventura Avenue.

Three days after the arrival of Mr. Strongfort's second letter, his third letter came. From this time on our correspondence became one-sided. In fact, I didn't write at all. Mr. Strongfort's communications were overpowering and not at all easy to answer, without money. There was, in fact, almost nothing to say.

It was wintertime when the first letter came, and it was then that I made up my mind to become the most powerful man in my neighborhood and ultimately, for all I knew, one of the most powerful men in the world. I had ideas of my own as to how to go about getting that way, but I had also the warm friendship and high regard of Mr. Strongfort in New York, and the mystical and furious guardianship of my uncle Gyko, at home.

The letters from Mr. Strongfort continued to arrive every two or three days all winter and on into springtime. I remember, the

day apricots were ripe enough to steal, the arrival of a most
charming letter from my friend in New York. It was a hymn to
newness on earth, the arrival of springtime, the time of youth in
the heart, of renewal, fresh strength, fresh determination, and
many other things. It was truly a beautiful epistle, probably as
fine as any to the Romans or anybody else. It was full of the
legend-quality, the world-feeling, and the dignity-of-strength-
feeling so characteristic of Biblical days. The last paragraph of the
lovely hymn brought up, apologetically, the coarse theme of
money. The sum was six or seven times as little as it had been
originally, and a new element had come into Mr. Strongfort's
program of changing me over from a nobody to a giant of tremendous strength, and extreme attractiveness to women. Mr.
Strongfort had decided, he said, to teach me everything in one
fell swoop, or one sweep fall, or something of that sort. At any
rate, for three dollars, he said, he would send me all his precious
secrets in one envelope and the rest would be up to me, and
history.

I took the matter up with my uncle Gyko, who by this time
had reached the stage of fasting, meditating, walking for hours,
and vibrating. We had had discussions two or three times a week
all winter and he had told me in his own unique broken-English
way all the secrets *he* had been learning from Yoga.

I tell you, Aram, he said, I can do *anything*. Eat ease wonderful.

I believed him, too, even though he had lost a lot of weight,
couldn't sleep, and had a strange dynamic blaze in his eyes. He
was very scornful of the world that year and was full of pity for
the dumb beautiful animals that man was mistreating, killing,
eating, domesticating, and teaching to do tricks.

I tell you, Aram, he said, eat ease creaminal to make the horses
work. To keal the cows. To teach the dogs to jump, and the mon-
keys to smoke pipes.

I told him about the letter from Mr. Strongfort.

Mohney! he said. Always he wants mohney. I do not like heem.

My uncle was getting all his dope free from the theosophy-philosophy-astrology-and-miscellaneous shelf at the Public Library. He believed, however, that he was getting it straight from God. Before he took up Yoga he had been one of the boys around town and a good drinker of *rakhi*, but after the light began to come to him he gave up drinking. He said he was drinking liquor finer than *rakhi* or anything else.

What's that? I asked him.

Aram, he said, eat ease weasdom.

Anyhow, he had little use for Mr. Strongfort and regarded the man as a charlatan.

He's all right, I told my uncle.

But my uncle became furious, releasing mysterious vital forces, and said, I wheel break hease head, fooling all you leatle keads.

He ain't fooling, I said. He says he'll give me all his secrets for three dollars.

I tell you, Aram, my uncle Gyko said, he does not know any seacrets. He ease a liar.

I don't know, I said. I'd like to try that stuff out.

Eat ease creaminal, my uncle Gyko said, but I wheel geave you tree dollar.

My uncle Gyko gave me the necessary three dollars and I sent them along to Mr. Strongfort. The envelope came from New York, full of Mr. Strongfort's secrets. They were strangely simple. It was all stuff I had known anyhow but had been too lazy to pay any attention to. The idea was to get up early in the morning and for an hour or so do various kinds of acrobatic exercises, which were illustrated. Also to drink plenty of water, get plenty of fresh air, eat good wholesome food, and keep it up until you were a giant.

I felt a little let down and sent Mr. Strongfort a short polite note saying so. He ignored the note and I never heard from him again. In the meantime, I had been following the rules and growing more powerful every day. When I say *in the meantime*, I mean for four days I followed the rules. On the fifth day I decided to sleep instead of getting up and filling the house with noise and getting my grandmother sore. She used to wake up in the darkness of early morning and shout that I was an impractical fool and would never be rich. She would go back to sleep for five minutes, wake up, and then shout that I would never buy and sell for a profit. She would sleep a little more, waken, and shout that there were once three sons of a king; one was wise like his father; the other was crazy about girls; and the third had less brains than a bird. Then she would get out of bed, and, shouting steadily, tell me the whole story while I did my exercises.

The story would usually warn me to be sensible and not go around waking her up before daybreak all the time. That would always be the moral, more or less, although the story itself would be about three sons of some king, or three brothers, each of them very wealthy and usually very greedy, or three daughters, or three proverbs, or three roads, or something else like that.

She was wasting her breath, though, because I wasn't enjoying the early-morning acrobatics any more than she was. In fact, I was beginning to feel that it was a lot of nonsense, and that my uncle Gyko had been right about Mr. Strongfort in the first place.

So I gave up Mr. Strongfort's program and returned to my own, which was more or less as follows: to take it easy and grow to be the most powerful man in the neighborhood without any trouble or exercise. Which is what I did.

That spring Longfellow School announced that a track meet was to be held, one school to compete against another; *everybody* to participate.

Here, I believed, was my chance. In my opinion I would be first in every event.

Somehow or other, however, continuous meditation on the theme of athletics had the effect of growing into a fury of anticipation that continued all day and all night, so that before the day of the track meet I had run the fifty-yard dash any number of hundreds of times, had jumped the running broad jump, the standing broad jump, and the high jump, and in each event had made my competitors look like weaklings.

This tremendous inner activity, which was strictly Yoga, changed on the day of the track meet into fever.

The time came at last for me and three other athletes, one of them a Greek, to go to our marks, get set, and go; and I did, in a blind rush of speed which I knew had never before occurred in the history of athletics.

It seemed to me that never before had any living man moved so swiftly. Within myself I ran the fifty yards fifty times before I so much as opened my eyes to find out how far back I had left the other runners. I was very much amazed at what I saw.

Three boys were four yards ahead of me and going away.

It was incredible. It was unbelievable, but it was obviously the truth. There ought to be some mistake, but there wasn't. There they were, ahead of me, going away.

Well, it simply meant that I would have to overtake them, with my eyes open, and win the race. This I proceeded to do. They continued, incredibly, however, to go away, in spite of my intention. I became irritated and decided to put them in their places for the impertinence, and began releasing all the mysterious vital forces within myself that I had. Somehow or other, however, not even this seemed to bring me any closer to them and I felt that in some strange way I was being betrayed. If so, I decided, I would shame my betrayer by winning the race in spite of the betrayal, and once again I threw fresh life and energy into my running. There wasn't a great distance still to go, but I knew I would be able to do it.

Then I knew I wouldn't.

The race was over.

I was last, by ten yards.

Without the slightest hesitation I protested and challenged the runners to another race, same distance, back. They refused to consider the proposal, which proved, I knew, that they were afraid to race me. I told them they knew very well I could beat them.

It was very much the same in all the other events.

When I got home I was in high fever and very angry. I was delirious all night and sick three days. My grandmother took very good care of me and probably was responsible for my not dying. When my uncle Gyko came to visit me he was no longer hollow-cheeked. It seems he had finished his fast, which had been a long one—forty days or so; and nights too, I believe. He had stopped meditating, too, because he had practically exhausted the subject. He was again one of the boys around town, drinking, staying up all hours, and following the women.

I tell you, Aram, he said, we are a great family. We can do *anything*.

William Faulkner

THE BEAR

The hunter stalks not only his prey:
he stalks his own fear as well.

He was ten. But it had already begun, long before that day when at last he wrote his age in two figures and he saw for the first time the camp where his father and Major de Spain and old General Compson and the others spent two weeks each November and two weeks again each June. He had already inherited then, without ever having seen it, the tremendous bear with one trap-ruined foot which, in an area almost a hundred miles deep, had earned for itself a name, a definite designation like a living man.

He had listened to it for years: the long legend of corncribs rifled, of shotes and grown pigs and even calves carried bodily into the woods and devoured, of traps and deadfalls overthrown and dogs mangled and slain, and shotgun and even rifle charges delivered at point-black range and with no more effect than so many peas blown through a tube by a boy—a corridor of wreckage and destruction beginning back before he was born, through which sped, not fast but rather with the ruthless and irresistible deliberation of a locomotive, the shaggy tremendous shape.

It ran in his knowledge before ever he saw it. It looked and towered in his dreams before he even saw the unaxed woods where it left its crooked print, shaggy, huge, red-eyed, not malevolent but just big—too big for the dogs which tried to bay it, for the horses which tried to ride it down, for the men and the bullets they fired into it, too big for the very country which was its constricting scope. He seemed to see it entire with a child's complete divination before he ever laid eyes on either—the doomed wilderness whose edges were being constantly and punily gnawed at by men with axes and plows who feared it because it was wilderness, men myriad and nameless even to one another in the land where the old bear had earned a name, through which ran not even a mortal animal but an anachronism, indomitable and invincible, out of an old dead time, a phantom, epitome and apotheosis of the old wild life at which the puny humans swarmed and hacked in a fury of abhorrence and fear, like pygmies about the ankles of a drowsing elephant; the old bear solitary, indomitable and alone, widowered, childless and absolved of mortality—old Priam reft of his old wife and having outlived all his sons.

Until he was ten, each November he would watch the wagon containing the dogs and the bedding and food and guns and his father and Tennie's Jim, the Negro, and Sam Fathers, the Indian, son of a slave woman and a Chickasaw chief, depart on the road to town, to Jefferson, where Major de Spain and the others would join them. To the boy, at seven and eight and nine, they were not going into the Big Bottom to hunt bear and deer, but to keep yearly rendezvous with the bear which they did not even intend to kill. Two weeks later they would return, with no trophy, no head and skin. He had not expected it. He had not even been afraid it would be in the wagon. He believed that even after he was ten and his father would let him go too, for those two November weeks, he would merely make another one, along with his father and Major de Spain and General Compson and the others, the dogs which feared to bay it and the rifles and shot-guns which failed even to bleed it, in the yearly pageant of the old bear's furious immortality.

Then he heard the dogs. It was in the second week of his first time in the camp. He stood with Sam Fathers against a big oak beside the faint crossing where they had stood each dawn for nine days now, hearing the dogs. He had heard them once before, one morning last week—a murmur, sourceless, echoing through the wet woods, swelling presently into separate voices which he could recognize and call by name. He had raised and cocked the gun as Sam told him and stood motionless again while the uproar, the invisible course, swept up and past and faded; it seemed to him that he could actually see the deer, the buck, blond, smoke-colored, elongated with speed, fleeing, vanishing, the woods, the gray solitude, still ringing even when the cries of the dogs had died away.

"Now let the hammers down," Sam said.

"You knew they were not coming here too," he said.

"Yes," Sam said. "I want you to learn how to do when you didn't shoot. It's after the chance for the bear or the deer has done already come and gone that men and dogs get killed."

"Anyway," he said, "it was just a deer."

Then on the tenth morning he heard the dogs again. And he readied the too-long, too-heavy gun as Sam had taught him, before Sam even spoke. But this time it was no deer, no ringing chorus of dogs running strong on a free scent, but a moiling yap-ping an octave too high, with something more than indecision and even abjectness in it, not even moving very fast, taking a long time to pass completely out of hearing, leaving even then somewhere in the air that echo, thin, slightly hysterical, abject, almost grieving, with no sense of a fleeing, unseen smoke-colored, grass-eating shape ahead of it, and Sam, who had taught him first of all to cock the gun and take position where he could see everywhere and then never move again, had himself moved up beside him; he could hear Sam breathing at his shoulder and he could see the arched curve of the old man's inhaling nostrils.

"Hah," Sam said. "Not even running. Walking."

"Old Ben!" the boy said. "But up here!" he cried. "Way up here!"

"He do it every year," Sam said. "Once. Maybe to see who in camp this time, if he can shoot or not. Whether we got the dog yet that can bay and hold him. He'll take them to the river, then he'll send them back home. We may as well go back, too; see how they look when they come back to camp."

When they reached the camp the hounds were already there, ten of them crouching back under the kitchen, the boy and Sam squatting to peer back into the obscurity where they huddled, quiet, the eyes luminous, glowing at them and vanishing, and no sound, only that effluvium of something more than dog, stronger than dog and not just animal, just beast, because still there had been nothing in front of that abject and almost painful yapping save the solitude, the wilderness, so that when the eleventh hound came in at noon and with all the others watching—even old Uncle Ash, who called himself first a cook—Sam daubed the tattered ear and the raked shoulder with turpentine and axle grease, to the boy it was still no living creature, but the wilderness which, leaning for the moment down, had patted lightly once the hound's temerity.

"Just like a man," Sam said. "Just like folks. Put off as long as she could having to be brave, knowing all the time that sooner or later she would have to be brave once to keep on living with herself, and knowing all the time beforehand what was going to happen to her when she done it."

That afternoon, himself on the one-eyed wagon mule which did not mind the smell of blood nor, as they told him, of bear, and with Sam on the other one, they rode for more than three hours through the rapid, shortening winter day. They followed no path, no trail even that he could see; almost at once they were in a country which he had never seen before. Then he knew why Sam had made him ride the mule which would not spook. The sound one stopped short and tried to whirl and bolt even as Sam got down, blowing its breath, jerking and wrenching at the rein while Sam held it, coaxing it forward with his voice, since he could not risk tying it, drawing it forward while the boy got down from the marred one.

Then, standing beside Sam in the gloom of the dying afternoon, he looked down at the rotted overturned log, gutted and scored with claw marks and, in the wet earth beside it, the print of the enormous warped two-toed foot. He knew now what he had smelled when he peered under the kitchen where the dogs huddled. He realized for the first time that the bear which had run in his listening and loomed in his dreams since before he could remember to the contrary, and which, therefore, must have existed in the listening and dreams of his father and Major de Spain and even old General Compson, too, before they began to remember in their turn, was a mortal animal, and that if they had departed for the camp each November without any actual hope of bringing its trophy back, it was not because it could not be slain, but because so far they had had no actual hope to.

"Tomorrow," he said.

"We'll try tomorrow," Sam said. "We ain't got the dog yet."

"We've got eleven. They ran him this morning."

"It won't need but one," Sam said. "He ain't here. Maybe he ain't nowhere. The only other way will be for him to run by accident over somebody that has a gun."

"That wouldn't be me," the boy said. "It will be Walter or Major or—"

"It might," Sam said. "You watch close in the morning. Because he's smart. That's how come he has lived this long. If he gets hemmed up and has to pick out somebody to run over, he will pick out you."

"How?" the boy said. "How will he know—" He ceased. "You mean he already knows me, that I ain't never been here before, ain't had time to find out yet whether I—" He ceased again, looking at Sam, the old man whose face revealed nothing until it smiled. He said humbly, not even amazed, "It was me he was watching. I don't reckon he did need to come but once."

The next morning they left the camp three hours before daylight. They rode this time because it was too far to walk, even the dogs in the wagon; again the first gray light found him in a place which he had never seen before, where Sam had placed him and told him to stay and then departed. With the gun which was too big for him, which did not even belong to him, but to Major de Spain, and which he had fired only once—at a stump on the first day, to learn the recoil and how to reload it—he stood against a gum tree beside a little bayou whose black still water crept without movement out of a canebrake and crossed a small clearing and into cane again, where, invisible, a bird—the big woodpecker called Lord-to-God by Negroes—chattered at a dead limb.

It was a stand like any other, dissimilar only in incidentals to the one where he had stood each morning for ten days; a territory new to him, yet no less familiar than that other one which, after almost two weeks, he had come to believe he knew a little— the same solitude, the same loneliness through which human beings had merely passed without altering it, leaving no mark, no scar, which looked exactly as it must have looked when the first ancestor of Sam Fathers' Chickasaw predecessors crept into it and looked about, club or stone axe or bone arrow drawn and poised; different only because, squatting at the edge of the kitchen, he smelled the hounds huddled and cringing beneath it and saw the raked ear and shoulder of the one who, Sam said, had had to be brave once in order to live with herself, and saw yesterday in the earth beside the gutted log the print of the living foot.

He heard no dogs at all. He never did hear them. He only heard the drumming of the woodpecker stop short off and knew that the bear was looking at him. He never saw it. He did not know whether it was in front of him or behind him. He did not move, holding the useless gun, which he had not even had warning to cock and which even now he did not cock, tasting in his saliva that taint as of brass which he knew now because he had smelled it when he peered under the kitchen at the huddled dogs.

Then it was gone. As abruptly as it had ceased, the woodpecker's dry, monotonous clatter set up again, and after a while he even believed he could hear the dogs—a murmur, scarce a sound even, which he had probably been hearing for some time before he even remarked it, drifting into hearing and then out again, dying away. They came nowhere near him. If it was a bear

they ran, it was another bear. It was Sam himself who came out of the cane and crossed the bayou, followed by the injured bitch of yesterday. She was almost at heel, like a bird dog, making no sound. She came and crouched against his leg, trembling, staring off into the cane.

"I didn't see him," he said. "I didn't, Sam!"

"I know it," Sam said. "He done the looking. You didn't hear him neither, did you?"

"No," the boy said. "I—"

"He's smart," Sam said. "Too smart." He looked down at the hound, trembling faintly and steadily against the boy's knee. From the raked shoulder a few drops of fresh blood oozed and clung. "Too big. We ain't got the dog yet. But maybe someday. Maybe not next time. But someday."

So I must see him, he thought. *I must look at him.* Otherwise, it seemed to him that it would go on like this forever, as it had gone on with his father and Major de Spain, who was older than his father, and even with old General Compson, who had been old enough to be a brigade commander in 1865. Otherwise, it would go on so forever, next time and next time, after and after and after. It seemed to him that he could see the two of them, himself and the bear, shadowy in the limbo from which time emerged, becoming time; the old bear absolved of mortality and himself partaking, sharing a little of it, enough of it. And he knew now what he had smelled in the huddled dogs and tasted in his saliva. He recognized fear. *So I will have to see him*, he thought, without dread or even hope. *I will have to look at him.*

It was in June of the next year. He was eleven. They were in camp again, celebrating Major de Spain's and General Compson's birthdays. Although the one had been born in September and the other in the depth of winter and in another decade, they had met for two weeks to fish and shoot squirrels and turkey and run coons and wildcats with the dogs at night. That is, he and Boon Hoggenbeck and the Negroes fished and shot squirrels and ran the coons and cats, because the proved hunters, not only Major de Spain and old General Compson, who spent those two weeks sitting in a rocking chair before a tremendous iron pot of Brunswick stew, stirring and tasting, with old Ash to quarrel with about how he was making it and Tennie's Jim to pour whiskey from the demijohn into the tin dipper from which he drank it, but even the boy's father and Walter Ewell, who were still young enough, scorned such, other than shooting the wild gobblers with pistols for wagers on their marksmanship.

Or, that is, his father and the others believed he was hunting squirrels. Until the third day he thought that Sam Fathers believed that too. Each morning he would leave the camp right after breakfast. He had his own gun now, a Christmas present. He went back to the tree beside the little bayou where he had stood that morning. Using the compass which old General Compson had given him, he ranged from that point; he was teaching himself to be a better-than-fair woodsman without knowing he was doing it. On the second day he even found the gutted log where he had first seen the crooked print. It was almost completely crumbled now, healing with unbelievable speed, a passionate and almost visible relinquishment, back into the earth from which the tree had grown.

He ranged the summer woods now, green with gloom; if anything, actually dimmer than in November's gray dissolution, where, even at noon, the sun fell only in intermittent dappling upon the earth, which never completely dried out and which crawled with snakes—moccasins and water snakes and rattlers, themselves the color of the dappled gloom, so that he would not always see them until they moved, returning later and later, first day, second day, passing in the twilight of the third evening the little log pen enclosing the log stable where Sam was putting up the horses for the night.

"You ain't looked right yet," Sam said.

He stopped. For a moment he didn't answer. Then he said peacefully, in a peaceful rushing burst as when a boy's miniature dam in a little brook gives way, "All right. But how? I went to the bayou. I even found that log again. I—"

"I reckon that was all right. Likely he's been watching you. You never saw his foot?"

"I," the boy said—"I didn't—I never thought—"

"It's the gun," Sam said. He stood beside the fence, motionless—the old man, the Indian, in the battered faded overalls and the frayed five-cent straw hat which in the Negro's race had been the badge of his enslavement and was now the regalia of his freedom. The camp—the clearing, the house, the barn and its tiny lot with which Major de Spain in his turn had scratched punily and evanescently at the wilderness—faded in the dusk, back into the immemorial darkness of the woods. *The gun,* the boy thought. *The gun.*

"Be scared," Sam said. "You can't help that. But don't be afraid. Ain't nothing in the woods going to hurt you unless you corner it, or it smells that you are afraid. A bear or a deer, too, has got to be scared of a coward the same as a brave man has got to be."

The gun, the boy thought.

"You will have to choose," Sam said.

He left the camp before daylight, long before Uncle Ash would wake in his quilts on the kitchen floor and start the fire for breakfast. He had only the compass and a stick for snakes. He could go almost a mile before he would begin to need the compass. He sat on a log, the invisible compass in his invisible hand, while the secret night sounds, fallen still at his movements, scurried again and then ceased for good, and the owls ceased and gave over to the waking of day birds, and he could see the compass. Then he went fast yet still quietly; he was becoming better and better as a woodsman, still without having yet realized it.

He jumped a doe and a fawn at sunrise, walked them out of the bed, close enough to see them—the crash of undergrowth, the white scut, the fawn scudding behind her faster than he had believed it could run. He was hunting right, upwind, as Sam had taught him; not that it mattered now. He had left the gun; of his own will and relinquishment he had accepted not a gambit, not a choice, but a condition in which not only the bear's heretofore inviolable anonymity but all the old rules and balances of hunter and hunted had been abrogated. He would not even be afraid, not even in the moment when the fear would take him completely—blood, skin, bowels, bones, memory from the long time before it became his memory—all save that thin, clear, quenchless, immortal lucidity which alone differed him from this bear and from all the other bear and deer he would ever kill in the humility and pride of his skill and endurance, to which Sam had spoken when he leaned in the twilight on the lot fence yesterday.

By noon he was far beyond the little bayou, farther into the new and alien country than he had ever been. He was traveling now not only by the compass but by the old, heavy, biscuit-thick silver watch which had belonged to his grandfather. When he stopped at last, it was for the first time since he had risen from the log at dawn when he could see the compass. It was far enough. He had left the camp nine hours ago; nine hours from now, dark would have already been an hour old. But he didn't think that. He thought, *All right. Yes. But what?* and stood for a moment, alien and small in the green and topless solitude, answering his own question before it had formed and ceased. It was the watch, the compass, the stick—the three lifeless mechanicals with which for nine hours he had fended the wilderness off; he hung the watch and compass carefully on a bush and leaned the stick beside them and relinquished completely to it.

He had not been going very fast for the last two or three hours. He went no faster now, since distance would not matter even if he could have gone fast. And he was trying to keep a bearing on the tree where he had left the compass, trying to complete a circle which would bring him back to it or at least intersect itself, since direction would not matter now either. But the tree was not there, and he did as Sam had schooled him—made the next circle in the opposite direction, so that the two patterns would bisect somewhere, but crossing no print of his own feet, finding the tree at last, but in the wrong place—no bush, no compass, no watch—and the tree not even the tree, because there was a down log beside it and he did what Sam Fathers had told him was the next thing and the last.

As he sat down on the log he saw the crooked print—the warped, tremendous, two-toed indentation which, even as he watched it, filled with water. As he looked up, the wilderness coalesced, solidified—the glade, the tree he sought, the bush, the watch and the compass glinting where a ray of sunlight touched them. Then he saw the bear. It did not emerge, appear; it was just there, immobile, solid, fixed in the hot dappling of the green and windless noon, not as big as he had dreamed it, but as big as he had expected it, bigger, dimensionless against the dappled obscurity, looking at him where he sat quietly on the log and looked back at it.

Then it moved. It made no sound. It did not hurry. It crossed the glade, walking for an instant into the full glare of the sun; when it reached the other side it stopped again and looked back at him across one shoulder while his quiet breathing inhaled and exhaled three times.

Then it was gone. It didn't walk into the woods, the undergrowth. It faded, sank back into the wilderness as he had watched a fish, a huge old bass, sink and vanish back into the dark depths of its pool without even any movement of its fins.

He thought, *It will be next fall.* But it was not next fall, nor the next nor the next. He was fourteen then. He had killed his buck, and Sam Fathers had marked his face with the hot blood, and in the next year he killed a bear. But even before that accolade he had become as competent in the woods as many grown men with the same experience; by his fourteenth year he was a better woodsman than most grown men with more. There was no territory within thirty miles of the camp that he did not know—bayou, ridge, brake, landmark tree and path. He could have led anyone to any point in it without deviation, and brought them out again. He knew game trails that even Sam Fathers did not know; in his thirteenth year he found a buck's bedding place, and unbeknown to his father he borrowed Walter Ewell's rifle and lay in wait at dawn and killed the buck when it walked back to the bed, as Sam had told him how the old Chickasaw fathers did.

But not the old bear, although by now he knew its footprint better than he did his own, and not only the crooked one. He could see any one of the three sound ones and distinguish it from any other, and not only by its size. There were other bears within those thirty miles which left tracks almost as large, but this was more than that. If Sam Fathers had been his mentor and the back-yard rabbits and squirrels at home his kindergarten, then the wilderness the old bear ran was his college, the old male bear itself, so long unwifed and childless as to have become its own ungendered progenitor, was his alma mater. But he never saw it.

He could find the crooked print now almost whenever he liked, fifteen or ten or five miles, or sometimes nearer the camp than that. Twice while on stand during the three years he heard the dogs strike its trail by accident; on the second time they jumped it seemingly, the voices high, abject, almost human in hysteria, as on that first morning two years ago. But not the bear itself. He would remember that noon three years ago, the glade, himself and the bear fixed during that moment in the windless and dappled blaze, and it would seem to him that it had never happened, that he had dreamed that too. But it had happened. They had looked at each other, they had emerged from the wilderness old as earth, synchronized to that instant by something more than the blood that moved the flesh and bones which bore them, and touched, pledged something, affirmed something more lasting than the frail web of bones and flesh which any accident could obliterate.

Then he saw it again. Because of the very fact that he thought of nothing else, he had forgotten to look for it. He was still-hunting with Walter Ewell's rifle. He saw it cross the end of a long blow-down, a corridor where a tornado had swept, rushing through rather than over the tangle of trunks and branches as a locomotive would have, faster than he had ever believed it could move, almost as fast as a deer even, because a deer would have spent most of that time in the air, faster than he could bring the rifle sights up to it, so that he believed the reason he never let off the shot was that he was still behind it, had never caught up with it. And now he knew what had been wrong during all the three years. He sat on a log, shaking and trembling as if he had never seen the woods before nor anything that ran them, wondering with incredulous amazement how he could have forgotten the very thing which Sam Fathers had told him and which the bear itself had proved the next day and had now returned after three years to reaffirm.

And he now knew what Sam Fathers had meant about the right dog, a dog in which size would mean less than nothing. So when he returned alone in April—school was out then, so that the sons of farmers could help with the land's planting, and at last his father had granted him permission, on his promise to be back in four days—he had the dog. It was his own, a mongrel of the sort called by Negroes a fyce, a ratter, itself not much bigger than a rat and possessing that bravery which had long since stopped being courage and had become foolhardiness.

It did not take four days. Alone again, he found the trail on the first morning. It was not a stalk; it was an ambush. He timed the meeting almost as if it were an appointment with a human being. Himself holding the fyce muffled in a feed sack and Sam Fathers with two of the hounds on a piece of plowline rope, they lay down wind of the trail at dawn of the second morning. They were so close that the bear turned without even running, as if in surprised amazement at the shrill and frantic uproar of the released fyce, turning at bay against the trunk of a tree, on its hind feet; it seemed to the boy that it would never stop rising, taller and taller, and even the two hounds seemed to take a sort of desperate and despairing courage from the fyce, following it as it went in.

Then he realized that the fyce was actually not going to stop. He flung, threw the gun away, and ran; when he overtook and grasped the frantically pinwheeling little dog, it seemed to him that he was directly under the bear.

He could smell it, strong and hot and rank. Sprawling, he looked up to where it loomed and towered over him like a cloud-burst and colored like a thunderclap, quite familiar, peacefully and even lucidly familiar, until he remembered: This was the way he had used to dream about it. Then it was gone. He didn't see it go. He knelt, holding the frantic fyce with both hands, hearing the abased wailing of the hounds drawing farther and farther away, until Sam came up. He carried the gun. He laid it down quietly beside the boy and stood looking down at him.

"You've done seed him twice now with a gun in your hand," he said. "This time you couldn't have missed him."

The boy rose. He still held the fyce. Even in his arms and clear of the ground, it yapped frantically, straining and surging after the fading uproar of the two hounds like a tangle of wire springs. He was panting a little, but he was neither shaking nor trembling now.

"Neither could you!" he said. "You had the gun! Neither did you!"

"And you didn't shoot," his father said. "How close were you?"

"I don't know, sir," he said. "There was a big wood tick inside his right hind leg. I saw that. But I didn't have the gun then."

"But you didn't shoot when you had the gun," his father said. "Why?"

But he didn't answer, and his father didn't wait for him to, rising and crossing the room, across the pelt of the bear which

the boy had killed two years ago and the larger one which his father had killed before he was born, to the bookcase beneath the mounted head of the boy's first buck. It was the room which his father called the office, from which all the plantation business was transacted; in it for the fourteen years of his life he had heard the best of all talking. Major de Spain would be there and sometimes old General Compson, and Walter Ewell and Boon Hoggenbeck and Sam Fathers and Tennie's Jim, too, because they, too, were hunters, knew the woods and what ran them.

He would hear it, not talking himself but listening—the wilderness, the big woods, bigger and older than any recorded document of white man fatuous enough to believe he had bought any fragment of it or Indian ruthless enough to pretend that any fragment of it had been his to convey. It was of the men, not white nor black nor red, but men, hunters with the will and hardihood to endure and the humility and skill to survive, and the dogs and the bear and deer juxtaposed and reliefed against it, ordered and compelled by and within the wilderness in the ancient and unremitting contest by the ancient and immitigable rules which voided all regrets and brooked no quarter, the voices quiet and weighty and deliberate for retrospection and recollection and exact remembering, while he squatted in the blazing firelight as Tennie's Jim squatted, who stirred only to put more wood on the fire and to pass the bottle from one glass to another. Because the bottle was always present, so that after a while it seemed to him that those fierce instants of heart and brain and courage and wiliness and speed were concentrated and distilled into that brown liquor which not women, not boys and children, but only hunters drank, drinking not of the blood they had spilled but some condensation of the wild immortal spirit, drinking it moderately, humbly even, not with the pagan's base hope of acquiring thereby the virtues of cunning and strength and speed, but in salute to them.

His father returned with the book and sat down again and opened it. "Listen," he said. He read the five stanzas aloud, his voice quiet and deliberate in the room where there was no fire now because it was already spring. Then he looked up. The boy watched him. "All right," his father said. "Listen." He read again, but only the second stanza this time, to the end of it, the last two lines, and closed the book and put it on the table beside him. " 'She cannot fade, though thou hast not thy bliss, for ever wilt thou love, and she be fair,' " he said.

"He's talking about a girl," the boy said.

"He had to talk about something," his father said. Then he said, "He was talking about truth. Truth doesn't change. Truth is one thing. It covers all things which touch the heart—honor and pride and pity and justice and courage and love. Do you see now?"

He didn't know. Somehow it was simpler than that. There was an old bear, fierce and ruthless, not merely just to stay alive, but with the fierce pride of liberty and freedom, proud enough of that liberty and freedom to see it threatened without fear or even alarm; nay, who at times even seemed deliberately to put that freedom and liberty in jeopardy in order to savor them, to remind his old strong bones and flesh to keep supple and quick to defend and preserve them. There was an old man, son of a Negro slave and an Indian king, inheritor on the one side of the long chronicle of a people who had learned humility through suffering, and pride through the endurance which survived the suffering and injustice, and on the other side, the chronicle of a people even longer in the land than the first, yet who no longer existed in the land at all save in the solitary brotherhood of an old Negro's alien blood and the wild and invincible spirit of an old bear. There was a boy who wished to learn humility and pride in order to become skillful and worthy in the woods, who suddenly found himself becoming so skillful so rapidly that he feared he would never become worthy because he had not learned humility and pride, although he had tried to, until one day and as suddenly he discovered that an old man who could not have defined either had led him, as though by the hand, to that point where an old bear and a little mongrel dog showed him that, by possessing one thing other, he would possess them both.

And a little dog, nameless and mongrel and many-fathered, grown, yet weighing less than six pounds, saying as if to itself, "I can't be dangerous, because there's nothing much smaller than I am; I can't be fierce, because they would call it just noise; I can't be humble, because I'm already too close to the ground to genuflect; I can't be proud, because I wouldn't be near enough to it for anyone to know who was casting that shadow, and I don't even know that I'm not going to heaven, because they have already decided that I don't possess an immortal soul. So all I can be is brave. But it's all right. I can be that, even if they still call it just noise."

That was all. It was simple, much simpler than somebody talking in a book about a youth and a girl he would never need to grieve over, because he could never approach any nearer her and would never have to get any farther away. He had heard about a bear, and finally got big enough to trail it, and he trailed it four years and at last met it with a gun in his hands and he didn't shoot. Because a little dog—But he could have shot long before the little dog covered the twenty yards to where the bear waited, and Sam Fathers could have shot at any time during that interminable minute while Old Ben stood on his hind feet over them. He stopped. His father was watching him gravely across the spring-rife twilight of the room; when he spoke, his words were as quiet as the twilight, too, not loud, because they did not need to be because they would last. "Courage, and honor, and pride," his father said, "and pity, and love of justice and of liberty. They all touch the heart, and what the heart holds to becomes truth, as far as we know truth. Do you see now?"

Sam, and Old Ben, and Nip, he thought. And himself too. He had been all right too. His father had said so. "Yes, sir," he said.

Copyright Acknowledgments